GRACE UNDER PRESSURE

**Center Point
Large Print**

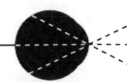

**This Large Print Book carries the
Seal of Approval of N.A.V.H.**

GRACE UNDER PRESSURE

JULIE HYZY

CENTER POINT PUBLISHING
THORNDIKE, MAINE

This Center Point Large Print edition
is published in the year 2011 by arrangement with
The Berkley Publishing Group,
a member of Penguin Group (USA) Inc.

The text of this Large Print edition is unabridged.
In other aspects, this book may vary
from the original edition.
Printed in the United States of America
on permanent paper.
Set in 16-point Times New Roman type.

ISBN: 978-1-60285-945-6

Library of Congress Cataloging-in-Publication Data

Hyzy, Julie A.
  Grace Under Pressure : a manor house mystery / Julie Hyzy. — Center Point large print
ed.
     p. cm.
  ISBN 978-1-60285-945-6 (library binding : alk. paper)
  1. Millionaires—Fiction. 2. Family secrets—Fiction. 3. Large type books. I. Title.
PS3608.Y98G73 2011
813′.6—dc22
                                                                        2010040912

This one is for you, Curtie

Acknowledgments

I am wildly excited to begin this new series and to introduce readers to Grace and her friends at Marshfield Manor. It is because readers like you have been so kind to Ollie (White House Chef Mysteries) and Alex ("Deadly" series) that I am able to launch this new adventure. Thank you so very much for all your e-mails, updates, and blog posts. You spread more sunshine than you may know.

Many thanks to my agent, Erin C. Niumata, for facilitating this new endeavor and for her unflagging good cheer. I am delighted to be working with Natalee Rosenstein of Berkley Prime Crime again. Thank you, Natalee, for taking another chance on me. I'm thrilled to be here.

Special thanks to George Pratt, illustrator extraordinaire, who provided artistic information on Raphael Soyer. Any errors in the story are mine.

As always, I couldn't do any of this without the loving support of my family and friends. You guys are the best.

GRACE UNDER PRESSURE

Chapter 1

THERE WERE AT LEAST SIXTY PEOPLE IN the Birdcage room this afternoon but not one of them made a peep. The animated conversations, gentle laughter, and musical *plinks* from the harp had gone suddenly silent, as though a giant thumb had hit the mute button.

And that giant thumb stood in front of me.

"Please keep your voice down," I said to him.

The big guy paced in circles, his untamed red hair ballooning like a lion's mane. He stopped moving long enough to glare at the crowd. "What are you all staring at?"

Guests, who moments before had been nibbling finger sandwiches, now exchanged awkward glances. They tried, and failed, to shift their attention elsewhere. But who could blame them? The heavyset fellow with the ripped jeans, dirty shirt, and wild eyes didn't belong in this serene setting. He made a show of looking around the room then shouted again, his voice echoing. "Huh? Whatcha all looking at?"

I tried to get his attention. "Sir, why don't you tell me how I can help you?"

He shot me a dirty look. Resumed pacing.

Next to me, our hostess, Martha, took a half step

back. She had called me down to help with a "problem guest." I hadn't expected 350 pounds of fury. The worst complaint we usually received about afternoon tea in the Birdcage was about it being too hot or too cool. Regulating temperature in an all-window room was always a challenge. I whispered to Martha to call security and she took off, clearly relieved to get away.

Trying again, I smiled at the big guy. "What's your name?"

He stopped moving. "Why do you want to know?"

"My name is Grace," I said, inching forward. "I'm the assistant curator here at Marshfield Manor."

"Cure-ator? What does that mean? They sent you here to cure me?" His angry look was replaced by confusion. "And you're, like, just an assistant? Where's the important people? I don't want to talk to some dumb assistant."

"Why don't you tell me what you need," I said, more slowly this time, "and I'll do my best to get the right person to help you."

Teeth bared, he spread his arms wide and lifted his gaze to the glassed ceiling as though begging the heavens for patience. Whatever biceps he might have once had sagged out from short sleeves, seams shredded to accommodate his arms' girth. He looked as though he'd slept in this outfit. All week. At about twenty-five, he was younger than I was, and a few inches taller than my five-foot-eight, but he outweighed me by at least two hundred pounds. A morbidly obese time bomb. I glanced over to the wall where we kept the defibrillator and hoped I wouldn't need to use it.

Still staring upward, he asked, "What do I have to do to get a cheeseburger around here?"

A nervous laugh bubbled up from the back of the room.

Snapping his attention toward the giggler, the guy yelled, "What, you think this is funny?"

Two of our plainclothes security guards eased in. Older guys, decked out to look like tourists, they didn't cut an imposing sight. I wished they'd sent a different team, but beggars couldn't be choosers. I moved into the big man's view, distracting him. "We don't serve cheeseburgers here, I'm afraid . . ."

"Why not?"

"This," I gestured, "is our tearoom." Maybe if I explained things, he might be encouraged to leave. "We serve light refreshments here, like savories and sweets. If you want a more substantial meal, our hotel offers a full menu." Not that our bellicose guest would fit any better there than he did here. "Or maybe you'd prefer to try one of the great little diners off property? We have a shuttle that can take you into Emberstowne, if you like."

He worked his tongue inside his bottom lip. "Don't want that," he said more to himself than to me. Grabbing the back of a nearby chair, he shouted, "I want a cheeseburger." He lifted the chair over his head and leaped sideways toward the outside wall. "Or I'll . . . I'll . . . throw this through a window."

He certainly had plenty to choose from. This room was called the Birdcage for good reason: Jutting out from the mansion to the south, the cylindrical room was a two-storied glass marvel. Each of the clear panes was framed by black support beams, which arched to meet at a buttressed central point. Though impressive, the Birdcage was just one more showstopper setting in this 150-room Gothic beauty. A giant museum as well as a home, each of its huge rooms showcased priceless artifacts. Stepping inside the manor always made me feel tiny, yet protected.

I kept my voice even and tried to smile. "Just put the chair down and we can talk."

His arms faltered. He bit his lip and glanced from side to side. I could only imagine what he was thinking. I had my back to the rest of the room, focusing completely on this wild-eyed, crazy-haired man in front of me.

"Tell me your name," I tried again.

"How come it's just you talking to me? I mean, shouldn't they, like, send security in here?"

I sincerely hoped the security guards would make their move soon. They must be waiting for backup. These two men were both over sixty, unarmed, and relatively small. The toughest assignments this team usually faced were stopping kids from entering roped-off areas or adults from using flash photography. I doubted these two could take down our sizeable guest. Not even working together. Not even if I jumped in to help.

The big guy waved the chair over his head again. I got the feeling his arms were getting tired.

"Come on," I said, "how can I help you if I don't know your name?"

He surprised me by answering. "Percy."

"Nice to meet you, Percy. Now why don't you put down that chair and we'll talk."

Without warning, he threw the chair to the floor and ran to my right. The two elderly security guards had rushed him but they were a half step too slow. Percy threw a fat arm against William, the smaller of the two guards, sending him sprawling onto the marble floor. When he hit the ground, I heard William *whoof* in pain.

Percy hustled along the room's perimeter, arms pumping, his mane of hair blocking his view as he glanced back at the guard sprawled on the floor. The big man didn't run out of the room, as I expected. Instead, he ducked between tables, grabbing the backs of patrons' chairs as he dodged the other guard, Niles, who was trying his best to corner the big man all by himself.

I pulled up my walkie-talkie and called for assistance, requesting an emergency team to help the fallen William. He'd managed to sit up, but I didn't want to take any chances.

People screamed. Some shouted. Those nearest the doors got out. Who could blame them?

Our young harpist, looking shell-shocked and too panicked to run, kept her arms protectively around her instrument. Nearby, an elderly woman with arthritic hands stared up at the big man. Her eyes were bright and wide. Just as I thought she might faint, she hurled her teacup at him. It bounced off his shoulder before crashing to the floor. Percy turned and ran past her, patting her blue-white hair more gently than I would have expected. "Good aim, lady," he said. Then, waving his arms over his head he skirted tables with surprising agility, crying out, "My kingdom for a cheeseburger."

Had this been a scene in a movie, I might have laughed. But this was Marshfield Manor. Outbursts like this didn't happen here. Our guests must not be terrorized. This magnificent, extraordinary haven should not be compromised. Ever.

I was not amused.

The rest of security finally stormed in. Although Percy's wild behavior had probably only gone on for about a minute and a half, it seemed ten times longer. Uniformed guards took positions at every exit and three tough officers—two men just hired by our head of security, and the top man himself—came in, hands on holsters. These men *were* armed but I knew they wouldn't draw their weapons with patrons present unless it became absolutely necessary.

The chief of security, Terrence Carr, sidled up. "What do we got? Talk to me," he said.

I gave him a quick rundown, adding, "I don't think the guy is dangerous. Just a little unstable."

Tall, black, and stunningly handsome, Carr had an Ironman triathlete's physique and—much to the disappointment of many female staffers—a wife and three kids. He didn't take his eyes off our unwelcome guest. "Mr. Percy," he called. "We will take you out by force if we have to. But I think it would be much better if you came out on your own."

"Yeah, right," Percy answered. A woman behind him leaned as far away as possible, the look on her face making it apparent she was too terrified to get up and run. As he backed up, Percy stumbled against her seat, knocking it sideways. She jumped to her feet, squeaking in fear. "Sorry," he mumbled. He offered a quick smile. "My fault."

An apology? This made no sense at all. I started feeling sorry for the big guy. Maybe he had just come in looking for a handout. Maybe he'd missed taking his meds.

When Carr's two men got within striking distance, Percy took off, nimbly avoiding further collisions with patrons, tables, and harp. I stepped back, letting the professionals do their job, sad to see this beautiful room suffer as Percy threw empty chairs into the officers' paths and knocked furniture to the ground. Abandoned meals crashed loudly and messily to the floor. I winced.

This was one of my favorite rooms in the entire mansion, and the only place in the actual home where guests could sit, relax, and grab a bite to eat. With its reproduction furniture—rattan chairs and settees with peach-, cream-, and pale green–striped cushions—potted palms, and a soaring ceiling, this was always the brightest place to be.

Sitting in this room, as I had as a young child with my family, always made me feel special. Like I belonged here. And now, as assistant curator, I really did belong here. I was as protective of the Marshfield Manor castle as I was of my own home.

I stepped forward instinctively as Percy grabbed another chair, using it to fend off the guards as a lion tamer might tease his quarry. I didn't know what I could possibly do, but I felt a powerful need to do *something*. With Percy's leonine appearance, watching him fight the guards with the upturned chair was a peculiar sight. Again, in another situation, I might have laughed. No one wanted to hurt this guy, but we couldn't let him get away with this behavior. Carr repeatedly ordered him to put the chair down.

Instead, wiggling the chair like a sword, Percy grinned, pointedly ignoring the officer's demands. Carr pulled out pepper spray. I hoped he was bluffing because pepper spray would affect everyone in the room if he used it. From the set of his jaw and the tension in his posture, however, I could tell he was itching to spring.

"Stop this nonsense!"

The unexpected voice, authoritative and deep, boomed from behind me.

I spun. Bennett Marshfield, owner of the manor, strode toward Percy with a bearing that belied his seventy-plus years. Bennett's perennially tanned face was tight with anger, and his white hair glinted brightly in the room's sunshine, making him look angelic and demonic at the same time. "This is my home and you will cease this ridiculous behavior at once!"

For a heartbeat, everybody stopped. Even Percy. The big guy's mouth dropped open. He recovered long enough to ask, "Who are you?"

That was all Carr and his team needed. A handful of guards rushed up, and in a sea of arms and legs, amid gurgling, angry noises that I could tell came from Percy, they tackled the big guy and wrestled him to the ground. The moment he was turned onto his stomach and handcuffed, the room erupted in applause. People stood and cheered.

The little old lady who had thrown the teacup clapped gleefully, her aged face wrinkling into a wide smile. "That'll teach you, you oaf!" she called.

As our patrons settled back into their seats, I

called for attention. "Your afternoon tea is on the house today," I said. Turning toward the doorway where some of the more skittish guests had disappeared, I welcomed them back in. "We are very sorry for the disturbance, and as our staff cleans up, we will refill your trays and bring you whatever you like. I hope our small treat this afternoon will help leave a sweeter taste in your mouth."

My announcement was met with another round of applause.

Four guards flanked Percy as they led him past me. Head down, the big man no longer resisted, apparently resigned to his fate. I suggested to Carr that they escort him out through the service doors and he nodded. In moments, they were gone.

Bennett made his way over. "Good move." He nodded toward the crowd. "Keeping the guests here for a little free food will help them remember the good and"—he glanced back the way the guards had gone—"forget the unappetizing."

"I didn't see you come in," I said. "I thought you were out all day today."

He grimaced in a way I didn't understand. "My morning appointment was . . . unpleasant to say the least. I was just on my way to meet Abe upstairs but decided to detour when I caught the call on the walkie-talkie. I was curious to see how you would handle the situation." His pale eyes were deep-set, but not too deep to dilute the power of his glare.

"You are still within your ninety-day probationary period, you know."

How could I forget? If Abe—my immediate boss, and head curator—wasn't constantly reminding me, our assistant, Frances, certainly was. I had been hired two months earlier because Bennett Marshfield's attorneys warned that he needed to inject fresh blood into the administration. Tourism was down, security was seriously outdated, and Marshfield, once the jewel of the South Atlantic region, had lost its edge. Exhibits had not been changed or refurbished in years. The current staff, most of whom had been with the manor for more than three decades, had grown complacent. If the estate were to retain its position as a vacation destination—moreover, if it wanted to increase its market share in the world of tourism—changes had to be made.

Head of security Terrence Carr was another new recruit, as were about a half dozen others. As new employees in key positions, we had been given a mandate: Bring Marshfield Manor into the twenty-first century. Not everyone was happy at our arrival. There were days I felt "Agent of Change" had been branded onto my forehead, causing staff members to either avoid me completely or go out of their way to explain just how important they were in the running of the mansion so I wouldn't consider cutting their jobs.

My title of assistant curator had come with an

understanding. When Abe retired—within the next year or so—I would be in the best position to be considered as his replacement. He not only served as museum curator, he was the mansion's director. As such, all staff members reported to him. And in a little more than a year, they might all report to me.

As long as I made it through this probationary period, of course.

Bennett apparently expected me to reply to his reminder. Instead I deflected. "Abe received another warning letter." I pointed upward, in the general direction of Bennett's private sanctuary on the fourth floor. "I think he's leaving it for you in your study right now, if you want to catch him."

Bennett straightened, taking a deep breath. "Trying to get rid of me, are you?"

"More like trying to ensure the manor's efficiency," I said, smiling to take the sting out of my words. According to the attorneys who had interviewed me, Abe had lost touch a long time ago. But they also warned me that Abe and Bennett were tight, and until Abe chose to retire, all decisions rested with him. This issue was non-negotiable.

"Abe gets worked up about these letters," Bennett said, waving his hand with a shoofly motion. "They're the work of a crank. I keep telling him that. But he worries about me." Casting a long glance around the Birdcage room, he added, "And about the manor."

I watched as our maintenance team restored the Birdcage. They righted chairs, fluffed cushions, and placed tables back where they had been before Percy's outburst. Waitresses carried out trays laden with sweets and savories, as busboys hurried out with replacement vases and fresh flowers for each of the distressed tables. While Bennett and I had been talking, the last of the fled guests had returned. Conversations resumed, china *clinked,* and I noticed a heightened, more jovial air than had been in the room before.

Danger as entertainment. Whatever worked.

I turned to Bennett. "A little excitement, and no one got hurt. I think we dodged a bullet here."

He was about to say something, but our walkie-talkies crackled to life, interrupting him. "Private channel," the dispatcher said, her voice strained. "All security switch to private channel."

Bennett and I moved in sync, grabbing our walkie-talkies and heading out the door. Only security and certain high-ranking staff members were allowed access to the private network. Bennett and I both switched over, and I was the first to open the line.

The dispatcher's voice was tense. "I repeat: Shots have been fired in the residence. Fourth floor. Private study. Authorities are on their way."

Bennett blanched. "The study. That's where I was supposed to meet Abe."

Chapter 2

I WAS TEN STEPS UP THE NEAREST STAIR-case when I thought about Bennett behind me. Although the man was in great physical shape, he *was* seventy years old. Running up four flights of stairs into possible gunfire was probably not a great idea. For him, or for me. But I hadn't been hired to run away from crises. I'd been hired to handle them.

I took comfort from the dispatcher's report: Shots had been fired. She hadn't said shots "were being" fired. I was betting this was a false alarm. And so I raced upward into the fray, convincing myself that my actions would do my career a lot of good. Especially during the probationary period.

I worried for Bennett, though. Slowing at the first landing, I turned. "Why don't you take the elevator?"

He growled an unintelligible reply. But I got the message.

"Okay," I said, resuming my race up the stairs. Although these were considered "back stairs" in that they were not open to the public, they were nonetheless ornate. My feet crushed into the thick carpet runner that spanned each step. As I cleared the third-floor landing, the stairway narrowed. We were getting into Bennett's private rooms here, an area of the mansion I was not privy to. Not yet.

My thighs burned as I hauled myself up the final set of stairs, panting. I wiped a thin bead of sweat from my hairline, thinking it had been too long since I'd hit the gym. Looking back, I wondered if I should wait for Bennett, but he was two flights behind me now. I pushed through the double doors at the top and walked into mayhem.

Rosa Brelke was sobbing. Our head of housekeeping sat on the floor of a wide wood-paneled corridor, her legs splayed out from her pale blue uniform skirt. She held her hands over her face, but there was no mistaking her cranberry red hair or her fireplug build. Next to her was one of our younger housekeepers. An attractive girl, her face was a pale mask of fear. For the life of me I couldn't remember her name. She was trying to comfort Rosa, crouching next to the sobbing woman, rubbing her back. Every second or two, the woman whose name I couldn't remember stole a glance across the hall. She looked as though she might throw up.

"Rosa," I called, but she didn't hear me. Her high-pitched wails went right up the back of my spine.

This was no false alarm. But I saw no blood. And except for her screams, she seemed unhurt. "Rosa!" I called again, as I crossed the floor toward her.

The crouching woman gently shook Rosa's shoulder and pointed to me. Rosa peeled her fingers away enough to look up. Her blotchy face expressed pain—loss—terror—and intense grief. All at once. Her wails became deep-throated moans and she pointed to her left across the corridor. A door was open.

As I reached the room, a door far down the hall banged open and four security guards rushed in, Terrence Carr at the lead. "What happened?" he shouted.

I had no words. Inside the room—Bennett's private study—Abe lay facedown in a puddle of blood. I started to move forward, but in the two seconds it had taken for my mind to process what I was seeing, Carr had reached me. He grabbed my arm. "No."

"But . . ." I pointed toward Abe. He wasn't moving. My words felt slow and hard to form. "We have to see if he's okay." That sounded stupid. He was definitely not okay. "I mean, if he's alive."

Carr met my eyes. "Stay here," he said and pushed me back a step. I complied.

By this time, Bennett had made it to the top of the stairs. He was panting worse than I had been and as he ran a hand through his white hair, I noticed him shaking. Striding slowly across the hallway, he stopped to talk to Rosa and the other woman, who were still on the floor. "Are you okay?"

Rosa's sobs had quieted to hard hiccups. She didn't answer. The other woman kept her hands on Rosa's shoulders, but her face turned toward the wall.

I backed away from the open door to allow security access to Abe. He lay in the room's center, as though he'd had his back to the windows when he fell. He was wearing a charcoal suit, but I could see the wet shine of blood between his shoulder blades. Carr crouched beside the elderly man, and reached around, groping for Abe's neck.

I held my breath.

The look on Carr's face told me all I needed to know.

A moan bubbled up from somewhere deep inside me. My vision went bright and sparkly. The room around me buzzed.

Struggling to catch his breath, Bennett grabbed my elbow just as my knees gave out. "Grace," he said. "Grace, what happened?"

The moment of weakness passed; I felt my body regain its strength. Still, I could do no better than Rosa had. I pointed into his study. "Abe," I said.

He let go of me. "Abe?" he asked, and started into the room.

One of the security guards stopped him. "Please, sir. It's best if you stay back."

"But this is my study." Bennett seemed more confused by an employee rebuffing him than by the body on the floor. "I must go in. Abe and I have a meeting planned."

"Sir," the guard said gently, stepping into the doorway to block Bennett's path. "If you could just wait out in the hall for a while." He flicked a glance at me and I tugged Bennett's arm.

Carr shouted to me. "Take Mr. Marshfield to his room. But wait until my guys secure the premises."

"Come on." I walked Bennett down the long corridor, the opposite direction from Rosa. "Let's let them do their jobs."

My boss's glower from earlier was long gone. He stared at me as though he had never seen me before. "Abe?" he asked. "Is he all right?"

Although I had never been in this part of the building, I figured I could find a place for Bennett to sit. Double doors at the end of the hall looked promising. "What's in there?" I asked, to distract him. "Can we find a seat?"

He nodded. "My room."

An officer jogged up behind us. "Wait," he said.

I didn't think Bennett would be steady enough to stand up much longer. "But—"

"Let me secure the area first."

Dutifully, Bennett and I waited until the young man came out and gave us the all-clear. I nodded my thanks.

I didn't care if I was breaking every level of protocol by escorting Bennett into his personal space. These were not ordinary circumstances. "Let's get you settled in there, okay?"

Like a little kid, he obeyed me. I held on to his arm while I propped open one of the doors with my behind. My breath caught the moment we were inside. Even in the dim light, I recognized its abundant splendor.

Bennett Marshfield was a chronic collector who had amassed treasures from all over the world and had adorned every nook and corner of Marshfield Manor with his finds. But in here, his accumulating had gone wild. There was not a single empty spot in the room. Racing vertically, horizontally, and in wide circles to take it all in, my eyes could not find a place to rest. It was too much—even for me. Could that be an original Rembrandt? No way to tell—there were too many trinkets piled in front of it, including a vase that looked suspiciously like a genuine Egyptian canopic jar. Books, maps, and papers covered and surrounded what might have been a Louis XIV chair. Unable to help myself, I gasped.

I couldn't leave him in here. There was nowhere to sit, even though this was clearly a sitting room. Two love seats placed opposite one another in front of a giant hearth were covered with . . . stuff. I glanced at Bennett and realized he wasn't focusing. "What's in there?" I asked. There were four sets of doors leading out of this room. I headed toward one of them.

He frowned. "What about Abe? When will they let me talk to him? I have to find out what happened."

"Let's get you settled," I said, hoping I'd chosen well. Gripping the knob, I pushed the door open to find Bennett's bedroom and breathed a sigh of relief. The clutter was minimal. There were places he could sit or even lie down. Bennett's bed was clear. I walked him to its side. "Why don't you just relax for a little bit. I'll get someone to stay with you."

As Bennett lifted himself onto his giant bed—a canopied monster with raw silk dressings in a muted butternut—I pulled up my walkie-talkie and requested medical assistance in the private rooms. The dispatcher asked if this was another emergency.

I spoke quietly, but Bennett had rolled over and had his back to me. I don't know that he even knew I was still there. "No," I said. "But Mr. Marshfield has suffered an enormous shock. I think it would be a good idea if the doctor looked in on him."

"Roger that," she said.

I was about to take a seat to wait for the doctor when I remembered the walkie-talkie Bennett carried. Fortunately for me, it was on his left hip and easy for me to slide off without his noticing. I had just gotten it pulled away when he twisted back, grabbing my forearm with both hands.

"Tell me," he said.

I took a shallow breath. "Tell you what?"

Letting go of my arm, he tried to sit up. "Abe. Is he . . ."

I bit my lip.

At that moment, our walkie-talkies came back to life, still broadcasting the private channel. "Security alert. Emergency shutdown. Homicide confirmed. One dead. I repeat: Emergency shutdown. Initiate Level One security protocols."

Bennett's eyes sought mine. Swollen red, they leaked rapid tears. He swallowed. "Abe was my friend."

I squeezed his hand. "I'm so sorry."

Chapter 3

"WAS THERE A LOT OF BLOOD?" BRUCE asked. He grimaced, exaggerating a shudder. "Except for my great-aunt Agatha, I've never actually seen anybody dead except in a casket. And definitely not bloody." He placed a hand on Scott's knee and turned to him expectantly. "Did you ever see a dead body? I mean, besides at a wake?"

On the love seat next to him, Scott nodded. "Yeah," he said, but didn't elaborate.

I was extraordinarily grateful for my roommates right now. When I'd gotten home, still stunned from the day's events, these two wonderful men had listened then comforted me as best they could. Leading me into the high-ceilinged parlor of our Victorian home, they sat me down on the sofa and pressed a glass of their finest Merlot in my hand, urging me to sip slowly. As the deep red liquid trailed down my throat and warmed my insides, I tucked my feet up under me and let the wine work its magic.

Handsome, buff, and tanned, my roommates could have played the Hardy Boys at thirty-five. A former Wall Street executive turned entrepreneur, Scott was surfer blond and had deep dimples that made women swoon. At least until they realized they were no competition for Bruce. For his part, Bruce was shorter, and though not nearly as elegant as Scott, he was no less handsome. He had broader shoulders, darker hair, and a nose that had been broken once. The two men owned and operated Amethyst Cellars, a darling little wine and tchotchke shop in town. Although always thoughtful and willing to help, right now they looked ready to leap into action if I so much as sighed.

Scott asked, "What happens now? I mean . . . your boss has been killed. Does that automatically make you the new curator?"

Down to the last drops of a second glass of wine, I'd calmed enough to converse without shaking. But I hadn't relaxed enough to consider what Abe's death meant for my career trajectory. "I doubt that," I answered slowly. "It seems awfully cold to be thinking about that, doesn't it?"

Scott leaned forward to pour me more Merlot, but I placed a hand over the top of my glass. "Come on," he said. "You've had a bad scare. One more glass and maybe you'll be able to sleep."

"I've had two. I'll sleep fine. A third would put me into a coma." I shook my head. "Remember, I have to go back there in the morning. Can you imagine how it would look if I called in sick?"

"That's what I'm trying to tell you, sweetie," Scott continued. "Somebody has got to take charge over there. Why not you? The place is going to be an insane asylum until they figure out who killed the old guy. You have to step into his shoes first thing in the morning, whether you feel ready or not. Show them what you're made of."

"It's not a question of being capable," I said. "For one, I've got more formal training than Abe had. And I've learned a lot about Marshfield Manor's specific procedures over the past two months, so I can probably hold my own. No." I shook my head again. "It just feels wrong to talk about taking over the job now. Abe was part of an extended Marshfield family. I'm still just an outsider."

"Outsider or not, they're going to need a steady hand at the helm," Bruce said. "And let me tell you, kid, you're the steadiest I've ever seen." He made a *tsk*ing noise. "The stuff you went through last year would've killed a lesser woman."

I upended my glass to finish my wine. "Thanks for the reminder, Bruce," I said.

"What?" he asked when Scott shot him a derisive look.

"Grace comes home from finding a murder victim and you cheer her up by talking about . . ." Scott's hands worked the air in front of him as though grasping for the right words, ". . . about *last year*?"

"I was just trying to give her a compliment. It isn't every girl who can lose her mother to cancer and her boyfriend . . ."

I held up a finger to correct him. "Fiancé," I said.

Bruce nodded, but didn't stop. ". . . her fiancé to another woman, and still be strong enough to build a life for herself in a brand-new town."

Scott interrupted. "Grace was born here, remember?"

He waved Scott off. "Yeah, but she was in New York before her mother got sick." Turning his full attention to me, he went on. "You had a whole life out there. An exciting life. And you left it all to care for your mom."

When he smiled beatifically, I reconsidered that third glass of wine. The guy was on a roll and wasn't about to let either of us thwart his dramatic narrative. Just what I wanted. To rehash all this. Tonight.

"Of course, with the benefit of hindsight," he continued, "I think moving here was one of the smartest moves you ever made. I didn't like that scummy Eric anyway. And Emberstowne didn't like him. I think the town scared him off, if you want to know the truth."

Emberstowne scare Eric off? I didn't think so. I had my own suspicions about the mystery woman who had caused Eric to dump me just weeks after my mother's funeral, but those feelings were too raw to put into words.

Scott sighed. "Let's talk about something happier, shall we?"

I held up my empty glass in salute. "I agree. What can we talk about?"

The room went silent. Bruce looked at me, then at Scott. Scott lifted his chin as though expecting Bruce to jump in. Bruce shook his head.

Scott opened his mouth then shut it again. As for me, I had nothing to offer. My body and mind were sapped of energy and the wine was making me drowsy. But like the elephant in the room, the murder couldn't be ignored. Nor could the memory of last year's disappointments. We all strained to not discuss either. I knew I didn't want to go through it all again. But what else was there?

Bruce was right about one thing: When Mom had first gotten sick, I'd left a plum position in New York to be with her in Emberstowne. My sister, Liza, claimed she couldn't break away, but promised to come help just as soon as she could. That hadn't surprised me. She'd finally made it into town a scant week before Mom died. And she'd stayed just long enough to collect her share of inheritance before she was off again to parts unknown. That hadn't surprised me either.

The thought of where my sister was now and what she might be doing depressed me. Needing a distraction, I glanced at my watch then reached for the remote. As I turned on the TV, I said, "Let's see if there are any updates on the Marshfield story."

We all watched together as the newscast led off with Abe's murder. From all reports there were no new leads in the case. The anchorwoman mentioned that the police were questioning a person of interest.

"You think they caught the guy?" Bruce asked.

"No," I said. "I bet they mean Percy."

"The fat boy who caused the ruckus? They think he's involved in the murder?"

I nodded. "The police have to assume so. The timing was just too precise to be ignored. They're keeping him overnight for questioning." I made a face at the TV. "And here I believed he was just some random troublemaker looking for food. He had me fooled. I sure hope they sweat the truth out of him tonight."

Scott and Bruce looked as convinced of that outcome as I felt.

When the murder news segment ended and the focus switched to that of the T. Randall Taft swindling scandal, I got to my feet. "I hate to break up this cozy evening," I said, "but I'm going to bed."

Bruce pointed to the TV. "Hey, look. Your boss. Twice in one night."

I turned, half-expecting to see another photo of Abe on the screen, but was surprised by footage of Bennett Marshfield instead. He waved cameras away, looking annoyed. The anchor's voice-over reported, "But the most incriminating testimony came from billionaire Bennett Marshfield, who took the stand first thing this morning. Marshfield told the jury how he began to suspect his former friend T. Randall Taft of creating a Ponzi scheme to lure innocent investors. Prosecutors are confident that Marshfield's testimony will be what ultimately delivers a guilty verdict in this case."

The footage continued following Marshfield as he stepped into a waiting limousine and the driver shut the door, effectively closing his employer off from the extended microphones and eager cameras. The anchor added, "Outside of the courtroom, Mr. Marshfield refused to comment on allegations against his former friend."

"Whoa," I said, half to myself. "I had no idea that's where he was today. No wonder he said it wasn't a good morning."

"Taft took a lot of bigwigs down," Bruce said as he started to clean up. "Marshfield is just the tip of the iceberg."

Scott said, "I've been following this since the story broke. Marshfield *is* the iceberg. Taft had already gotten a lot of wealthy folks on board. It was Marshfield who was his undoing. He's the guy who turned him in."

When the news broke for a commercial, I was ready to hit the sack. The day had tired me out, but the evening had, too. At some point in the conversation, things had shifted from my roommates trying to cheer me up, to me trying to convince them I was sufficiently cheered.

Scott took my wineglass. "I'll clean up. You take care of you."

"Thanks," I said, grateful to head upstairs and put my spinning head to rest. I couldn't even blame it all on the wine. There was just too much in there for one brain to keep straight.

With a hand on my carved oak banister I took a moment to stare up the wide staircase, wondering if life would look brighter when I headed back down. Poor Abe. There would be no tomorrow morning for him. "I have to go in early," I called over my shoulder. "Try to beat the reporters in, y'know. So I probably won't see you guys until evening."

Scott had two wineglasses in his hand and was just about to walk past me.

"Oh my gosh," I said, suddenly remembering. "Today was the interview!" I felt like a jerk for forgetting. I often stopped by their Amethyst Cellars shop on the way home, but after today's events, it just wasn't possible. Spinning to face them, I spoke fast, as though to make up for lost time. "Did the woman like the store? How did it go?"

Scott's face lit up and Bruce stepped up behind him, the two looking the happiest I'd seen them all night. Scott's voice held unmistakable glee when he said, "It went . . . well."

Bruce boomed, "That's an understatement! The woman spent over two hours in the shop sampling things and asking questions. Good questions, too. She kept complimenting us on our displays and especially on our wines. She was pretty sure that she'll be able to convince *Grape Living* to feature us. She said they would send out a photographer and everything."

"That's wonderful! Why didn't you tell me earlier?"

Scott shrugged. "We thought about it. But we didn't want to step on Abe's grave with our good news. Bad karma, you know?"

I smiled at the two of them. Having *Grape Living* do a feature on their wine shop was a coup beyond their wildest dreams. Such national exposure could drive lots of new business to their little store, where they were currently just making ends meet. A boost like this would be a godsend.

"No bad karma," I said. "Good news is good news. Now let's just hope it can carry us into a better day tomorrow."

Chapter 4

MY WINDSHIELD WIPERS BEAT A SOLEMN rhythm as I made the early drive in to Marshfield the next day. Each blade swipe cleared the blurry window so briefly, I didn't dare blink. I concentrated on the shadowy road as I drove—at half the speed limit—hoping for relief from this relentless rain. Dark gray clouds somersaulted overhead and I glanced at my dashboard clock just to reassure myself that it was, indeed, morning. The sky cracked with lightning, and thunder shook my little red car, the only vehicle on this twisty highway at five A.M.

I could have turned on my radio for company but at times like these I preferred to focus without distraction. How strange life was. Abe had been murdered in what should have been a safe place on a bright sunlit day, as different from this one as could be imagined.

Lightning zinged in front of me and I jerked away, swerving instinctively. The car's back end fishtailed and its tires hydroplaned as I fought to steer out of the oncoming lanes. My heart beat louder and faster than the wiper blades and I was glad there had been no one else on this narrow stretch of road.

Today seemed more appropriate for murder than yesterday had. And this lonely stretch of forest seemed a far better venue. This was the sort of setting I might expect for so vile a crime. And yet I knew from personal experience that life was never exactly as we expected it to be. Why should death be any different?

Involuntarily, I shuddered. Emberstowne was a sweet, safe haven. At least, it had been up until recently. Among us, we now not only had a swindler who targeted friends. We had a murderer in our midst.

We all felt safe, I supposed, until we didn't. When tragedy struck, it shattered everything. The trick was learning to put the pieces back together again.

By the time I pulled up to the employee gate, the rain had lessened enough for me to decrease my wiper speed. I reached up to press the remote clipped to my visor and the cyclone gate jerked to life, rolling open to allow me entrance. For the first time I saw this barrier for what it was: nothing. The Marshfield estate was so sprawling that a mere fence—even with its barbed-wire crown—was no match for an intent trespasser. Heck, whoever had killed Abe could very well have been a guest at our hotel. I hadn't considered that last night when I gave my statement, but I imagined the detective I'd spoken with had. I hoped so.

I followed the employee road to the mouth of the

underground parking lot. The red-and-white-striped barrier tucked between trees looked a lot like the entrance to the Batcave. I pressed my remote again and the arm raised to admit me. Years ago, when staff members no longer lived in and began driving themselves to work, this underground lot was created to keep the landscape clear of unsightly vehicles. Now golf carts, and the occasional limousine, were the only motorized means of transport allowed aboveground in the mansion's perimeter.

I caught sight of several squad cars parked along the walking path. Well, today was an exception, I guess.

I parked and got out. A single tunnel ran between the garage and the house. I waved hello to Ned, a security guard standing at the tunnel's entry. This was a change since yesterday. We all usually just came and went without notice. Ned nodded acknowledgment from his new station. The tunnel ahead, with its low, curved ceiling and concrete walls, reminded me of the ones in movies where rats scurry and the hero sloshes through puddles, a fiery torch his only means of illumination. The difference here, however, was though the tunnel was dank, the floor was dry. Fluorescent lights buzzed above, more than adequately lighting my path. My heels skip-tapped my nervousness as I hurried through. After yesterday, nothing felt safe.

Another new addition: a guard at the basement entrance. He stopped me long enough to check my ID. We planned to eventually install ID card readers throughout the mansion, but retrofitting such a system into an historical building took a great deal of effort and planning. I knew Carr had already begun seeking bids for the job, but the added security would come too late for Abe.

I made my way across the building to the far west wing, then up three flights to the anteroom I shared with my assistant, Frances. The room was dark and though the thunder was fading, rumbles from outside still shook the glass in the next room. There were no windows in this anteroom—we were landlocked here, with Abe's quiet office just beyond the carved oak doors. At one time, this combined space served as sitting room and bedchamber for Marshfield guests and I appreciated the opulence that remained from that more genteel time. Winged cherubs floating in a pastel sky graced the ceiling. I wondered what the little chubbies thought when they looked down and saw the filing cabinets, the copier, and assorted business furniture that replaced the gracious living of yore.

Leaving my purse and jacket at my desk, I headed back out to the corridor, passing other similarly outfitted offices to get to the back stairway and up to the fourth floor.

One of Carr's deputies—a young man of about

twenty-five—met me at the top landing. "No admittance," he said.

I held up my badge. "I'm . . . I *was* Abe's first assistant," I said. "Now that he's gone, there's no one to oversee management of the estate. Until they appoint someone else, that responsibility falls to me."

He looked skeptical, until I added, "That means I'm your boss. At least for now."

Carr had come up behind the young man and placed a hand on the kid's shoulder. "She's right, Cubbie. Let her through." To me, he said, "I wanted to talk with you anyway. Glad you came early."

"Cubbie?" I asked, when we were out of earshot. "Is that really his name?"

Carr's eyes crinkled as he smiled. "Nah. We call him that because he's this huge Chicago Cubs fan. His locker's covered with stickers and he's always wearing a jersey or jacket and talking about how many days until their opener."

"What did you want to talk about?"

"We're going to have people in and out all day. My team has been on duty overnight and they're starting to fade. I called in everybody, but we're still going to wind up shorthanded for this kind of coverage."

"The mansion is closed to visitors today," I said.

He nodded, as though he'd expected as much. Lowering his voice, he stopped walking. "This team wasn't ready for an emergency of this magnitude. They need training, support, and . . ." he glanced around the area to make sure we weren't being overheard, ". . . sophistication. I knew when I started here that I had a big job ahead of me, but I never expected this."

I started to say that no one had, but he interrupted. "I got caught unprepared. My fault." The smile was long gone. "And I'm going to need your help."

"Of course."

"As the detectives clear my team for duty, I want to put them to work up here and in other key areas of the residence. We're going to need all the eyes and ears we can get. I can only work with a skeleton crew at the moment; security personnel I can vouch for myself, but as soon as I get relief for them, I'm going to take it."

"What about the local police? Aren't they willing to help out?"

Carr frowned. "Their resources are limited, too."

"I thought they were bringing in a task force."

He started walking again, gesturing me to follow. "Did you see the news last night?"

"Part of it."

"You heard about the bank robbery in Springfield?"

"No . . ."

"Five people shot." His face was grim. "And the guy got away with less than ten thousand dollars.

46

What a waste." He shook his head. "Any task force we might have hoped for has been pulled away to handle that. We're stuck with what we have. Between you and me, a little hamlet like Emberstowne doesn't have the kind of police force you'd find in a big city because we don't usually get big-city crime. The detectives assigned to us have probably never even investigated a murder before. Couple of robberies, some assaults, but nothing as big as this."

"Well, just let me know what you need," I said.

"Thanks."

We stopped outside Bennett's study, which was cordoned off with bright yellow crime scene tape. There were two uniformed officers standing guard at the door; inside the restricted area, two evidence technicians were cataloging samples and taking pictures.

"I thought this was supposed to be done last night."

Carr gave me an I-told-you-so shrug. "Yeah, but it took this long for them to get here from the state crime lab."

Two plainclothes armed men were down the hall, talking with another security guard. "Where's the detective from last night?"

"Which one?"

"I didn't get his name," I said. "Fifty-ish maybe? Average height. Maybe a little paunch?"

"You've just described half the people in here

yesterday." He grimaced. The long hours were obviously taking their toll on Carr. "Some of them are still here. Some of them went back to the station to sweat out that fat guy, Percy. You see what I mean? I haven't been able to establish any sort of structure here. I don't have any control over who's coming or going."

"We've got a lot of priceless antiques here."

"Tell me something I don't know."

I knew Carr would do his utmost to protect the mansion, its people, and its treasures so I decided to change the subject. "Did they find the letter yet?"

"What letter?"

Surprised the police hadn't bothered to share this crucial piece of information with our head of security, I brought Carr up to date with regard to the threatening letters Marshfield had received. "I didn't know anything about them until the most recent one arrived," I said. "I opened it and took it to Abe. That's when he told me he'd received several others before that one. He was taking the newest threat to show Bennett when he was killed."

Carr swore under his breath. "No," he said, his disgust evident. "I don't believe any letters were found on Abe's body. But I will look into this."

"That's the main reason I came up here this morning," I said. "The detective I talked with said he had to wait until the evidence technicians cleared out."

Carr's brow tightened. "Hmph."

I tilted my head toward the two plainclothes fellows down the hall. "I should probably go talk to them."

Cubbie called to Carr.

"In a minute," Carr said. Then to me: "You're right. The local cops and the task force will need to talk with the entire staff. Even people who weren't on-site yesterday. You're going to have to make sure that everyone cooperates."

"Got it," I said. As he trotted toward Cubbie, I made my way to the detectives. They chose that moment, however, to head eastward down the hall toward Bennett's room. That would be a tough interview. Deciding not to interrupt, I moved into the study's doorway, my fingers skimming the slick, yellow tape as I stared in. Except for the large bloodstain on the area rug, and one small table that had been turned on its side, the room looked ordinary. They had removed Abe's body last night after I'd left. The far windowed wall overlooked the south grounds, which were beginning to brighten. I sighed. Despite the low chatter of the professionals around me, I had never felt so lonely.

Shaking myself as though to dispel the melancholy, I headed toward the stairs, and my office. I had no doubt the detective I spoke with would be back for more today—which is why I'd gotten in so early. I wanted to be sure the mansion was running as smoothly as possible, before my time was no longer my own.

Chapter 5

FRANCES, OUR ADMINISTRATIVE ASSIS-
tant, had arrived while I was upstairs. Wide-set,
with a neck that cascaded over the top of her
lavender turtleneck, she looked up when I walked
in. Her carefully penciled eyebrows always
reminded me of fat tadpoles. Right now they were
raised high over half-moon glasses. Whether that
was an expression of anticipation or annoyance, I
couldn't tell. "We've never closed Marshfield
before," she said by way of greeting. "This is a
first. Except for Christmas and Thanksgiving
every year, we don't ever close the manor."
Making a clucking sound, she added, "There's
going to be trouble. You'll see."

I was perturbed, both by her tone and by her
apparent lack of concern after yesterday's murder.
"There already has been trouble," I said. "Didn't
you hear about Abe?"

For a woman who prided herself on knowing
everything that went on at the mansion at any
given minute, I'd pushed a button. She shot me a
withering glare. "Who hasn't?" Continuing to
press her point, she said, "Just wait. I predict that
by nine o'clock this morning we won't be able to
handle all the calls. People make plans, you know.

They come here for their vacation. They spend good money. Why should we refuse to let them tour the mansion today? The murder didn't take place in any of the public rooms." She made another noise of disgust as she glanced at her watch. "Complaints to high heaven. Just as soon as we open the switchboard. Mark my words."

She stared as though daring me to disagree. After two months of dealing with Frances's roadblock attitude, I knew better than to continue this conversation. A Marshfield employee since before I was born, she was convinced it was she who ran the place, and that the manor would be lost without her. She had no patience for those who didn't agree with her every proclamation. Abe had cautioned me that Bennett intended to keep her on until she retired. No negotiation. Surprise, surprise.

I scratched my head. How in the world were we new people supposed to bring this business into the twenty-first century with such millstones around our necks? Frances's grimace warned me she was poised to strike if I dared open my mouth. Rather than grant her the pleasure, I smiled and crossed the room we shared. Instead of taking a seat at my desk, however, I changed my trajectory and headed for Abe's office. I had my hand on the doorknob when Frances stood up, tugging the sweater down over her midsection where it had ridden up. "Where are you going?"

Last time I checked, Frances reported to me, not

the other way around. "Lots to get done before all those phone calls start. We need a plan for making good on all the admission tickets issued for today. Why don't you come up with a script for our switchboard?"

Her mouth set in a line and she sat back down behind her desk, spinning in her chair to face forward—pointedly away from me.

"Run it past me before you give it to them, okay?" I didn't wait for acknowledgment, but mused aloud. "Today's Wednesday."

"Uh-huh. All day," she said sing-song.

Ignoring her tone, I continued. "Good thing. Wednesday is one of our slower days." Being early spring meant we weren't in high season yet. That time would come just after Memorial Day. "Chances are, most of our guests are on multiday tickets. They can still have access to the grounds and enjoy all the amenities of the hotel and outdoor attractions. We can offer to extend their hotel stay by an extra day, or we can offer them entrance tickets again at any time of their choosing."

Arranging her already neat desk—aligning paper corners and reshuffling pens—Frances made a show of not listening. But I knew better. Despite all her guff, she excelled at her job. If a detail needed to be remembered, you could be sure Frances remembered it. She spent the mansion's money as if it were her own, and she guarded the place and its people with unsurpassed vigor. She was not, however, a woman prone to displays of sentiment and I wondered how much Abe's death had really hit her. They had known each other since they both started here, almost forty years ago. She couldn't be as unfeeling as she came across.

I started toward Abe's office again.

Frances asked, "What about guests who can't stay or can't come back?" I moved closer to her desk and she finally looked up. "What if this was a family's onetime trip and they can't extend it an extra day. What then?"

"Let's deal with those situations on a case-by-case basis," I said. "In the meantime, do whatever it takes to keep our guests happy."

"Happy. *Pheh*." Her mouth twisted downward. "They wouldn't know happy if it came up and bit them. All they ever do is complain."

I refrained from making a comment about pots and kettles, and entered Abe's sanctuary without further resistance.

Closing the door behind me, I leaned against it for a long moment. Abe's office was as spartan as Bennett's room had been cluttered, but it was stunning nonetheless. Enormous mullioned windows spanned one wall, and I gasped in awe at the endless vista before me. I had been in this room before, of course, but today—for the first time—spring had taken hold of the estate, creating a feast of color as though to dispel the mansion's overwhelming sadness. The rain had worked wonders, creating a panorama of shocking green. Grassy fields, ornamental gardens, and a maze of evergreens were brighter in hue than they had been since I began working here. As a child, I'd walked the grounds with my hand tucked firmly in my mom's but I had never seen the change into spring from this vantage point before.

Just as I stepped away from the door it opened behind me, smacking me in the back. Hard.

Frances's voice was high, agitated. "Why are you standing behind the door? You scared of getting too close to the desk? Afraid Abe's ghost will come back and haunt you for messing with his things?"

"I'm fine, thanks," I said, massaging my left shoulder.

"I hope you're not expecting me to knock every time I come in. Abe never did. Of course, he never stood right behind the door either." She made a face. "Were you spying on me?"

"What did you need, Frances?"

Thrusting a sheet of paper at me, she cocked one of her tadpole eyebrows. "Here's that script you wanted."

"But I asked you for it less than a minute ago."

With an exaggerated shrug she turned back to her desk. "Guess maybe I knew exactly what you needed before you did, huh?"

She was absolutely right. She had anticipated our

exact needs. I watched her settle herself back at her desk, squirming into her seat with a self-satisfied grin. We would get along so much better if she could pair her expert efficiency with a smidgen of friendliness, but today wasn't the best time to suggest that. I read over the transcript she'd prepared. "Thanks," I said, "this is great."

She glanced up. "Anything else you need right now?"

"I'll let you know."

This time when I closed the door, I crossed the room immediately. Abe's massive oak desk was set at an angle in the far corner so that the windows were to his left and the fireplace to his right. A coffered ceiling of carved teak provided a mix of beauty and gravitas—the perfect setting for serious curator and directorial work.

Right now, however, instead of appreciating the view or the décor, I needed to find the threat we'd received yesterday afternoon. Since the police hadn't found the letter Abe intended to show Bennett, it had to be here. Unless, of course, the killer had taken it with him when he fled.

Either way, we now knew the threats were real. Bennett had pooh-poohed that idea, but he had been proven horribly wrong. I stared upward at the ornate ceiling, thinking about Bennett one floor above. I hadn't seen him since leaving him in the doctor's care yesterday.

Returning my attention to the desk, I flipped

through Abe's calendar and searched through the papers on his blotter. There were so few, it didn't take long. No letter. The one that had arrived yesterday wasn't the first we'd received, so I decided to think like Abe. He would have created a file. And he would have kept it nearby.

Taking a seat in his soft leather chair, I bit my lip. "Sorry, Abe," I said aloud. "But I need to see what you've got here."

The man was organized. His desk, an antique from America's colonial era, had relatively small drawers, and in them he had chosen to store items most people keep on top of their desks. Paper clips, tape, stapler, pens. All these were tucked away in neat, sectioned compartments.

I twirled to my left to face the windowed wall. Under the wide sill at the base of the paned glass were filing cabinets that had been custom fitted to utilize the space. These were relatively new and had been designed to accommodate everything from letter- to legal-sized documents. Most of the mansion's files were stored in the office I shared with Frances, but I imagined Abe kept a great deal here, out of the nosy assistant's curious reach.

"Good morning, Grace."

I spun. Bennett Marshfield stood before me, looking as though he hadn't slept much. While he generally favored pastel blues and khakis, today he wore black slacks and a matching long-sleeved shirt with an open collar. The dark color accentuated the shadows under his eyes.

I stumbled over my return greeting as I stood.

"Frances tells me you're eager to take over Abe's position."

Frances stood in the doorway, gloating.

"I thought it would be helpful to find that letter," I said. Feeling like a kid caught Web-surfing when she should be doing her homework, my face flushed hot and my words came out fast. "Abe intended to bring you the latest threatening letter. I know he must have had it on him yesterday when he . . . when he came to see you."

Bennett rubbed his eyebrow. "That letter is long gone. I'm sure of it. Whoever . . . whoever . . ." He worked his jaw. "That letter is gone."

"Yes," I began, "but—"

"You young people are always in such a hurry." His voice was low but emotion trembled behind it as he continued. "Abe hasn't been gone for twenty-four hours yet. Is it too much to ask that we wait a respectable amount of time before we erase all that he was?"

"I'm not trying to erase anything—"

"Oh no?" Bennett tilted his head toward the office I shared with Frances. She'd remained in the doorway. The better to listen in, I supposed. "I can see no reason for you to be rooting around in here."

I took a breath, keeping my gaze steady and my

voice calm. "Abe was very thorough. You *know* how thorough he was. Even if the original is gone, I'm sure he would have kept a copy."

I could tell the thought hadn't occurred to him. He gave a brief nod. More acknowledgment than apology. "You're right, of course. I should have thought of that."

"I can help," I said. "Abe taught me a lot. I can keep things running here the way he would. That is, if you'll let me."

Silence hung between us for a long moment. Finally, he nodded. "For now I will expect you to act as liaison between the manor and the police." This was a directive, not a request. I nodded, and he turned toward the door.

There was a flash of lavender behind him— Frances scurrying back to her desk before he could catch her eavesdropping.

"Before you go . . ." I said. "Could you tell me just a little more about the letters you received before the one yesterday?"

Aiming for one of the office's red leather chairs, he took a faltering step. Instinctively, I started around the desk to help, but he warned me back with a look. While he had always been the picture of vitality and could have been a poster boy for AARP, today his height made him look gaunt and his black clothing rendered him pale. "Sit," he said as he settled himself in one of the two wing-back chairs. I sat.

Bennett stared out the mullioned window. "I have a similar view from upstairs."

Not knowing what else to say, I murmured, "It's gorgeous."

He kept his attention on the grounds. "Yes."

For a moment I was afraid Bennett might break down. He wasn't just seeing the grounds outside this window, of that I was certain. Abe had been hired here a long time ago, back when he and Bennett were young. From what I'd heard, Abe's parents worked on the estate, too, so just like Bennett, Abe had grown up here. Losing Abe had to be like losing a best friend.

As Bennett's eyes grew red and he worked his jaw again, I realized that that was probably exactly what had happened. As an only child of privilege, he may have had friends among the children of his parents' friends, but here at home, who did he have?

I stared out the window to give Bennett time to compose himself.

No wonder Abe had become the curator-director. Of all positions on staff, this was the most prestigious, the most important. In other countries, such a position is referred to as the "palace manager," because in addition to maintaining all the museum-quality artifacts, the "palace" must be managed, like a business. Whoever is in charge must be able to wear ten hats and juggle a hundred crises at once.

Although Abe took care of Marshfield Manor to the best of his ability, there was no doubt he had not kept up with new and better efficiencies. As a result, the place had developed a patina of neglect. From what I understood, Bennett had initially fought the idea of bringing on someone new—he preferred to promote from within. A great concept, except for the fact that most of those qualified to take over the position at Marshfield were near retirement age themselves.

Bennett's anger at seeing me invade Abe's space made sense. I understood how important it was to him to keep things static—for now. But I wanted this job. I wanted it more than anything else in my life.

Even Eric? My brain taunted me with the question and the sudden, unbidden memory of his departure made me frown.

"What are you thinking about?" Bennett asked.

I gave a wry smile and a vague reply. "It's a day for sad memories, I guess."

He seemed to understand my reluctance to share. Straightening his shoulders, he asked, "What did you want to know about the other letters?"

"You don't happen to have copies, do you?"

He shook his head.

"I'm sure I'll find them here somewhere," I began. "Do you remember when they started?"

"No. When Abe showed me the first one, I laughed. Told him to throw it away. Just silliness, I was sure. People are always trying to get something from me." He ran his gaze around the room, as though seeing it through new eyes. "I suppose I don't blame them." His voice grew soft. "They believe I have so much more than they do."

Frances was probably having a hard time hearing our conversation. I liked that thought.

Keeping Bennett on topic, I asked if they had taken the letters to the police.

"I told Abe not to," he said, swallowing. "Maybe if I had—"

"It's possible the letters have nothing to do with . . ." Why was it that none of us could say the actual words? "Nothing to do with what happened yesterday. We may find that the letters were just silliness and whoever . . . whoever broke in yesterday was completely uninvolved with that."

He nodded, but I could tell he didn't agree. It was as though he'd aged a decade overnight. Pain lined his face, deepening his scowl. "What the hell happened to our security? I thought we were improving that."

I nodded. This wasn't the time to argue, but I couldn't throw Carr under the bus either. "That's one of the projects we've been working on," I said. "Terrence Carr has been implementing excellent changes . . ."

Bennett's eyes glittered. "But he didn't protect Abe, did he?"

"Installing a new system is a huge undertaking.

With such an enormous expense, we want to make the right decision . . ."

"A big expense?" Anger nearly propelled Bennett out of his chair. "Do you think there is any expense I would refuse to protect my people?"

I held my hands up and spoke very quietly. "Of course not. But no one could have anticipated this."

Bennett nodded absently. "A big expense," he said again. "That's why Abe argued against upgrading our security. He said we were adequately covered, adequately staffed. I believed him." His voice trailed off and I waited. "We were wrong about that."

"Honestly, we don't know who was behind all this," I said. "But I think figuring out the timeline will help. And finding the old letters." Not for the first time, I wished I'd been brought in on this issue from the start.

Bennett made a so-so motion with his head. "Maybe."

He turned to face the window again, the blue of his eyes aglow with memories. I hated to interrupt him, but it didn't take long for him to snap back to reality. "I'm sorry," he said, getting to his feet. "You go ahead and do what needs to be done." Was it my imagination or was he relieved to be able to rely on me? "If you need anything from me, I'm right upstairs."

I stood when he did, reluctant to broach the next

topic—but it had to be done. "Abe told me he had direct contact with you. Anything I needed, I went through him. Since that's no longer an option, how can I best get in touch with you?"

He twisted his lips and turned toward the fireplace, his face a mask. I couldn't read him. Was my question so out of line? Staff members had been forbidden to contact Bennett Marshfield without routing through Abe. While the master of the castle possessed a walkie-talkie to monitor the premises as desired, we were never to contact him without permission. Abe had made that clear.

If Abe had done nothing else, he had insulated Bennett. Asking to breach that chasm was a big deal and I knew it. It was as though I was asking for Bennett's de facto permission to completely take over where Abe had left off.

Dragging his attention back to the question, Bennett sized me up. Again. He rattled off his phone extension. "You will have questions. You may call as needed." He licked his lips. Buying time—coming to a decision. Finally, he added, "I will provide you a set of keys. These will grant you access to some private areas. We will discuss the keys' usage at a later date."

His face crumpled and he stared out the window for a long moment to compose himself. "I haven't thanked you," he finally said, "for all you did for me last night."

"I was glad to help."

Without making eye contact, he gave a curt nod and headed for the door.

I wanted to press him, to ask about his involvement in the Taft scandal, but this was not the right moment. To bring up the pain of his swindling friend's legal troubles would be to kick a man when he was down.

As Bennett made it through the doorway, he addressed my assistant. "How's the eavesdropping business today, Frances? Learn anything new?"

Chapter 6

FRANCES APPEARED IN THE DOORWAY the moment the outer door closed. "Do I still call you Grace, or are you going to insist on Ms. Wheaton now?" I was still in Abe's office, trying to think of where he might have kept the threatening letters.

"Grace will be fine."

Frances had one thick fist jammed into her hip, while the other hand waved about, making a jingling sound as the dozen brass bracelets encircling her wrist jockeyed for position. "You sure don't waste time."

I ignored the bait. "Do you know where Abe kept those letters?" No need to pretend she hadn't overheard.

"'Bout time you asked me." Pivoting, she marched back into our shared office. I followed her to a tall filing cabinet on my side of the room. She wagged her head as she spoke. "Of course he asked me to file them. Abe understood I keep tabs on everything that goes on around here. I knew exactly where to put them."

"Why didn't you tell me this sooner?"

"You never asked. If you hadn't been talking so loud in there, I probably still wouldn't know what you were doing." She stared at me with a saccharine smile, bringing those tadpole eyebrows together. "You have to trust me," she said. "It's the only way you'll get things done around here." She pulled out a manila folder from a purple hanging file labeled "Old applications." The smile was still frozen in place as she handed it to me. "Here you go."

"You didn't think to pull these out yesterday?"

Her forehead creased and I realized she really hadn't thought to do that. "How was I supposed to know these might be connected to what happened? Bennett sure didn't think they were important."

Yeah, I wanted to say. And now someone's dead. Instead I asked, "Why was it filed with applications?"

"Because nobody would think to look there," she said with a shrug. "Abe believed in being careful. It's a lesson worth learning."

"But he trusted you?"

Oblivious to my sarcasm, she nodded. "Of course."

Letters in hand, I beeped Carr on the security channel and asked him to have the police stop by as soon as they were able.

"Roger that," he answered.

That done, I eased into my desk chair and shook out the file. It was a slim folder, with four individual sheets inside. Abe hadn't kept the envelopes, so I had to guess the order in which they'd arrived.

Three originals, four copies. All in twelve-point Courier font, the letters had been typed in all caps on cream-colored construction paper that appeared slightly water damaged. Odd. These days, everything was done on standard office paper. If I were sending a threat, I'd be sure to use the most plain, widely available materials around. Much tougher to track down when everyone owns the same stock. This gave me hope that the authorities might be able to glean clues from these sheets.

I read the photocopied note—no doubt the most recent one:

FINAL WARNING
   PAY TODAY OR SUFFER CONSE-
QUENCES

Well, wasn't that succinct?

For an extortion letter, it was woefully short on direction. Pay what? And to whom? I was about to scan the other three missives for clues when I stopped. There was no telling how many fingerprints had already marred the originals, but I sure didn't want to add mine to the mix. I pulled a pair of white cotton gloves from my desk drawer and put them on. I always kept extra gloves handy just in case I needed to inspect a valuable artifact. This mansion was home to thousands of treasures, some of which could be harmed by coming in contact with skin oils.

Safely snug in my gloves, I took the letters over to the copier and made duplicates for my files. Frances watched me, her confusion apparent. "Two sets of copies?" she asked. "What do you need two copies for?"

Instead of answering, I glanced at the grandfather clock near the door. "It's almost nine. Are the switchboard operators ready with that script?"

"Of course."

How the woman maintained such efficiency even as she eavesdropped was beyond me. "Good." Making a bold decision, I gathered originals and copies and made for Abe's office. "I'll go over these in here," I said as I reached for the door. "When the police arrive, show them in, please."

She scowled.

Two seconds later, Abe's desk phone beeped with an interoffice alert. I picked up the handset. "Yes, Frances?"

"Should I start moving all your personal items in there?"

I stared out the window at the sea of greenery below, forcing myself to remember that I was still relatively new and that Frances would naturally feel protective of the mansion and all who worked here, living and deceased. I didn't care for her surliness, and we would definitely address her attitude in an upcoming review, but for the next few days until we settled into our new roles, I decided to cut her some slack.

"No, thank you," I said with patience I hoped communicated through the phone.

She clicked off, and just as she did, the phone's base began lighting up with the flicker of incoming calls. We had an old-fashioned corded system, with push-button access to different lines. I glanced toward the fireplace, where a gleaming gold mantel clock ticked one minute after nine. Here come the complaints. Right on time. I just hoped most of our disappointed patrons would be mollified by our efforts. We had some of the nicest, most personable staffers on our switchboard. I had faith in them.

Finally able to get a good look at the warning letters, I studied them one at a time. What I guessed to be the first letter was also the most verbose:

YOU WILL DEPOSIT $500,000 IN THE ACCOUNT BELOW BY NEXT FRIDAY. DON'T ASK QUESTIONS. DON'T CALL POLICE.

PAY NOW OR YOU WILL BE VERY SORRY. YOU MAY HAVE EVERYTHING BUT YOU ARE NOT UNTOUCHABLE. YOU WILL LOSE ALL UNLESS YOU ARE SMART. KEEP YOUR MOUTH SHUT AND PAY.

There was information regarding a bank account number in another country and specific directions as to how to wire funds into it. Five hundred thousand was a lot of money, but apparently not enough of a threat to worry Bennett. I wondered if he would have taken it more seriously if the extortionists had asked for more.

I got my answer in the next letter.

YOUR DEADLINE PASSED AND YOU DID NOT DEPOSIT.
NOW YOU WILL PAY $5,000,000 BY FRIDAY THE 20TH, OR WATCH OUT.

Five million certainly upped the ante, but still Bennett hadn't seen fit to take these missives to the police. Not to speak ill of the dead, but it occurred to me that Abe should have taken the situation into his own hands and alerted the cops whether or not Bennett approved. This was serious. And yet Bennett had believed that, if ignored, the problem would go away. The letter gave the date of Friday, the 20th. I leafed backward through the calendar and decided that this one probably referred to either February or March. At least we were narrowing down the time frame.

The third letter was cryptic.

DON'T BE STUPID.
NEXT WEDNESDAY.

Okay, I mused, leafing through the calendar again. A Wednesday after February or March twentieth. I got up, opened the door, and waited for Frances to complete her phone conversation before asking, "Did anything happen here at the manor during February or March? Anything bad? On a Wednesday?"

"Nope."

"You're sure?"

"Abe made sure to keep an eye open that week. And the next week, too."

That week? I felt a tingle of excitement. "So you remember the date these letters started arriving?"

"We got the first one on January eighteenth."

Why did I keep forgetting that Frances was the oracle and that I should always consult her first? "Thanks, Frances," I said, grateful for the information. I jotted dates down. "This may help."

"Anything else?"

"As a matter of fact," I said, "there is."

She folded her hands on her desk, but kept one eye on the flashing phone lights. "That call is for you."

"In the future," I began, "I would really appreciate if you wouldn't always wait to be asked. When you have pertinent information, please share it."

Bright eyes blinked at me a couple of times. Her fingers spidered over to the phone. "Your call is on line four."

As I returned to Abe's office, I heard her say, "Ms. Wheaton will be with you in a moment."

Chapter 7

"I UNDERSTAND, MR. CASSANO," I LIED. Rubbing my brow while enduring the angry man's diatribes over the phone was not a new experience for me. Not that I thought I'd ever get used to it.

The estate's closest neighbor, Frank Cassano, had been my very first assignment. "Make him go away," Abe had told me. "He doesn't have a legal leg to stand on and he knows it. He's just hoping to make enough of a nuisance of himself that we'll give in." With a look meant to inspire, I supposed, Abe had added. "We won't."

"Is it too much to ask?" Cassano shouted again, making me pull the receiver away from my ear. "All's I'm asking is to be treated fair."

He had been treated fairly. More than fairly, if truth be told. But the man wouldn't listen to reason. Ever. We had gone over this at least twice a week for a month. When he'd insisted on speaking with Abe the other day, I'd assured him I was authorized to handle his complaint. He pushed hard to be connected to the mansion's director but I refused, unwilling to be defeated on my first real challenge in the new job. Cassano would deal with me, and only with me. I'd made that clear. Now I bit the insides of my cheeks. "Today really isn't a good day for this discussion—"

"Oh yeah? Why don't you tell me exactly when you *will* feel like discussing it? Huh? You're giving me the runaround."

"That's not true—"

"You calling me a liar?"

"Mr. Cassano," I began again, working as much empathy into my voice as I could muster. "Maybe you haven't seen the news. We had a tragic incident here yesterday. Abe Vargas—you've talked with him in the past—he was shot." Getting the words out was harder than I imagined it would be.

"What?" The incredulity in his voice was unmistakable. "Is he okay?"

I swallowed. "No, Mr. Cassano. I'm afraid he's not okay."

Understanding quieted our unruly neighbor. But only momentarily. "Wow," he said. "That's really something. I'm sorry he's dead, but that doesn't fix my problem. Your boss there, Marshfield, cheated me and I'm going to make him pay. You got that?"

Before I could answer, he hung up.

And before I could put the receiver down, Frances was announcing my next call.

A dozen complaints later, I was ready to promise the next unhappy guest an all-expense-paid trip to Europe, if only I could get back to studying the threat letters. But it was not to be. The phone beeped again—this time, it was Frances on the intercom.

"Yes?"

"You wanted to speak with the detectives when they arrived?"

"Thanks, Frances, please send them in."

The door to Abe's office opened and Frances held the knob. "Would either of you care for coffee?" she asked sweetly. "We have iced tea, if you prefer."

The two men demurred, and Frances, still smiling, nodded. "If you change your mind, please feel free to let me know." She didn't close the door behind her.

I stood to welcome my visitors, who introduced themselves and showed their badges. They were the same two men I'd seen upstairs this morning. Detective Rodriguez was older, taller, and rounder than his companion. What was left of his hair was more salt than pepper, and even though it was morning, he already had sweat trickling down the sides of his face. His pale green short-sleeved shirt must have been purchased thirty pounds ago, because the buttons looked ready to spring. He eyed the leather chair and sat down as soon as I invited him to do so.

By contrast, Flynn was lean, buff, and fidgety. Looking just as Hispanic as his partner, despite the Irish surname. He rolled his shoulders and neck, maintaining his balance on the balls of his feet, poised to run a marathon, shoulder holster and all. When Rodriguez gestured for him to sit, the younger man's eyes flashed. "This is the victim's office, isn't it?" he asked me. I nodded, about to answer when he continued. "Where is your office?"

I pointed toward the door. "Just outside."

"Why are you in here, then?" He shot a look toward Rodriguez. "Has this room been processed?"

Rodriguez smiled, teeth bright, holding up a pinkie-ringed hand. "I went through everything last night," he said slowly. "Don't worry, amigo."

"Already?" Flynn's head twisted as he took in all corners of the room. "There's no fingerprint dust anywhere. And I don't remember seeing any pictures of this room in the file."

"You wouldn't have. We didn't take any photos in here." Squeezing his eyes shut for a moment, Rodriguez took a deep breath. "If you remember from all your studying, we are working under the assumption that . . ." He pulled out a pair of reading glasses and consulted his notes. "That Mr. Abraham Vargas was killed in a botched robbery attempt."

"We shouldn't close off any paths until we've exhausted all possible options."

To me, Rodriguez said, "My friend here is just transferred in from a big city up north. He is not used to our pace yet."

Nor was I. Maybe it was all the years I'd spent in New York City before coming back here to live, but Rodriguez already struck me as a little too laid-back for a murder investigation. Although they proceeded to ask me all the questions I'd anticipated—how long I had worked here, where I had been during the time of the murder, did I know anyone who had a motive to kill Abe—their manner led me to believe that I'd been eliminated as a suspect already. At least in Rodriguez's view.

To me, the botched robbery theory didn't fit, so I floated my own hypothesis. "Did you consider that Abe might have been killed in a case of mistaken identity? He's similar in size and coloring to Mr. Marshfield. And after all the threatening letters, it's possible that whoever targeted Mr. Marshfield found Abe in the private residence and shot him by mistake."

Flynn's eyes widened and I thought he might leap across the desk to grab me, but Rodriguez waved him down. Licking his lips, he recited and scribbled into his notebook at the same time. "The deceased bears a resemblance to Bennett Marshfield, owner of the estate. Possible anyone attempting to break into mansion's private rooms expected to find Mr. Marshfield. Got it." Focusing on me, he said, "Now, what about these letters? Why didn't we hear about them last night?"

I was dumbfounded. To me, these letters were the most important clue of all—why wouldn't the entire department have this information? "I explained, last night, that I didn't know where they were. That's why I called you. I found them this morning."

Flynn again looked ready to jump up, eager to do something—anything. I could relate. Rodriguez nodded again. "Gonna let me see them?"

I'd taken my gloves off during the plethora of phone conversations, dropping them on the desktop where I'd noticed Flynn eyeing them suspiciously ever since he'd walked in. Now I pulled them back on and answered his unasked question.

"As assistant curator here, I regularly deal with precious artifacts. These . . ." I held up my gloved hands and wiggled my fingers, ". . . are standard operating procedure for me. Nothing weird about it."

"Why would you say that?" Flynn asked. "Why do you feel the need to make excuses?"

Rodriguez shut his eyes tight for another half second before he confirmed my suspicions. "Flynn, we are not investigating the lady. She isn't a suspect."

Flynn seemed more disappointed than he had any right to be. I tried ignoring his eager scrutiny as I opened the folder and turned it to face the two detectives. The originals were here, my copies safely tucked in a file drawer. I could have predicted the first words out of Flynn's mouth.

"Where's this original?" he asked, lifting the newest threat and scrutinizing it.

"I don't know. Abe told me he intended to show it to Bennett . . . that is, Mr. Marshfield. When I left him, Abe was heading up to Mr. Marshfield's study. I assumed he took the letter with him, but from what I understand, it wasn't found on Abe's body."

Fidgety Flynn asked, "No one told us anything about this last night when we were here. We thought we talked to every one of the witnesses. Where were you?"

Rodriguez again held up his hand. Although still in his relaxed position in the chair across from me, I could see his ire growing. He flipped back through his notes. "We interviewed two housekeepers, Rosa Brelke and Melissa Delling," he began. "That Rosa's eyesight's not so good," he said with a pointed look. "She says she thought she saw a man in there, but he disappeared when she looked back."

"Disappeared?"

"So she says. But like I said, the woman's eyesight's terrible. I asked her to look at some mug shots. I think it confused her."

"What about Melissa Delling?"

"I would consider bringing her in for a lineup if we ever get that far. She saw someone, too." Back to consulting his notes: "Said he was between thirty-five and fifty, under six feet, slightly overweight, wearing dark clothing. With that description, it could be just about anybody. She says she got a look at his face, but didn't recognize him."

"Well, it's something, at least," I said.

"We also interviewed your head of security, Terrence Carr. When we asked to speak with Mr. Marshfield, we were told he was indisposed and would see us in the morning." Rodriguez made a so-so motion with his head and gave me a pointed look. "In most circumstances, we would not wait until the next day, but Mr. Marshfield is well respected here in Emberstowne. We made an exception." Returning his attention to his notes, he added, "But I see no mention of you. Who did you talk to last night?"

I couldn't remember the officer's name. "It was very hectic," I began, aware of Flynn squinting at me. "I had helped Mr. Marshfield to his room when the call came out that Abe was . . . dead."

Rodriguez nodded, urging me on.

"Mr. Marshfield was understandably distraught, so I decided to stay with him even after the doctor administered a sedative." I shrugged. "The drug took a while to take effect." I remembered feeling at odds as I'd sat there next to the bed. It seemed wrong to leave Bennett all alone but it seemed equally wrong not to oversee the goings-on in the study. I'd reasoned that Carr would handle the mechanics of the investigation, and I would handle Bennett.

When I'd finally emerged a couple of hours later, the corridor was still bustling with activity. An officer had spied me approaching and escorted me to a far corner of the hall with an admonishment to not get too close to the crime scene. He'd taken my statement and then urged me to leave the area immediately. During my interview, I'd made it a point to mention the threats we'd received. "The officer I spoke with asked me a bunch of questions about the letters, but assured me the matter was already being handled." I shrugged. "I assumed that meant he told the detectives in charge . . . You."

Rodriguez and Flynn exchanged a look I didn't understand. "Was the officer in uniform?"

"No," I said slowly. "He was in plainclothes, but wore a shoulder holster." I pointed to Flynn. "Just like yours."

Rodriguez rubbed his temple. "Can you describe him?"

A funny feeling began to form, like my stomach curling in on itself. I spoke more quickly, eager to get the information out as fast as I could. "He was about my height, maybe five-foot-eight or -nine. A little paunch right here . . ." I indicated the love handle area. "His hair was thinning—I'd put him at about fifty. Ordinary face. Not bad looking, but not handsome either. Does that help?"

Flynn muttered what might have been an expletive.

"What?" I asked.

Rodriguez pointed to an area just above the bridge of his nose. "Did he have a mole, a dark one, right about here?"

"I don't remem . . ." I started to say, then stopped myself. "He did. Yes."

Flynn punched a fist into his palm.

My twisting gut tightened. "What did I do? Who did I talk to?"

Flynn shook his head, but Rodriguez ignored him. "His name is Ronny Tooney."

I must have made a face because Flynn said, "The guy's a real weirdo."

"He's not part of your department?"

Rodriguez harrumphed, looking suddenly tired. "Took an online course and thinks he's a private detective. He must have been monitoring calls again." This time, when the older detective wrote in his book, he scribbled hard. "The idiot keeps showing up at our crime scenes. Nine times out of ten we find him and toss him before he does any damage." Looking up at Flynn, he added, "Let's bring him in for questioning. See what he has to say." He tapped a thick finger on the folder in front of us. "Dollars to doughnuts Tooney is out right now trying to find these letters. He thinks if he solves one case he'll be in business for life."

Rodriguez pulled a plastic evidence bag from his belt and asked me to place the original letters inside. After I did, I removed my cotton gloves.

"How did this guy get into the mansion?" I asked.

Pushing himself to his feet, the detective shot me a wry smile. "You saw how it was yesterday. People don't know what to do when there's a crime. They panic. Folks are coming and going and nobody is really sure who's who. We don't get many murders in this little town, thank God, but I've seen it happen even with car accidents or break-ins. Victims spot someone who looks official and it's natural to trust them. Broke my heart once when a young couple's car got broadsided by a drunken idiot. Miraculously everyone was okay, but the woman's purse got stolen in the aftermath. Who took it? No idea. There were paramedics, cops, bystanders in and out of the car. Lots of people stepping forward to help. But one of them was a thief. And nobody ever figured out who." He stopped a moment. "Couple was on their honeymoon, too. Half their spending money in the wife's purse." He raised his eyebrows. "Makes a good case for carrying plastic, you know. Can always cancel those."

Flynn looked reluctant for our interview to end. I got the impression he wished he could interrogate me one on one. But Rodriguez was making for the door and Flynn had no choice but to follow.

"What about Percy?" I asked. "Did you find anything out about him?"

"The fat guy who caused the disturbance?"

Rodriguez was shaking his head even before I could answer. "Full name Percy Lepore. He don't know squat. We tried sweating it out of him, but all we could get was that some guy—a guy he never met before, of course—offered him a hundred dollars to raise a ruckus. The timing was pretty specific, so we know the two events are connected, but other than the lame description Percy gave us, we've got nothing to go on."

"What did the guy look like?"

Flynn narrowed his eyes at me. "Average guy. Average weight. Twenty to fifty years old. Wearing a dark baseball hat, dark jeans, and a navy blue T-shirt."

"That's it?" I asked. "No other description, like skinny? Heavyset?"

Flynn snorted. "Everybody looks skinny next to that guy."

Almost out the door, Rodriguez started when he bumped into Frances in her favorite eavesdropping position. Recovering, he twisted to talk to me. "The fat kid was a patsy. He saw a way to make a quick buck and he took it. Dumb as a box of rocks, that one. We'll keep an eye on him but until we come up with a suspect and a chance for a positive ID, there's no reason to hold Mr. Lepore. We got everything out of him we're going to get." Rodriguez started to walk away, then turned back. "For now, that is."

For the first time all morning, I sensed

determination in the relaxed detective's demeanor. His eyes sparkled when he added, "Do me a favor, Ms. Wheaton. Look around, speak with your staff. See if there's anybody we need to talk to who we might have overlooked. We'll be in touch." He tapped his notebook to his temple and turned to Flynn. "Let's go upstairs," he said. "Have another walk around the crime scene."

Flynn gave me one last glare—warning or confusion, I couldn't be sure—and sauntered off to follow his partner.

Chapter 8

THE MINUTE THE TWO MEN LEFT, I headed for Frances's desk. "What do you know about Bennett's involvement with the T. Randall Taft case?"

She shrugged as if to say "not much," but her eyes glittered. "Why? You think Randall Taft hired a hit man? I heard what you said about Bennett and Abe looking alike from the back." Folding her arms across her ample chest, she nodded sagely. "I was thinking the exact same thing. Why don't the cops look into possibilities like that? I mean, *pheh*, a robbery? Give me a break. If they were smart they'd take a look at Frank Cassano."

"Cassano?" I said skeptically. "Capable of murder?"

"Did you know he's divorced because he got caught cheating on his wife?" In her element—gossiping—Frances didn't take a breath. "He probably would've gotten away with it, too, except the woman he was seeing had a mean little dog who jumped up on the bed and bit him in a . . ." she wagged her eyebrows, ". . . *very* sensitive spot. How do you explain that to your wife?" Looking pleased with herself, she added, "Brings new meaning to the term *lapdog*, don't you think?"

"Thanks for sharing, Frances," I said, wishing she hadn't. "But Cassano doesn't really strike me as a killer. More like an angry blowhard."

"A man who cheats on his wife is probably capable of murder, too," she said. I didn't quite understand how one followed the other, but I kept my mouth shut. "And he's a pain in our backsides. The Mister really doesn't have any enemies except him."

A man in Bennett Marshfield's position often had adversaries he didn't even know existed. I couldn't discount Cassano completely but I believed the timing with the Taft news was more than coincidence. That was the angle I wanted to explore. "How long have Bennett and T. Randall Taft known one another?"

She considered that. "Long time. Twenty, thirty years, I'd say. Bennett's older than Randall by quite a bit, but I seem to remember hearing their names together a lot. Their wives were good friends, too."

"Bennett's first wife, or second?"

"Second," she said sadly. "The first wife, Sally, died young. Then came Marlis." The look on Frances's face told me exactly what she thought of wife number two. "Sally was barren—or so everyone said. I think Bennett was so desperate to have kids that he married the first woman who looked fertile. Marlis already had Hillary, proving she was capable of giving birth, so he snapped her right up. Big mistake. No babies here."

"Do you know anything about Randall Taft's Ponzi scheme?"

"Only that I'm glad Taft didn't come knocking on my door. These days, who's got money to lose? Not me."

"Why wasn't I told that Bennett was scheduled to testify in court yesterday?"

She shrugged. "The Mister keeps a lot to himself. Especially personal stuff. I think he talked to Abe . . ."

We both let the thought hang.

"You're a resourceful woman," I said.

Frances looked confused. "Sometimes."

"Do me a favor. We pay a service to keep us updated on all news and articles that are published about Marshfield Manor, right?"

She snapped her fingers. "You want me to ask them to clip news on Randall Taft, too?"

"Yeah, and have them backtrack. I want to know everything about this from the time the story hit."

"That's a good idea." Frances reached for the telephone. "I should have thought of that."

I started for the door, patting my hip. "I've got my walkie-talkie if you need me. But it looks like the complaint calls have died down, so you should be okay here for a little while."

"Are we opening tomorrow?" she asked.

"Won't know until this afternoon at the earliest."

"Where are you going?"

I'd called most of the department heads to check in, striving to be the voice of calm in this storm, letting them know we would reopen just as soon as the police gave us the all-clear. There were, however, a couple of departments I couldn't reach—probably because staffers were busy doing their jobs rather than sitting idly by the phone. I decided to visit these departments in person. "Outside, first, then down to the basement to talk with some of the staff."

"I could call them to come up here."

Sure, I thought. So you can listen in.

"No thanks," I said. "While I'm gone, though, would you do me a favor and pull out any information we might already have on T. Randall Taft?"

I left her and headed down the back stairs. I called Carr on my walkie-talkie to alert him about the uninvited Ronny Tooney—a problem we needed to address quickly. But he cut me off before I could even broach the subject.

"Hold up on any sensitive communication via radio," he said. "What's your location?"

I told him.

"I'll meet you outside in twenty. In the meantime, keep the lines as clear as possible."

"You got it."

He clicked off, leaving me further worried. Was there another security breach? I blew out a breath and hurried the rest of the way, but as I cleared the final landing, I stopped for a moment to gaze out the window. Teams of garden professionals dotted the south lawn, busy trimming, cutting, weeding, and planting under the soft sun. Though a gauzy mist hung overhead, the day had cleared up nicely. Outside the mansion suddenly seemed the safest place to be.

I made my way down the expansive corridor, with only the ticking clocks to keep me company as my shoes *tap-tapped* along the tile. This area was usually filled with happy, chatty tourists at this time of day, and the home felt empty without their energy. As I entered the silent Birdcage room, I paused a moment. Yesterday's fracas with Percy had been the beginning of Marshfield Manor's worst day. I replayed scenes in my mind and realized how flawlessly we had been set up.

And yet . . . the fact that an intruder had made it into the house during the melee should not have surprised me. Our security protocols were outdated, and our force largely untrained. Changes were in the works, but they hadn't come soon enough for Abe. But who would have expected violence in such an idyllic location? I was as guilty as the next guy of never expecting a major crime to happen here.

My footsteps beat a lonely pace across the Birdcage's marble floor as I made my way to the back garden exit. There was a chill in the room that had nothing to do with the temperature and I was happy to push the tall glass door open and step into the hazy sunshine.

Immediately outside the Birdcage was a massive tile patio, with umbrella-topped tables provided for tourists to sit while they waited to be seated indoors or just enjoy a view of the grounds. To the west, our hotel was just visible over a low rise. Beyond that were the stables, where guests could schedule trail rides. To the east, more than a polo field away, was our forest. And to the south were our gardens, so beautiful it almost hurt to take it all in.

These tables were a recent addition—and even better—they had been my suggestion. I'd gotten the idea after a visit to *Cà d'Zan*, the John and Mable Ringling mansion in Sarasota, Florida. The terrace, overlooking Sarasota Bay, was one of my favorite places on the property. I loved the sense of belonging created by the area, and I sought to re-create that feeling here at Marshfield. This would be our first spring and summer with a welcoming patio, and I looked forward to seeing how it would be received.

I thought about Abe. While he hadn't been the most accommodating individual I'd ever known, I was surprised when he'd agreed to the patio plan and further surprised when he allowed me to get started immediately. "Why wait?" he'd asked.

"That's what you were hired for, isn't it? New ideas. If that's what they want, that's what they'll get."

The furniture had been delivered and set up two weeks later. Amazing what could be done in a short period of time when money wasn't an object. I sighed as I ran my hand along the back of a rattan chair. Crafted in a similar style, they were a lighter color than those in the Birdcage and sturdier for outdoor use. Abe and I thought it best to have both areas matching in theme.

Although I hadn't known Abe long, I already knew I would miss him. He'd always been gracious and kind to me. And he'd been an effective buffer where Frances was concerned. Maybe he'd simply gotten used to her, but her attitude hadn't seemed to bother him at all.

I crossed the patio toward the low wall border, looking for Old Earl, the head groundskeeper. Like so many of the staff members, Old Earl had been in Marshfield's employ for a very long time. I even remembered him from when I used to visit as a child. He always hid a plastic bag filled with Starlight mints in his pocket, and would hand them out to those of us who knew they were there. He and I hadn't had much opportunity to work together since I started here, but I was eager for that to change.

These days, Earl moved more slowly. With his slouched posture and weakened right knee, he used a cane to make his way around the grounds and complained—loudly—about everything that wasn't getting done. We all knew it was just his frustration talking. Earl just wasn't able to keep up with the grounds as well as he once was. I spotted him carrying a tiny potted pansy in his free hand, shuffling past one of the outbuildings.

We all referred to these outbuildings as sheds, although the term was a misnomer. These structures housed garden equipment and other sundry landscape items of course, but "shed" wasn't a sufficient description. Outfitted with running water, heat, and refrigeration units, these lovely cabins—which dotted the estate's landscape—kept our groundskeepers from needing to return to the main residence for food and other basic needs. There were families in this world who would be happy to live in such sheds.

"Earl," I said, hurrying over. "Do you have a moment?"

His ruddy face had a drapey look that crinkled into a smile—like a cheerful shar-pei—when he recognized me. "Hey there, Ms. Wheaton," he said touching the pansy pot to his khaki hat in a mock salute. But then his smile faded away almost immediately. "Can't rightly say good mornin' now, can I? Not this mornin', at least."

"How are you holding up?" I asked.

His cane made soft indentations in the damp ground as we made our way to one of the planting tables next to the outbuilding. "All right, I guess." He shook his head in direct contradiction to those words. "I suppose I'll get by." He placed the pansy pot on the tabletop, and fished into the pocket of his canvas coveralls, as he tilted his head toward the house. "How's the Mister?"

"Bennett is . . . holding up," I answered, realizing how lame such things sounded. Weren't we all holding up? What else was there for us to do? Falling apart wasn't an option. Not with so much responsibility ahead.

Earl pulled a crinkled plastic bag from his pocket, fished out a Starlight mint, and offered it to me. "Peppermint helps you think," he said as I unwrapped the candy and popped it into my mouth. He joined me, then took back my empty wrapper. "I'll make sure these don't end up on the lawn."

Working the mint into the side of my cheek, I said, "I wanted to ask you about yesterday, Earl. Were there any members of your team out back when the break-in occurred? The detectives will be talking to everyone today, but I thought I'd try to help them corral witnesses to streamline things a bit."

He hung the handle of his cane on the tabletop and dragged over an old stool, lowering himself to sit. Just as he did so, he stood up again and dusted off the seat. "Sorry, I wasn't thinking. Ladies should sit."

I declined. "But you go ahead, please."

He smiled his thanks, his dirt-encrusted fingers working the soil around the pansy to free it from its tiny pot. "You know Jack, don'tcha?"

I shook my head.

Concentrating on the pansy, he reached down under the table, pulled up a larger pot, and dragged over a bag of dirt. "This one's needing some TLC," he said. "Jack's not one of the gardeners on staff, he's a landscape architect. He don't work here regular. Got his own company in town. But he helps us out."

"He's a consultant?"

He stopped working long enough to answer. "Yup. And I like to think I helped him get where he's at. I used to talk to him about growing things back when he was just a little tyke. Now he's the one teaching me. I guess that's what's called enjoying the fruits of my labors." Working the pansy into the new pot, he continued. "Jack's a good kid. Got real talent, and he's a local boy." Squinting outward, he pointed toward the gardens. "We don't only grow plants here at Marshfield; we grow family, too. Been doing that for years. That's how all of us started here way back when." He gave me a sad look. "Sorry, don't mean to put you city folks down."

"I'm not 'city folks,'" I said. "Well, not originally. I was born in Emberstowne."

His draped eyes twitched with skepticism. "You

94

don't talk like you're from around here. How's come I don't know you?"

"I spent a lot of time up north," I said, then pointed to the minty bulge in my cheek. "But I remember how you used to sneak these to me when my mom wasn't looking."

He grinned but still looked confused. "Wheaton, eh? I don't know that name. You married?"

"No," I said, "but you might be more familiar with my grandparents' name. My grandma used to work here, in fact. Her last name was Careaux."

He straightened. "Sophie? You're Sophie's kid?"

"Granddaughter."

"Shee . . . yeah. Granddaughter. Wow. Time flies."

A voice from my left interrupted. "Good morning, Earl. What do you have for me today?"

Earl said, "Speak of the devil." Jerking a thumb at the newcomer, he said, "This here's Jack Embers. Mark my words: Him and his company are the ones going to take over when I retire."

Although the day was cool, Jack had evidently been hard at work for most of the morning. Perspiration trickled from his dark hairline and splotches of sweat covered most of his gray T-shirt. He was tall—a full head taller than me—and that was saying something. With military-short hair, he was muscular though not ripped, carrying an extra ten pounds. The added weight suited him, but then again, I always preferred a sturdy build. His skin

95

suggested an adolescent battle with acne and the jagged white line slicing across the left side of his face suggested a battle of another kind. Where had he gotten that scar? An accident? A fight?

Jack sidled close enough to clap Earl on the shoulder. "Nobody can replace you, buddy. Not in a hundred years."

Clearly pleased, Earl's face reddened even more. He waved Jack away. "Oh, go on."

"I'm Grace Wheaton," I said, extending my hand.

Jack took a step toward me but before we could shake, he gave his right hand a look of disgust. "Sorry," he said, holding it up for me to see. "Been playing in the dirt. But I know who you are." He raised his chin to indicate the expansive grounds. "Talk about grapevines," he said with a wink, "out here word travels fast."

"I'll bet."

"I was very sorry to hear about Abe Vargas," he said. "He was a good man. They catch the guy yet?"

"Not yet."

"You heard I might have seen the guy?"

That took me by surprise. "No, I didn't. You saw the killer?"

Jack shrugged. "Might have. I talked to the police about it yesterday."

"They asked me to ask around. You'd think they might have mentioned a witness."

"Yeah, well, I get the impression the cops in this town are in over their heads," Jack said. "The guy I talked with yesterday didn't even ask for my contact information. He was in the middle of questioning me when he just took off."

Uh-oh. "Did he have a mole right about," I pointed to the area just above the bridge of my nose, "here?"

"How did you know that?"

Just as I was about to tell him about Ronny Tooney, Carr joined us outside. "Let everyone on staff know that no one gets near Mr. Marshfield without prior clearance from me," he said by way of greeting.

I started to interrupt, but he stopped me.

"I've got two armed guards keeping watch over him 'round the clock. Nobody's getting past them." He pointed to Jack and then to me. "You both wanted to talk with me about something. Who wants to start?"

Jack made a "ladies first" gesture so I jumped right in and told them all about my encounter with Ronny Tooney, explaining how I'd given my statement to him, erroneously believing he was a plainclothes detective. As I spoke Jack worked his jaw, probably feeling the same combination of frustration and stupidity I was experiencing. "I didn't realize," I said. "He looked so official."

Carr squeezed his eyes shut and massaged his brow. "Great," he said through clenched teeth.

"This is just great." Opening his eyes, he glared at Jack. "And what about you?"

"I gave the guy my statement, too," he said. "How the hell could this guy have gotten away with this? Didn't you check credentials?"

Carr took a step forward. "Have you met the team I inherited? Not one of them has actually been trained in security. They've been instructed on pointing out the washrooms and keeping kids from climbing on the furniture. There are no emergency protocols set up. Nobody here has any experience on the street, and this place has never even run a safety drill. How many times do you think any of these people have had to deal with a murder? Zero. Nobody knew what the hell to do yesterday, and we're just damn lucky that no one else got hurt." He held a finger up close to Jack's face. "I admit that mistakes were made. And I take responsibility. But it wouldn't hurt to pay closer attention yourself. Next time somebody questions you, maybe you ought to check before spilling your guts."

Eyes tight with anger, Jack edged forward. A tiger ready to leap.

From behind me, Earl spoke up. "If this Ronny fellow sneaked in here because he's trying to help figure out who killed Abe, then I don't see what's so wrong about that." He turned his back to us, resuming work on his pansy. "Maybe he'll get the job done before the cops do."

Addressing the elderly gardener, Carr modulated his tone. "What we all need to realize is that by interfering, this Tooney idiot is hampering the real investigation. If you see him around, Earl, call me on the radio. Okay? He doesn't belong here."

Turning to Jack I asked, "So what happened—what did you tell the fake detective?"

I could tell Carr had been about to ask the same question.

The defensive fury in Jack's eyes slipped away. He rolled his shoulders and took a breath before answering. "There are people going in and out of the mansion all the time," he began. "So at first I didn't think anything of a man in coveralls walking behind the western section of the house."

"You saw him?" Carr asked. "What did he look like?"

"He was pretty far away, and the sun was in my eyes." Pointing eastward, he continued. "I was up there, in that little gorge. I thought it was Kenny at first—which is why seeing him around the grounds didn't bother me. But then I noticed Kenny was standing about fifty feet away from me. I called to the guy. He turned and started to run. I ran after him. But the guy was fast—I lost him in the trees."

Carr had been jotting notes as Jack spoke. Now he looked up, gesturing with his eyes toward the hotel. "The trees? The ones closer to the road, or the ones behind the hotel?"

"Road," Jack said. "And before you ask, I did call it in. But by the time I got ahold of the dispatcher, all hell had already broken loose."

"Come up with me. I want the detectives to hear this."

Jack patted Earl on the shoulder. "You gonna be okay for a little while out here by yourself?"

"I been running these grounds since before your daddy could crawl," he said without looking up. "You go on ahead."

"I'm going in, too," I said. "I have a few other people to talk with."

The three of us strode to the house and parted company at the back entrance. Carr and Jack headed up while I took the stairs down to the basement.

Bennett Marshfield's grandfather, Warren, Sr., hadn't spared any expense when building his mansion. Even this belowground level was filled with decorative detail. Although less opulent than the upper stories, the hallways and rooms—which formerly housed staff living quarters—were cheerful and bright. The high windows allowed shafts of natural sunlight to bounce down onto the polished floors. Paintings—though not any of the real masters—adorned walls at regular intervals, each piece of artwork accompanied by a small plaque explaining the style, the medium, the time period. Warren Marshfield had been known for his penchant for educating others. Staff included.

I mulled over my discussion with Jack Embers. Embers, as in Emberstowne, I assumed, since Earl had referred to Jack as a hometown boy. The municipality had been founded shortly after the Civil War by the Embers family who had—briefly—been the town's most important people. That is, until the Marshfields discovered the beautiful area and moved in. I was mildly surprised the town name hadn't been changed to honor them. I wondered if Jack was a direct descendant of the original Embers family.

None of this mattered today, however. What mattered was finding the killer, and once Jack told the real police about the man he'd seen, maybe the authorities would put out an all-points bulletin. Or whatever it was they did these days to apprehend criminals.

So far, Emberstowne's finest hadn't impressed me overmuch. I hoped they were more astute than they appeared. They had demanded that all personnel report to the mansion today, whether scheduled to work or not. That was something, at least. Maybe now with the place on virtual lockdown there would be little chance of Ronny Tooney sneaking in to gum up the works.

I took yet another flight of steps down to one of the sub-basements. These areas housed the massive laundry room; miscellaneous storage areas; and the clunky machinery required to keep the house warm, cool, and properly humidified.

The scent of hot cotton and bleach hit me at the entrance to the laundry room. Although the door was wide open, I knocked at the jamb. Eight hair-netted women leaned against washers, dryers, and folding tables. Most held mugs in their hands. At my knock, they straightened. "Wait," I said as they quickly scattered. "I need to talk with you."

They eyed me suspiciously. Our head of housekeeping, Rosa Brelke, sat on a folding chair. She'd evidently been holding court.

"I understand that we've all suffered a major shock," I said to the group. "It's natural to want to talk about it. It's good that you're doing so."

Melissa Delling stood behind Rosa, clearly uncomfortable. For her part, Rosa seemed recovered enough from yesterday's trauma to shoot me a knowing look. She lumbered to her feet and made her way over with a pronounced waddle. "You want me to come talk to the police again, yes?" she asked.

"I'm sure the police will be down here later but for right now, I want to ask you a few questions, myself." I nodded toward Melissa. "Both of you."

The younger woman looked surprised but it was the reaction of the rest of them—rushing out the door as quickly as possible—that made it clear I had interrupted a coffee klatch. A thirty-something woman with four inches of black roots in her white blond hair and undisguised anxiety in her eyes tapped me on the arm as she walked past. "No harm done. Just talking here."

"I understand," I said. "What's your name?"

The fear in her eyes sparked. "Yvonne."

"It's been rough for all of us the past couple of days, Yvonne," I said. "I'm not down here to double-check on you. I'm here to talk with Rosa and Melissa."

Clearly, these people had been affected by the death of a colleague, but when it came down to it—in an economy as volatile as this one—they were more concerned about how Abe's death affected them personally.

Rosa and Melissa eyed me warily. "Thanks for staying," I said when everyone else was gone.

Rosa grunted as she settled herself onto her folding chair with Melissa standing next to her. For the first time, I got a good look at the younger woman. I put her in her late twenties, although her hands, rough and red, looked as though they belonged to someone much older. She wore a silver claddagh ring—facing inward—on her wedding finger. Her pale face was freckled and lovely. She watched me as warily as the other women had, but with a sadness in her eyes that seemed out of place in someone so young. That's what finding a dead body will do to you.

I glanced around and noticed several more metal chairs leaning against a nearby wall. I dragged two of them over and squeaked them open, inviting

Melissa to sit. She looked as though she would prefer to be anywhere but here. Was I so frightening? I suppose I might be. No one knew that until I had a better sense of the big picture, I didn't intend to initiate any personnel changes. That would come later, if at all. But there was no assuaging the fear I sensed in every single staff person's demeanor when they interacted with me.

"I'd like to ask you just a few questions about yesterday. You both gave the police your statements, didn't you?"

Rosa shrugged. Melissa nodded.

"I understand you both saw someone in the study."

"He was there." Rosa raised her hands and clapped them in the air. "Then he gone!"

"What did he look like?"

Rosa frowned. "Dark pants. Dark shirt. I no see his face."

"How old, about?"

Another frown. "I not know so good ages. Young kid. Maybe like you," she said to me. Turning to Melissa, she asked, "That right?"

Melissa made a face. "Not so young," she said. "But I only got a quick look. I told the police that. It all happened so fast."

I nodded, trying to encourage her to talk more. When allowed to ramble, people often reconnected with memories they'd forgotten they had. "Were you outside the room when you heard the gunshots?"

"Yes." Melissa clenched her eyes as though trying to banish the memory from her mind. "I hate this," she said, her voice shaky. "This is so hard."

I patted her arm. "It's okay. I don't mean to bring it all back."

Rosa pointed upstairs. "We always clean study first. But we no clean when the Mister is there. He no like that. We hear somebody in study—we start on bedroom instead." Her eyes widened. "Then we hear popping noise and something fall down."

"So you ran to the study?" I asked, thinking that most people might have gone for cover.

"Yah, of course. I think maybe something get broken, you know?" Rosa held her hands to her crimson red hair. "Oh my, my, then I see body on the ground. I sure it's the Mister." She pointed to Melissa. "She think so, too."

I turned to the young woman. "What happened next?"

Rosa looked peeved to have the attention taken away from her, but Melissa answered, speaking slowly. I got the impression she was a simple girl. "Just like she said, right off we was both sure it was Mr. Bennett layin' on the floor. I really thought it was. But we called for help right away. We really did."

"That's when the man took off?"

"He disappear," Rosa said. She snapped her fingers. "He just . . . gone."

I turned to Melissa. "Disappeared?"

She gave a slight headshake. "I grabbed Rosa and we ran back for our radios because we left them in the bedroom. But by the time we got back, the guy was gone."

"Could he have gotten out of the room and down the hall without you seeing him?"

"No way," Rosa said, pointing to her eyes and winking. "I see everything."

Melissa seemed to consider that. "Yeah. We weren't gone long, but it was enough time for sure."

"Did you *hear* anything else?"

Rosa shook her head, but Melissa perked up. "Now that you mention it, I think I did hear running." Her sad eyes brightened slightly. "Sort of loud. Like a heavy person, you know? It sounded like he went toward the back stairs. And I heard a door slam."

"A door? Where?"

Her brows came together and she stared at the floor as though trying to remember. "Can't say for sure. Maybe downstairs one floor? I don't know. Maybe two? Kinda far enough away that I couldn't tell."

"Thanks, Melissa. I know this has been hard on you."

Her eyes welled up. "Abe was always nice to me," she said, her voice unsteady. "I really wish he wasn't dead."

I patted her arm. "We all do."

Chapter 9

WHEN I GOT BACK, FRANCES WASN'T there. I peeked into Abe's office, wondering if I would catch her rummaging through his files, but the place was empty. Well, except for the pile of notes she'd left on my desk. I thumbed the edge of the small stack. At least a dozen calls to return. I cast a longing glance at my computer and noticed I had no new e-mails. There were times I felt Marshfield Manor was caught in a time warp. Most discussions were held over the phone or in person. Memos—when they were written at all— came out on paper. As much as I would have liked to send out updates via the Internet, I had come to the realization that almost no one in-house ever checked their e-mail.

My stomach growled just as the grandfather clock chimed one. Where had the morning gone? The cup of coffee and handful of almonds I'd had for breakfast wasn't doing it for me anymore. Unfortunately, I'd forgotten my lunch.

I took another look at the pile of pink papers on my desk. We really needed to go green around here. So much wasted paper.

The top message was the oldest—it had come in just minutes after I'd gone downstairs. Frances always made sure to arrange them chronologically so that I wouldn't mistakenly return the most recent call first. I thumbed the edge of the stack again. Grabbing food versus returning these calls. My stomach made its preferences clear, but I thought about how disheartening it would be to come back to all this, and decided to get through at least a few of them first.

Rather than return calls in order, I decided to shuffle through the pile and prioritize. Frances would have a fit.

Two of our suppliers had called with expressions of sympathy. That was very nice, but I could wait to call them back later. One of the assistant managers of our on-site hotel wanted approval to provide a complimentary appetizer buffet for the guests tonight. I thought that was a great idea and called immediately to tell him so. A few more messages, most from the media asking for a statement. I pushed those aside.

When I picked up the next message, I almost laughed. This one was from Frances. "Your cell phone kept ringing. I didn't think it was appropriate for me to answer, but you should probably check it." She'd added at the bottom. "Can you change that ring tone? It's really annoying."

Dragging my purse up, I flipped open my cell. Frances wasn't kidding. Seven missed calls. One text message. My heart gave a hard skip when I read it. My sister, Liza. Her note was brief: "Advice needed."

Advice? That was a joke. Except it wasn't ever funny. I slapped my phone shut.

For as long as I could remember, Liza's repeated requests for advice were thinly disguised pleas. Always for money. Sometimes for bail.

What was it this time? She had snatched up her portion of the inheritance and promised she wouldn't blow it. She swore she would stay in touch and that she was alone. No man in her life to take advantage of her.

I desperately wanted to believe my sister. But my gut told me differently. I wished our mom would have placed Liza's share of the inheritance in trust, where it could be doled out on an as-needed basis. But my sister was an adult. One who chafed at being called out on her lifetime of bad decisions. Nothing was ever her fault. When the going got tough, Liza took off running.

What in the world could she want now? She couldn't have possibly gone through all that money in just a few months.

My throat hurt as I swallowed again. I picked up the receiver on my desk then put it down again, like I had been scalded. I couldn't call her from here—then she would have this number in her caller ID. When Liza left, I hadn't yet gotten this job—hadn't even told her that I planned to apply. I didn't know why I felt it necessary to keep my job secret, but I'd learned the hard way to protect myself from my younger sister. I opened my cell.

Liza answered on the third ring.

"Grace," she said with forced enthusiasm. "You called me back."

"Where are you, Liza?"

She laughed. Stalling.

Anger welled up in me. "Liza, tell me you haven't lost all of Mom's money. Tell me you haven't blown it all already."

"It isn't Mom's anymore. It's mine. And for your information, no. I haven't blown it all. In fact, I'm starting my own business."

Elbows on my desk, head in my hands, I stared down at the blotter, the cell phone pressed close to my ear. "What kind of business?"

The giggle was back in her voice. "That's the part I'm not sure about yet," she said. "But I know how much you worry about me and I know you always keep telling me to be smart with money . . ."

"How much do you have left?"

Liza didn't like being interrupted. "A lot. Some."

"Define 'some.'"

"Enough to start my own business, okay?" she said, evading the question as only Liza could.

I waited.

"If I *invest* what I've got here," she continued, "I could turn a few thousand dollars into millions."

"My God," I said, "you're down to just a few thousand?"

"Aren't you listening? I can turn this money into a fortune."

"Doing what, Liza?" I asked, my voice rising dangerously high. "Exactly what are you good at? Beside breaking people's hearts, that is."

She hung up on me.

I closed my eyes in frustration.

My fingers were still curled tight around my cell phone when I heard Frances walk in.

She hefted a small blue cooler up onto her desk and patted its handle. "You hungry?" She gave what, for Frances, constituted a smile. "I figured you'd be so busy today you might forget to eat."

Speechless, I nodded.

Turning her back to me, she opened the cooler and began pulling things out.

Ten minutes later, I had devoured half of my portobello mushroom sandwich, while Frances daintily picked at her turkey club. She'd allowed me first choice of the two, surprising me with her thoughtfulness. In addition to the sandwiches, Frances had picked up two fruit salads and two slices of carrot cake from the hotel's kitchen. We sat at our respective desks, quietly enjoying the bounty.

About halfway through dessert, Frances started in: "So who was that calling your cell phone so many times this morning?"

I should have expected this, but the good spirits that resulted from a full tummy put me off my guard.

Frances used a corner of her napkin to wipe a tiny bit of cream cheese from the side of her mouth. "Boyfriend, I bet. Am I right? Men are so impatient. Everything is always about them."

"Not a boyfriend," I said, covering up the remaining dessert to take home.

Frances speared a final forkful of carrot cake. "But you do have a boyfriend?"

I didn't answer.

"If it wasn't your boyfriend calling you all those times, who was it?"

"Why do you need to know?"

"Just making conversation," she said and popped the last bite into her mouth. She chewed that cake a whole lot longer than it deserved, finally swallowed, and put down her fork. "Nothing wrong with that."

"Nothing at all," I said blandly. Changing the subject, I asked, "Can you pull some personnel files for me?"

Eyebrows shot up. "You going to fire somebody?"

"Hardly. I thought I might take a look at the records of all the people on staff." Although I wasn't counting on taking over for Abe, if I did get the nod, I needed to be prepared. "I prefer to work ahead."

"Yeah, you seem that type."

I didn't have the chance to ask what she meant by that. The momentary lull offered her opportunity to jump in with more updates on other employees and she clearly couldn't resist temptation. I was learning very quickly that, more than food, gossip was what fueled Frances's energy levels. "So, the housekeeping staff thinks you're out to get them," she said.

"Where did you hear that?"

"You spooked Yvonne by showing up there unannounced. She's an interesting one, that girl. Did you notice all her piercings? Ears, lip, eyebrow . . . we make her take them out while she's working but you can see . . ." Frances wrinkled her nose in clear distaste, ". . . all the little holes all over her. She used to be such a pretty girl, too. What a shame. She's got a tramp stamp, too."

I was surprised Frances knew what that was.

"Imagine what that will look like when she's forty," she continued. "Saggy, baggy. I'll bet she's sorry then. The things girls will do for their men."

At that, my assistant got such a gleam in her eye that I was afraid she'd start quizzing me on my love life again. "I talked mostly with Rosa and Melissa," I said to hold her off. "They were outside the study when Abe was killed."

"Sad stories there, both of them."

I wondered if Frances knew any happy stories. "I guess I'll find out soon enough when I go over their personnel files."

"Those are the ones you want?"

"Who did you think I meant?"

"You seem to spend a lot of time talking with

Terrence Carr," she said with a sly grin. "Let me warn you: He's happily married."

I knew that. "He took the job here even though big-city departments were courting him. He said he wanted a safe place to raise his three kids. I wonder what he thinks now, after this murder."

She seemed disappointed. "Then I don't know what else you might be looking for. We keep only the basics in there. If you want to know anything important about the people who work here, you should ask me."

"For now, I'll be fine with the personnel files. Do you know if the detectives are still on the property?"

"They set up a command post on the fourth floor." She raised her eyes to the ceiling. "The Mister isn't going to be too pleased about that. He likes his privacy." Now it was she who changed the subject. "Most of the hotel guests and the people with passes have been pretty understanding. Those calls we got this morning were the only real complaints." She picked up a note from her desk. "Except this one."

From the light in her eyes, I knew I wouldn't wait long for an explanation.

"This woman," she began, waving the note, "is a real piece of work. She terrorized poor Tricia on the switchboard, who sent her over to me. There's just no pleasing her."

"Who is she?"

"Name is Geraldine . . ." She spelled the last name.

"Stajklorski," I said, offering my best guess at a pronunciation. "That's a mouthful."

"And a handful." Frances went on to explain that the woman had called to complain about the snippiness of the hotel staff. "She claims that Twyla was intentionally rude to her. "

"Twyla?" I repeated. "That's impossible." The manager of the hotel, Twyla was one of the smartest, most patient women I'd ever met. I couldn't picture her being purposely unkind to anyone.

Frances waved the paper again. "Here's what gets me. This nasty Geraldine checked out yesterday. After she left, she found out we were giving perks like free nights to guests to make up for their inconvenience. She wanted in on it. People who take advantage of situations like this make me sick."

I nodded. I could see where this was going.

"Geraldine called the hotel a little while ago to ask why she didn't get her room comped. Twyla explained that that wasn't how it worked. Geraldine pitched a fit, and Twyla naturally put the call through to us." Frances's mouth curled downward. "Except the woman was on her cell and the call got dropped. When she called back, she went through the switchboard. By the time she got to me, she was steaming."

"Was this Geraldine one of the guests evacuated from the mansion yesterday? Was she unable to complete her tour?"

"That's the thing. The woman was in town all day. Took the mansion tour the day before and checked out before all the excitement. There was absolutely nothing here that affected her. And when I made that clear, she started coming up with reasons why she should get her hotel room refunded. Her biggest complaint was about Twyla's attitude." Frances sniffed. "And we know that's bogus."

My eyebrows shot up. Frances using the word *bogus* surprised me.

"So where do we stand right now? Do I need to call this Geraldine back, or are we done?"

"For now, there's no need to call her back. I made our position clear. But I don't think we're done yet. People like her always turn up again, just when we least expect them."

Chapter 10

WHEN THE HOUSE PHONE RANG THAT evening, I leaned across my kitchen countertop to get a look at the caller ID on the wall phone. Aunt Belinda, calling from Florida. "I'll get it," I shouted to my roommates upstairs. Although we all had our private cell phones, we shared this common number, just in case. This used to be my parents' number and I didn't have the heart to drop it. Having a landline often came in handy.

My aunt Belinda lived alone in a tidy one-level home near Tampa. My mom's only sibling, Belinda and her late husband, Fred, had lived in the Sunshine State for as long as I'd known them. My parents had taken us down to visit several times, but Belinda and Fred hadn't ever come up here to stay with us.

Aunt Belinda called me about once a month just to keep in touch. Childless by chance, not choice, she saw herself as a stand-in for Mom, to watch over me and to impart her wisdom as she saw fit. I was the sole beneficiary of her regular contact—Liza managed to escape this family obligation, too. I knew I should call my aunt more often, and guilt occasionally prompted me to do so. That, and knowing that if I didn't call her, she would undoubtedly call me at the worst possible time. Like tonight.

I picked up the phone and blew out a breath before answering.

"How are you, Aunt Belinda?" I asked, knowing exactly what her answer would be.

She didn't let me down. "Not so well," she said in the defeated tone she always affected. "I've been sick."

"I'm sorry to hear that."

She surprised me then by eschewing our standard conversation wherein she explained to me, in detail, which medical tests she'd recently undergone. Always, she was found fit as a woman her age could hope to be, yet she always seemed disappointed by the results. But not today.

"What's going on there at Marshfield Manor?" she asked. "The newspaper had a story about a murder there. They said the curator was killed. Did you hear anything about it?"

"Yeah," I said slowly, trying to decide whether to come clean. Not only had I kept the Marshfield job secret from my sister, I'd kept that information from my aunt as well. "I knew the man."

"You did? How in the world?" Her surprise was tinged with accusation. "You're not spending all your free time just hanging around that place anymore, are you? Your mother, I swear, that's all she ever wanted to do. What is it about that Marshfield Manor that keeps you so enthralled? I never understood it. Rich people. Who cares about them?"

Knowing she was good for a ten-minute speech on why the Marshfields were the worst thing to happen to Emberstowne, I interrupted.

"I work there."

I heard a sharp intake of breath. "Come again?"

"I took a position at Marshfield. I'm the assistant curator. The man who was killed was my boss."

Aunt Belinda wasn't often rendered speechless, but I'd thrown her a doozy this time.

"So they got their hooks into you, too, did they?" she finally said.

"I've always wanted to work there." That was true enough. Although I thoroughly enjoyed my time in New York, I'd always intended to move back to Emberstowne and seek out a position at Marshfield. Admittedly, I hadn't expected to make that change until much later in my career. Mom's illness had accelerated my plans. And here I was.

"What you find so intriguing about that place, I'll never understand. Those people stayed hidden in their castle and wouldn't give us townies the time of day. No way. And your mother didn't have a problem with that. She spent so much time there, I swear she believed she lived there. That's one thing I'll say about Amelia. She had delusions of grandeur."

"Not at all," I answered, annoyed. "Mom

appreciated beauty. I do, too. That's why I'm thrilled to work there. I get to be part of history."

She made an unpleasant noise. "I guess I can't blame you and I can't blame Amelia either," she said.

Here it comes.

"It's all our mother's fault. She was the one feeding us lines about how great the Marshfields were. Amelia bought into the great Marshfield mystique, hook, line, and sinker. But I was too smart for that. I saw the place for what it really was—a way for the rich to get richer at the expense of poor people who had to pay ten dollars just for the privilege of saying 'Oooh' and 'Ahh' over some old pieces of junk."

I had heard versions of this more times than I could bear to remember. I didn't intend to waste any more time listening, especially since I knew the inevitable second half was about to launch.

"I better get going," I said.

As though she hadn't heard my attempt to disengage, Aunt Belinda segued into her favorite rant, one I could almost recite by heart. "My mother thought the sun rose and set on Amelia. Your mother was the golden child." Belinda *tsk*ed. "*I* was my father's favorite. But he died first and then it was up to my mother to make decisions about who gets what. Just because I didn't see the appeal of the Marshfield millions, our mother didn't think I was worthy enough to inherit the house you're living in. No, she left that to your mother. What did I get? A piddly insurance policy."

That insurance policy and a few additional savings accounts, I knew, had netted Aunt Belinda a substantial sum. More, in fact, than the house had been worth at the time of our grandmother's death. The fact that Belinda had spent it all right away seemed a detail she always managed to forget. The house had naturally increased in value over the years. Yet my aunt insisted on comparing apples and oranges.

I thought about my sister, Liza. She'd gotten the cash, I'd gotten the house.

History repeats itself. Would Liza eventually hassle my children about how unfairly she believed she'd been treated? Would I ever have children? The pain of Eric's sudden departure was still raw, as if it had happened yesterday. As was the hurt I felt from my sister's quick exodus right around the same time. I had no proof, but . . .

As if reading my mind, Aunt Belinda asked, "You hear from your sister lately?"

"No."

"That girl is a pistol. She sure knows how to live. When you hear from her, tell her to call me."

"Sure." I was getting good at lying.

We finally signed off, with my aunt promising to call again soon.

Bruce and Scott were still upstairs. I'd stopped

by Amethyst Cellars earlier on my way home. With its cherrywood décor, recessed lighting, namesake-colored sparkling crystal, and ever-changing displays, the shop was more a destination than simply a place to pick up a bottle of wine. In addition to their range of vintages, the boys also offered a variety of gourmet chocolates, and an assortment of gift baskets. Browsing there felt like being on vacation, and every time I stopped by, I told them so.

Right now they were in the upstairs office hunched over a laptop, oblivious to anything else going on in the house as they came up with display designs and future plans for their store. I didn't know the details of how or when this magazine feature would come through. I did know that there would be considerable lead time. But once their little shop was introduced to the readers of *Grape Living*, success was practically guaranteed. The two men were excited about plans for expansion and how to use the magazine's article as a springboard to national distribution.

These two very enthusiastic businessmen were now in the enviable position of devising growth plans for the next two years and beyond. I was happy for them. And from a purely selfish point of view, I knew that the bigger their shop's business, the more likely they both would stay here with me, sharing expenses in this big house. Helping me keep it maintained.

There were too many things going wrong lately. I couldn't imagine handling all this myself.

When I'd moved here to take care of my mother, I'd been shocked by the house's state of disrepair. As I nursed my mother—with help from the hospice folks, thank God—I'd discovered a talent for improvising and jury-rigging. I also talked my mom into taking in boarders. When Scott and Bruce applied for the spot, I knew they were a gift from heaven.

All these months later, leaky toilets and dripping faucets were no challenge at all. I could shore up a fence post, change a light switch, and repair drawers that wouldn't close. Scott knew his way around power tools and Bruce around cars. The three of us managed pretty well, most days. We did, however, call in help for the big projects. The next one on the list, a new roof, would have to wait until I saved up quite a bit more. Until then, we kept a couple of buckets in the attic placed in strategic spots.

That reminded me. I trudged up to the third floor, pulling open the trap for the foldaway stairs, which led to the uppermost area. The attic smelled of old books and rotting wood. Dark beams rose steeply overhead, and at the room's center, a tower rose high above all its neighboring structures. Though there were tiny windows up there, I couldn't see anything in the dark. I just prayed that there were no bats in my belfry. This place was the stuff of which suspense novels were written. Gabled in four places with only the raw wood for a ceiling, the huge room boasted lots of dark corners where Mom had shoved old records and papers she hadn't ever had time to sort through. Apparently that job now fell to me.

Another day. Maybe another year.

We kept a stack of empty five-gallon buckets near the top of the stairs. I pulled out two and slid them into place, gingerly removing the two that were already half full. They had predicted more rain tonight, and as I stared upward into the dark rafters, I realized I couldn't let this repair go much longer. My salary was good but not so good to allow me to afford such extravagances like repairing my roof.

The wind buffeted the side of the house, rattling the nearby windows. Such a lonely sound. Taking creaky steps across the rough-hewn floor, I made my way to the room's far side, to stare out one of the windows. From up here everything looked small. I was four stories above the ground looking down on treetops and other homes.

Emberstowne had been an idyllic place to be a child—I wondered what life would have been like had I grown up here. Sitting in the shadow of Marshfield Manor, we'd enjoyed the prosperity of tourism and the quiet of small-town life. Aunt Belinda, eight years older than my mother, had seen fit to run off and get married as soon as she turned eighteen. She hadn't been back.

The wind pushed one of the trees so far sideways it almost touched the ground. At the same time, the sky rumbled and a gust of chilled air worked its way between the window and frame to swirl the fresh smell of wet green around me. We were in for another storm.

Chapter 11

I ALWAYS PARKED MY CAR ON THE DRIVE-way next to the house. The detached garage was so chock-full of junk and half-completed projects that no cars would fit inside. Fortunately for my two roommates and me, we had a sizeable driveway and we used it as a parking lot, much to our neighbors' dismay. A couple of them had pulled me aside to mention how unsightly it was to leave cars outdoors all the time. They also took the opportunity to point out a drooping eave on the house and places where the paint was peeling. As if I didn't know.

I was always very polite and thanked them for their concern, but vowed that next time I would sweetly suggest they could help pay for all these improvements if they wanted them so badly. But that next time never came. I cringed every time I was caught by one of these criticisms. Didn't they realize I wanted my house to look as pristine and beautiful as theirs? Didn't they know I was trying my best to get there?

The neighbors were relentless. And lately their complaints were coming more often.

So when I *whoosh*ed open my umbrella to dash to my car, I wasn't surprised to see someone waiting there for me. With his face obscured by the swoop of his umbrella, I couldn't make out which of my neighbors it was. But I put money on it being Chuck.

I hit the "unlock" button on my remote and called, "No time to talk today, Chuck," as I opened the driver's side door and slid in. No easy feat while trying to close an umbrella in slicing rain. Even though I wore a lined trench coat today, I shivered as I pulled my door shut.

To my surprise, Chuck opened the passenger door and sat down, closing his umbrella in a smooth move. When he turned to me, I was even further surprised. Not Chuck.

It took me a minute to place the face.

"You're Ronny Tooney," I said, my heart jumping in alarm. "Get out of my car."

The morning was dark, and I could barely see across the street. My roommates were sound asleep upstairs. There was no one to help me if I called out.

The half second it took me to process that *I* should get out of the car—now—was enough for Tooney to get ahead of me. He locked my doors from the control on his side. "I need to talk with you."

I unlocked the door on my side, and reached for the door handle.

Too late. Tooney locked it again. "I'm not going to hurt you."

It was like we were playing a stupid game. But I wasn't having fun.

"I don't care what you want," I said. "Unlock the damn door." At that I used the remote in my right hand to unlock the car, and my free left hand to grab the handle. This time I was fast enough. I leaped out of the car, not caring about the wind and rain whipping at me as I ran up the steps to my back door.

"Wait!" he called.

I had my keys out and was fumbling to get the right one into the dead-bolt lock, but Tooney was right there. He tapped me on the arm. "I just want to talk to you."

I spun to face him. "Get off my property."

At that he stepped back. Neither of us had our umbrellas out, but while I was covered by my small porch's overhang, Tooney had no protection whatsoever. "I'm sorry I startled you. It was wrong of me to get into your car." He held his hands outstretched. "But it's miserable out here. I'm sorry."

The guy didn't look so scary. In fact, with his plastered hair and soaked trench coat, he looked like a drowned rat. "I'm not coming anywhere near you," I said. "You've got a gun."

"I don't," he said, opening his coat to expose the front of his shirt and slacks. The shoulder holster he'd been wearing the other day was gone. He widened his coat and stood sideways, then turned to show me his other side. "See? No gun." Squinting in the rain, he let the edge of his coat drop. "Please, just a couple questions?"

I looked at my watch. "I have to get to work."

"Five minutes?"

The last thing I needed to do was to complicate an already difficult situation by cooperating with the man who had led me to believe he was a real cop. With no umbrella—I'd dropped it just outside my still-open car door—but with the security of knowing that he at least wasn't armed, I pushed past him. "Not a chance."

Within seconds, I was back in my car with the doors locked. As I started the engine, Tooney ran out in front of it, pressing both hands on the front of my hood. Like he thought he was Superman trying to stop a speeding locomotive. "I'll call you later," he said. "I can help you."

He stepped away, holding up a hand as I drove past, looking soggy, sorry, and ridiculous. I needed help, all right. But I wasn't about to get it from the likes of him.

"Is the manor opening today?" Frances asked the moment I walked in.

I dropped my purse on the desk, frustrated by the early morning altercation with Ronny Tooney. "As of last night, I couldn't get an answer from our detective friends. I hope so. But I owe them a call on another matter."

"What happened to your hair?"

I pushed back my damp locks and checked out my reflection in the glass of the grandfather clock. "Ick."

"It's all indoor parking here," Frances reminded me unnecessarily. "How in the world did you get so wet?"

Today she had on another turtleneck sweater—a virtual duplicate of the one she wore yesterday—except this one was pale blue. "I don't have an attached garage," I said.

She laughed. "Oh that's right. You live in that old monstrosity on Granville."

Her comment set me off-kilter. Why the personal attack? It was bad enough that I didn't seem to have anywhere to turn, but now Frances was taking potshots at where I lived. What major faux pas had I made in karma-ville to deserve such consistently rotten treatment?

Whatever it was, I'd had enough.

"You are talking about my home," I said. "And you will stop. Now."

The tadpole eyebrows arched upward, but she didn't say a word.

"Now," I said, changing the subject. "What have you learned about Bennett Marshfield's involvement with T. Randall Taft?"

Even as she protested, "It's only been twenty-four hours," she reached around to her credenza and pulled out a file. "They sent me some recent notices to get us started." She handed it to me. "These are copies of articles that appeared over the past few days."

"You received these via e-mail?" I asked, impressed. "It's about time somebody on staff became Internet savvy."

She shook her head. "Fax."

I bit back my disappointment. "Soon," I said. "We will rectify this, soon."

Frances moaned her familiar lament. "I don't like computers. I don't like the idea of a machine being smarter than I am."

I held up my hand. Unbelievably, it stopped her.

At that, realization dawned. No one was going to come down from on high and promote me into Abe's job. If I wanted to be the manager of this enormous estate—if I wanted the title of curator/director—I was going to have to start acting like one. And that meant assuming all responsibilities. At least until I was ordered to stop.

I tapped the file folder against my palm. "Two things," I said. "First, I've seen the job you do around here. We both know you are perfectly capable of mastering a computer. Second," I squared my shoulders and nodded toward Abe's office, "effective immediately, I will be moving in there. If there is anything you need before I move all my things in, this would be a good time to recover them."

Frances didn't react. I wondered if it was hard for her to maintain that poker-faced expression.

"Any questions?" I asked.

"No, ma'am."

"Good, then please get Detective Rodriguez on the phone for me. We need to find out if we're opening our doors this morning."

Ten minutes later the intercom buzzed, startling me out of my reading. I had opened the file and found about fifteen articles, most of which delivered a version of the same basic story but worded a little differently under each individual byline. The best, most comprehensive, had been written by a staff reporter for a major financial publication. I saved my place as I hit the intercom to reply.

"Yes, Frances?"

"The detective says he'll be by shortly."

"Did you ask him about opening the mansion to visitors?"

"He said he would cover that when he gets here."

"Great." It was already almost eight o'clock. We'd instructed the entire staff to be in position, poised to act just in case we got a last-minute all-clear. It was looking increasingly likely that we would be sending a significant portion of our staff home.

I was about to verbalize my disappointment, but stopped myself just in time. What was wrong with me? The manor would stay closed for as long as the detectives needed us to keep it closed. Abe was dead and his killer was still on the loose. Although we had a business to run, what we needed to keep uppermost in our mind that one of our own was dead and the detectives were doing their level best to find the guilty party. I had fallen into the trap of being so concerned about overseeing the tourist trade, that I'd begun treating Abe's murder as an inconvenience—an obstacle to getting things done.

I'd lost sight of what was important.

Uncharitably, I wondered if this was how my sister, Liza, felt all the time.

"Thank you, Frances," I said, finding my voice. "By the way, have you heard what arrangements are being made for Abe? Do you know when his family will be having the wake?"

"Abe didn't have any living relatives," she said. "The Mister is taking care of everything. There won't be a wake. And the funeral will be private. Just those of us who knew him best."

"I understand." Rather than making me feel left out, this disclosure made me glad that Abe had his Marshfield Manor family to say good-bye. "Thanks."

I returned to reading the financial article. The story not only provided significant background on Taft, it also clearly explained how Ponzi schemes worked. The pyramid was an apt example. The swindler, in this case, T. Randall Taft, promised significant returns to eager investors. When certificates of deposit and bonds were paying less than 5 percent, Taft promised his people 14 to 17. Unheard of in this market. But people believed him. They gladly handed their investment portfolios to Taft based on his promises to multiply their wealth.

According to this article, the folks who invested with Taft were, by and large, sophisticated men and women who should have known better. The victims mentioned in the piece read like a who's who of the entertainment world. That Taft had managed to entice them into his financial lair was beyond belief. And yet—there it was, in black and white.

The intercom buzzed. "Detective Rodriguez is here," Frances said.

I stood to greet him as he entered, inquiring about Flynn. Rodriguez scratched the back of his neck. "The kid's tracking down a couple of leads."

"Leads?" I asked. "That sounds like good news."

Rodriguez waved down my enthusiasm as we sat. "Don't get excited. We couldn't hold Percy any longer, so my partner is shadowing him. Hoping the guy who hired him pays him another visit."

"So, you're no further along than you were yesterday."

His brown eyes met mine and I caught a glint of steel in their depths. "We've got all our samples sent to the state crime lab, experts going over the threatening letters, and every available man canvassing the area—including interviewing your hotel guests—working 'round the clock. Maybe we don't have anyone in custody yet, but it won't be long." He narrowed his eyes. "Trust me."

I knew the police had been questioning all our guests. We had received a number of complaints—people asking why their vacations were being interrupted and held hostage to this murder investigation. I supposed they expected the guilty party to be found and brought to justice in an hour—just like on TV.

Rodriguez worked his tongue inside his mouth. "You wanted to see me? What's up?"

"That fake detective came to visit me this morning."

"Tooney?"

"The same." I told Rodriguez about the altercation on my driveway.

As always, the detective took copious notes. "I wouldn't be so worried about that guy," he said, scribbling. "Tooney's harmless. He's just a frustrated wannabe."

Sounded like a cop-out to me—but I kept that observation to myself for the moment. No sense in antagonizing a man with a gun.

"Will we open today?" I asked. "Not that I want to rush your investigation. I'm just curious. The sooner we have an idea of our opening, the better prepared we'll be."

"My team will maintain presence in the fourth-floor study where the murder took place, but otherwise, I think we're okay. You can probably open up for business this morning."

Probably. That wasn't much of an answer.

In order to pin him down, I picked up the phone. "I'll call my assistant now and give her the all-clear. You're good with that, right?"

He nodded and I made the call. When that was done, he started to push himself out of his chair. "Was there anything else, Ms. Wheaton?"

"As a matter of fact, there is."

He reluctantly settled himself again, looking at me with an expectant expression.

"Did you get to talk with Jack Embers?"

"Yeah, we got a description from him, too." He made a face of disgust as he hoisted himself to his feet. "Not much to go on." At the doorway, he stopped, looking up at the ornate ceiling and across the walls, past the artwork and other treasures. "You live in a place like this . . ." he gestured out the window, ". . . in a little haven like Emberstowne, and you think nothing bad is ever going to happen. That's the problem, y'see? Nobody here knows what's really out there. Everybody is just content to go about their business. Nobody has the edge they need to fight. Why? Because we don't usually have criminals here."

"It's a nice way to live," I said.

"Yeah, well," he said, mouth twisting into a rueful smile, "it was."

Chapter 12

"LOOK AT THE COLORS, WOULD YOU?" Lois said, awe dropping her voice to a whisper. "I had no idea RH Galleries would do such a marvelous job."

Lois was an assistant curator, which is to say she now worked for me. When I'd been hired, I'd asked for a departmental organization chart only to be told such a thing didn't exist. Marshfield's staff had grown over the years, but there were no clear lines delineating who reported to whom. The only mandate that seemed clear was that everyone eventually reported to Abe.

Lois had been on staff for about fifteen years. Early forties, chubby, with blond hair and a quick smile, she was one of my favorites, even from my first day. She worked on the second floor of the administrative wing, one level below my office. We had three people in that area, all of whom were assistant curators. When I'd been hired with that title, I had asked about the reporting structure. Were these three other assistants my peers or subordinates? And how did Frances fit into the picture? I was told, vaguely, that it would all work out and not to worry. So eager was I to work in the palace of my childhood dreams that I accepted Abe's promise at face value.

And now that he was gone, I realized I would have to sort all this out on my own.

We stood amidst a musty collection of junk in one of the second-floor bedrooms in the mansion's east wing. With a view to the north and an adjacent bath, this had once been a busy guest room. Now it served as a staging area for our discoveries. In a place as big as Marshfield, there were many areas left unexplored. We were forever finding trinkets and treasures in hidden niches and little-used rooms.

This former bedroom was being used to store items we hadn't yet decided where to place, and for items as they waited to be picked up for repair. Well lit, trimmed in dark oak, as was most of the rest of the manor, this room had been stripped bare of any ornamentation. Good thing, because it was as cluttered with artifacts and artwork as Bennett's private room had been.

I took a step closer to the portrait of Warren Marshfield, Jr., understanding the basis of Lois's admiration. The painting had been brought back to vibrant life after spending decades in dusty storage. "Wow," I said. "Looks like we made a good decision, huh?"

For the first time since Marshfield Manor opened as a museum, we had chosen to have one of its treasures restored at an Emberstowne establishment rather than send it out to one of our regular restoration experts. The reason for this was twofold. One: We liked the idea of supporting our local merchants; and, two: the owner of RH Galleries, Roxanne Heath, had been begging us for months to give her a try. We finally had with this painting discovered in the attic. With dozens of family portraits lining the walls of this grand castle, the risk of sending one insignificant piece was small. It had been so covered with grime that we hadn't even been able to discern the artist's name.

But now . . .

"Take a look at this," Lois said, handing me a note.

Roxanne's stationery was embossed with a gold lowercase *rh* on the front. I opened the crisp vanilla vellum and read:

Words cannot express my thanks to you for entrusting me with such a valuable piece from your collection. Thank you for allowing me to work with this treasure.

Sincerely,
  Rox

I turned to Lois who grinned. "Is she being sarcastic, or is she really this excited?"

"I think she means this." Lois pointed to the signature on the painting's lower right.

"No way," I said.

"Way."

I twisted toward the room's desk, but Lois was quicker. She grabbed the brass-handled magnifying glass and handed it to me, her smile getting wider by the moment. "I couldn't believe it when I saw it."

Carrying the painting closer to the window for natural light, I stared down at the signature, guiding the magnifying glass up and down until the name was clear. "Wow," I said, looking up at her. "And this gem was tucked away in the attic all these years?"

"Getting grungier by the day."

I felt my smile grow as big as Lois's. "We rescued it," I said, then looked more closely. "Now we just have to verify that this is, indeed, a genuine Raphael Soyer."

"You doubt it?"

"I take God on faith," I said. "All others pay cash."

She laughed. "Can you imagine how much this is worth if it's real?"

I nodded. "I'll put it in one of the safes. At least until we call in an expert to verify its authenticity. Can you arrange for that?"

"I'll get right on it."

I walked back to my office via the public corridors, carrying our happy discovery, pleased to see the manor teeming with visitors. Some carried a digital playback device hanging from a sturdy lanyard around their necks and wore buds in their ears. These audio guides were provided to narrate the mansion's history at whatever speed the guest preferred. This experience was relatively new— we'd just begun offering it a month ago but already demand was far outstripping our supply. I made a note to confirm delivery of the next order of players. They couldn't get here quick enough.

Docents roamed the area as well. Some were stationed inside rooms to prevent people from crossing the velvet rope barriers; some stood in the hallways, eager to answer questions or provide directions. All of them, male and female, wore the same standard-issue uniform: navy blazer with the Marshfield coat of arms embroidered on the chest pocket, tan slacks, white shirt, and red tie. I nodded hello as I passed, smiling at the individuals who smiled back, clearly pleased to be back at their posts.

I turned the corner, headed toward the back stairs. As I approached, a male docent just ahead of me twisted away suddenly as though responding to an unexpected noise. I hadn't heard anything. He froze in that position then trotted down the corridor, away from me.

"Hello," I called to his departing figure. "Is something wrong?"

He didn't turn. Rather, he picked up his pace.

I called to him again.

He had to have heard. But still he ignored me.

The mansion had back stairs that the staff used when not escorting guests, more or less hidden from view by doors that looked like regular room doors. The guy ahead of me bypassed these and ran down the wide, main staircase—weaving from side to side as he dodged visitors trudging up.

With the painting in my hands, I was unwilling to break out into a full run. "Wait, please," I called again.

As he turned at the stair's landing, I finally got a look at his face. "You!" I shouted, surprise bringing me to a halt.

People turned at my exclamation. Reluctant to cause a scene, I bit my lip, grabbed my walkie-talkie, and called for security as unobtrusively as I could manage while resuming a more sedate pursuit. The last thing we needed was for our guests—with the recent murder on their minds—to stampede out the door in panic.

My quarry stopped at the bottom of the stairs long enough to give me a sheepish wave, then Ronny Tooney took off for the back exit, as fast as his sneaky legs could carry him.

"WHAT IS IT WITH THIS GUY?" I ASKED Terrence Carr when we met in my office later. "How is he getting in?"

Carr didn't sit. He paced the office, stopping to stare out the windows before answering. "I thought we'd covered every possible entrance point. And how the hell did he get out?"

I couldn't answer that. "Your guys were on the scene in seconds."

"And yet he disappeared." Carr's voice held a mixture of disbelief and disgust. "Again." He turned from the window to face me. "When you saw him, did you notice if his blazer had the embroidered crest on the pocket? Or was it plain?"

I thought back to the run through the corridors. The only good look I got was when he'd been one flight below me. I'd been concentrating on his face, not his apparel. "Can't say for sure."

"Have laundry do an inventory of uniforms. I want to know if any have gone missing." Carr's nostrils widened as he took a deep breath. "Could be he was just wearing the right colors and nobody noticed it wasn't regulation. We're going to have to train everyone on staff to be more alert."

"What do you think Tooney wanted?"

"He wants to be part of the process. Badly."

I'd watched plenty of cop shows in my day. "Isn't that usually the mark of the guilty party? To try to insert himself into the investigation?"

Carr was about to answer when Frances walked in. Without knocking.

"You'll want to see this." As she handed me an envelope, she gave Carr a meaningful glance. "You'll want to see it, too. We got another one."

I held the plain, white business envelope by its

edges and peered into the open top. The paper inside appeared to be cream-colored construction paper. Frances wasn't kidding. This was another threat. "You didn't touch the letter, did you?" I asked.

She flashed a look of disdain. "What do you think?"

Carr sprinted around the desk and by the time I opened my drawer, he'd pulled a pair of latex gloves from his belt and donned them. "Allow me," he said.

"Hang on."

I handed him a pair of extra-long tweezers. "We handle a lot of delicate things in this office. I like to be prepared. Here, take my seat."

He sat, nodding a distracted thanks, focused entirely on the envelope. Before pulling out the sheaf inside, he shot a glance to Frances. "Call Detective Rodriguez. He'll want this for evidence."

As she reached for the phone on my desk, Carr snapped, "Use your phone. I don't want to feel crowded here."

Frances wrinkled her nose at the directive—clearly miffed to be ordered out.

As she crossed the threshold, I whispered to Carr, "How much you want to bet she'll be back in under a minute?"

He broke concentration long enough to grin. I'd positioned myself to his left, one hand on the desk, the other on my hip. If he felt as though I was crowding him here he didn't mention it and I wasn't feeling particularly polite. All I wanted was to get a look at this new message before the police whisked it away.

He laid the envelope on the desk facedown with the slit side facing right. Gingerly, he lifted the back of the envelope and grabbed the letter inside with the very tips of the tweezers. He swallowed, and though the room was comfortable a tiny trickle of sweat formed directly in front of his left ear.

"Should we call Bennett down?"

He stopped his maneuvers and squinted off into the distance. "Let's wait. He's got plenty of time to get worked up again. No sense in bringing that on too early."

"Somebody is with him, right? Keeping an eye on him?"

Carr nodded. "Two guards every moment he's not in his rooms, and two others as often as possible when he is. Mr. Marshfield is not happy with this arrangement and keeps kicking the guards out. Frustrating." Licking his lips, Carr returned his attention to the process at hand.

I held my breath as he tugged at the construction paper. The coarseness of the document made it difficult to slide and Carr hissed his frustration when a corner of the page caught for the third time.

"The envelope was mailed and postmarked," I

said, intending to be helpful. "Can't we just rip that open because it's probably covered with fingerprints already?"

He shook his head, not looking at me. "You never know what you might need," he said. "You never know what evidence may turn up, or be required as the investigation progresses. Treating evidence with care is a good habit to develop. And one we try never to compromise, even when it seems obvious that extraordinary caution is unnecessary."

As he spoke, the page inside came free. Using the tweezers to turn the single sheet, Carr took a deep breath before gently unfolding it.

Frances returned. "What does it say?" she asked.

I leaned in close enough to get a whiff of Carr's spicy aftershave. This letter was longer and I read silently.

TO BENNETT MARSHFIELD:
YOU GOT LUCKY, OLD MAN. DON'T THINK YOU WILL BE SO LUCKY AGAIN. ABE'S DEATH WAS AN ACCIDENT. THIS MUST BE UNDERSTOOD. YOU WILL NEVER BE SAFE AGAIN UNLESS YOU GIVE US WHAT YOU OWE. THE STAKES ARE TOO HIGH. DELIVER THE FUNDS AS DESCRIBED BELOW OR THIS TIME WE WILL NOT MISS. YOU WILL PAY OR YOU WILL DIE.

"Whoa," I said, leaning back. "Did you notice the word *we*?"

Carr nodded. "But psychopaths often refer to themselves in the plural. It could mean nothing."

Frances moved closer. "What does it say?" she asked again.

But Carr folded the letter before she could get a glance. He stood, placed the document in a clear plastic evidence bag he withdrew from his belt, and headed for the door. "I'll get this to Rodriguez right away."

Frances blocked his path, her arms folded. "Why don't I get to read it?"

Carr stopped long enough to answer, "You don't need to."

Pointing at me, Frances frowned. "But she does?"

"Yeah," he said.

I interrupted. "Can we make a copy before you take it? I'll want to show this to Bennett."

Carr snapped his fingers. "Good idea."

I led him to the copier and he placed the letter on the glass. Frances hovered. Within seconds he'd made two copies, handed one of the still-warm sheets to me, and rebagged the evidence. "Thanks," I said.

He left without another word.

I wouldn't have been surprised to see steam radiating from the top of my assistant's head. "Who does he think he is?" Turning back to me, she asked, "What does it say?"

"More of the same," I said, keeping it vague. I pulled out my file with the other letters and added this one to the group. Frances strained for an upside-down look.

"What did you mean when you said 'we'?"

I took a deep breath and sat down, closing the manila file. "I just thought it could be a clue. An insight into the killer's identity," I said. "The letter-writer referred to 'we' rather than 'I,' but Carr is right. That might not mean anything at all."

"You think that Ronny Tooney guy could be involved?"

"He strikes me as more of a nuisance than a danger."

"Quite the nuisance," Frances agreed. "Turns out Melissa and Rosa might have talked to Tooney the night of the murder. They thought he was a real cop, too."

"At least the real police talked with them both later."

"Speaking of detectives," my assistant continued, "you think that young buck, Flynn, is married?"

"No idea."

"He might be a good catch."

Why Frances was so interested in my personal life was beyond me. Or maybe she was just one of those people who couldn't keep her nose out of other people's business. "He's not my type."

"Not you. I meant Melissa, the housekeeper. She

could use a stand-up man in her life. That Flynn's a cutie."

In my opinion Flynn was a pompous ass. "I thought Melissa was married."

"*Pheh*. I think they're separated. After that husband of hers pulled his stunt, I think she had enough and kicked him out."

"What stunt?"

In her element, Frances beamed. "About a year ago the husband told Melissa she could quit work so they could start a family. You never saw a girl so happy. We threw her a going-away party. Next thing you know, *boom*. She's working back here again."

Despite my better instincts, I asked, "What happened?"

"He changed his mind." Frances's eyes brightened. "I think he took off, leaving her without a job or any money. So she came back to work here. Melissa doesn't talk about him anymore. Doesn't smile much anymore either. Used to be all she could talk about was her Samuel, but after she started working back here again, she went mum. Poor kid."

I thought about Liza running off. And Eric not so far behind. "Yeah, well there's a lot of that going around," I said.

"Sad," Frances agreed, not having any clue what I meant. "And Rosa's story is even worse. Her granddaughter got into some big trouble doing drugs. The granddaughter has been hitting Rosa up for money right and left. It's getting ugly. But you know what the worst part is?"

I'd reached my gossip limit for the day. "I'd better get in touch with Bennett to let him know about the new letter," I said. "Some other time."

She made a noise of disgust and started for her office. "Used to be around here people appreciated me," she said.

I ignored that and lifted the phone.

Chapter 13

BENNETT ARRIVED IN MY OFFICE ABOUT ten minutes later, accompanied by two security officers, who waited in the anteroom with Frances. I shut the door.

I didn't know exactly what to expect from Bennett when I showed him the newest letter, but what I hadn't anticipated were the swift tears that filled his eyes.

"I'm sorry," I said, instinctively pulling the copy toward me. "I just thought you should be kept informed."

He swallowed noisily, his nose reddening. He averted his eyes to stare out the window but I could tell he wasn't seeing anything. When he blinked, tears streamed freely down his weathered cheeks. "No," he whispered, "I'm the one who's sorry."

For several minutes there were no sounds in the room except for the rush of the air in the vents and the ticking of the mantel clock. I watched the secondhand step around the face, each soft *thck* an urge for me to say something, anything, to ease Bennett's pain. But there was nothing anyone could do.

I cleared my throat.

As though reminded of my presence, Bennett turned to face me. He wiped his eyes, not trying to hide it. "I should have paid," he said. "Maybe if I had, Abe would still be here."

"Criminals don't operate by the same rules you and I do," I said. "There's no predicting that."

Watery blue eyes met mine with skepticism. Truth was, as much as I believed it would have been wrong to pay this extortion, I also assumed that the killer would not have broken into the mansion if the money *had* been paid.

"You're new," Bennett said. "You don't know this town like I do."

I opened my mouth to argue, thought better of it, and listened instead.

"People knew that Abe and I were friends. Good friends. He and his family have been with my family for generations. When my wives died, Abe was there for me. When his wife died, it was I who held his hand and walked him through the arrangements. We grew up together. Became men together." Bennett's Adam's apple bobbed. "Abe used to joke that he would take a bullet for me." The tears sprang again to his eyes. "And now he has."

I didn't know what to say to that.

Bennett continued, "Whoever killed Abe knew how much it would kill me. I don't believe this was an accident. I believe whoever did this meant to do so. They meant to make me suffer."

"You're assuming it's someone from Emberstowne?" I asked gently.

He blinked at me in annoyance. "Who else could it be?"

"The way things are these days," I said, keeping my voice low, "it could be anyone angry because you have so much and they have so little. The mansion is featured in documentaries and magazines all over the country. You're an international celebrity. Everyone knows who you are."

"And see where that's gotten me." The irritation in his eyes lessened, but only slightly. "With a target on my back and the backs of my dearest friends."

"The detectives will be going over this newest letter," I said in an effort to return to the matter at hand. "I have a feeling this one holds the answers."

Again the skepticism. "You're so young."

"Look," I said, turning the sheet sideways so we could both read it. "It refers to 'we' and it claims you 'owe' them."

Bennett seemed unimpressed but let me continue.

"Maybe," I broached the subject as benignly as I could, "this is related to your testimony against T. Randall Taft."

Bennett reacted as though the thought had never occurred to him. "No," he said, but the denial in his voice wavered. His gaze roved the room, seeking answers in its corners. "Randall would never . . ."

I said nothing.

"It's too terrible to contemplate," he said. Answers were apparently not to be found in our surroundings, and he clenched his eyes. "Randall understands why I turned him in. He must."

I silently wondered how a man as sophisticated as Bennett could be so naïve. Bennett had been the instrument of Taft's ruin. People killed one another over matters more trivial than this every day.

"Look at the timing," I said. "These letters started arriving fairly soon after Taft was indicted. I don't think we can discount him as a suspect. I'm pretty sure the detectives consider him a person of interest."

"Can't be." Bennett shook his head with effort. "No."

I focused on him. "How are you?" I asked. "I know this has been hard. How are you holding up?"

He jerked a thumb at the door. "I wish they'd release the damn babysitters. I'm not an invalid, you know. I can't even walk around without company. Two of them. Night and day. The only time they leave me alone is when I'm asleep in my bed and only because I insist. A man needs his privacy," he said in a way that dared me to contradict.

"You have to understand . . ."

"No," he said, vehemence overtaking his voice. "Everyone *else* needs to understand. I am Bennett Marshfield. I own this home. Why should I suffer under the rules of those who work for me? Shouldn't I be the one making the rules here? Do you all believe I'm incapable of handling myself?"

If the intruder who killed Abe had outdistanced our landscape consultant, Jack Embers, I ventured to guess that he was in good enough physical condition to overpower Bennett. Instead of voicing that opinion, I said, "No one is suggesting you're incapable. But we are worried for your safety. For our collective safety. You are clearly a target. If we're able to make it known that you're protected, then we all benefit. No one will attempt to get in with guards surrounding you. And that makes it safer for everyone here."

He gave grudging acknowledgment.

I decided to broach the swindling subject once more. "Let's talk about Taft. I just want to understand how he got away with his money scheme for as long as he did."

Bennett faced me straight on and leaned forward, placing his elbows on the desk. "I'll tell you why he was able to get away with it—because people are greedy. It's the truly blessed man who can be content with what he has and who isn't always longing for that elusive 'something more.'"

I thought about the wealth that surrounded me every moment I spent at Marshfield Manor. I thought about my leaky roof, and the back fence, which needed shoring up. I thought about the myriad of things I needed and the luxuries I did without.

"*You're* that blessed man," I said, thinking about how little he knew of the desperation others experienced throughout their lives. He lasered a glare at me, but I plunged on. It was ridiculous for him to pontificate about the nature of greed from his comfortable perch in the crown of luxury. "You have everything you've ever wanted."

"Did I know you were this impertinent when I hired you?"

"I'm only suggesting that maybe that's why you were able to see Taft's scheme for what it was. You don't need his help to get rich."

He leaned back ever so slightly. "True. Randall and I go way back. He was always taking the shortcut, always trying to compare himself with me. But for what purpose? I'm not bragging when I say that my family owned a thousand times what his family did. That's just how it was. It never bothered me and I couldn't understand why it bothered him. But it did."

"Maybe that's why Taft tried to entice you into investing with him."

Bennett nodded slowly. "I asked him for a prospectus and for a few other key items. And he provided what he had, poor bastard." He looked up at me. "Why would he do that?"

"Maybe he hoped you would lose everything? Maybe he hoped to bring you down with the rest of his clients when the house of cards collapsed."

"No," Bennett said. "I believe Randall was tired of the charade. He wanted to be caught and he expected me to turn him in. That's why I know Randall can't be behind Abe's killing. No matter how much he lost for himself or for his clients, Randall would never hold me personally responsible. And even if he did, he and I go back too far for him to try to harm me or my staff."

I thought that little speech spoke less to Taft's loyalty and more to Bennett's naïveté.

We'd stayed on this subject too long. Bennett started to rise, but I hadn't had half of my questions addressed. I stopped him with, "Did you hear about our find this morning?"

Lowering himself back into the seat, his eyes twinkled. The first glimmer of interest I'd seen from him all day. "What do you mean by 'find'?"

I told him about the Raphael Soyer painting we'd just had restored. "But before we can truly celebrate, we'll have to wait for final authentication."

"That portrait of my dad used to hang in his sitting room. I always wondered what happened to it." He smiled then—warm, real happiness bringing life to his face. "Keep me updated."

I promised I would.

When I tried veering the subject back to Taft, Bennett pushed himself out of his chair. Clearly, this was a signal for me to cease and desist. But there were too many unanswered questions and I believed Bennett held the key to some of their answers. I stood, too.

"If you don't think Taft had anything to do with Abe . . ." I began.

"I don't."

"Then who do you think is after you?" I pointed at the copy of the most recent letter on my desk. "Who else is out there who might believe you owe him something?"

"If I had any idea, I would tell you, and the detectives." Bennett turned away, but stopped just before the door. "Everyone wants a part of me. Everyone wants assurances that they will be provided for when I die. But I've set it up so that no one person will profit from my demise. You haven't asked, but you will eventually. And I will tell you now what I have told everyone else: Upon my death, this estate becomes the property of Emberstowne. With its income and the trust account I've set up, there should be plenty of money to keep the estate running indefinitely. No one wants me dead, because as long as I'm alive, I retain the power to change my will." He laughed, but without humor. "It's almost like having an insurance policy."

I thought of his commentary about the blessed

man who never wanted for anything. Bennett was not that man after all.

"I plan to do some digging of my own," I said.

Hand on the doorknob, he turned. "Do you, now? Don't you have confidence in our detective friends?"

"I think they're inexperienced in situations this serious."

"And you believe you can do better?"

"No, of course not," I said with a little asperity. "But I do believe I have the capacity to help."

One corner of Bennett's mouth curled upward. "Update me as needed," he said. "But do be careful." He shuddered and the lightness of his mood flashed away. Pulling open the door, he said softly, "I wish I could have been there for Abe."

As he left, I realized I'd forgotten to remind him about those keys he'd mentioned. I was curious as to how much access he planned to grant me with regard to the private rooms.

Frances didn't waste any time. The moment Bennett and his escorts were gone, she swung into my office. "Did the Mister say anything about you taking over Abe's office?"

"How is the mansion operating today?" I asked, ignoring her. "Are we caught up with all the complaints from yesterday?"

"All but that Geraldine woman. She's relentless."

"You predicted she'd turn up again."

Frances smiled at the implied compliment. "Bit

quicker than I expected. Now she's threatening to sue us for emotional aggravation."

"What? That's nuts."

"*She's* nuts."

"What will it take to make her go away?"

Frances's mouth dropped open. "You're not going to give in to her?"

"We're in the middle of the worst crisis this place has ever experienced. We need to focus on that first. The last thing we need is some crazy guest initiating a frivolous lawsuit. We pride ourselves on keeping our guests happy." I held up my hand to stave off Frances's objections. "So, again, what will it take to make her go away?"

Wiggling her shoulders in a way that made her displeasure clear, Frances said, "She wants to come back and stay here for free."

"Fine," I said. "She can have her free night."

"She wants two."

"Two?"

Frances nodded. "And she wants to stay on the concierge floor."

"This woman really is a piece of work, isn't she?"

"Told you."

I sat up. "Give me her number."

Chapter 14

PASTING A SMILE ON MY FACE, WHICH I hoped would be conveyed over the phone line, I prepared to do polite battle with the avaricious Geraldine. I was confident I could turn this situation into a positive—and was eager to have a go at her.

Unfortunately, her phone went directly to voicemail. After debating the wisdom of leaving a message, I simply said, "This is Grace Wheaton from Marshfield Manor. I'm sorry to have missed you. I'll call back again soon." I didn't invite her to return the call. Better I should choose when to make contact.

Thwarted from getting that small task done, I consulted my to-do list. This list was often all that came between me and certifiable insanity. Keeping the mansion running smoothly was paramount. And with that mandate, I knew I had to put the kibosh on any more intrusions by Ronny Tooney.

Tooney was more nuisance than threat. But I didn't like the idea of the guy skulking around here, able to drift in and out without anyone noticing.

I opened the door, catching Frances in the middle of a personal phone call. I held up a hand. "Let me know when you're done," I said, about to start back into my office.

She said, "Gotta go," into the phone, and hung up. "Sorry."

Sorry? From Frances? "No problem," I said. "I just wanted to ask what you know about Ronny Tooney."

"Never met the man," she said. "But I think he's related to somebody on staff." She tapped her fingers on the desk. "Yvonne, maybe. Can't remember. Want me to find out?"

"Absolutely." If someone on the inside had helped Tooney gain access to the house, I needed to know about it. "And while we're at it, can we get a list of everyone Taft swindled?"

"Why do you want that?"

"The timing is just too coincidental. All these threats, Abe's murder, they all came on the heels of Taft's indictment. I want to learn more about the guy and I figure I might find clues in his client list." I pointed to her telephone. "I'll bet Bennett's attorneys can get their hands on a copy."

Her eyes lit up as she reached for the phone. "Not a bad idea."

JACK EMBERS WAS PUSHING AN EMPTY wheelbarrow across one of the garden paths when I stopped him. Although he'd claimed to be "playing in the dirt" last time we met, I assumed that as a consultant, he would be more involved in management than in actually participating in the physical labor. Interesting. "Hey," I called to him.

The day still held a wet chill. I should have brought my sweater with me. When I shivered, Jack raised an eyebrow. He was dirty, clad in a sweat-stained gray T-shirt and green shorts. His legs were long, lean, and shiny with perspiration.

"So?" he asked, "Caught the guy yet?"

"No, but I almost caught that fake detective." I told him about chasing Ronny Tooney down the stairs, then losing him in the crowd when he turned the corner. "Have you seen him again anywhere?"

Jack worked his jaw, staring at some middle distance. "No, but if I do, there will be hell to pay."

My face apparently broadcasted my alarm, because he smiled then. "Don't worry. I'm not going to beat him up or anything. What kind of person do you think I am?"

Too startled to blurt anything but the truth, I said, "I have no idea. I really don't know anything about you."

My statement hung there for an awkward moment. I realized I'd given him an inadvertent lead-in for the inevitable "Then maybe we should get to know one another better" response.

But he didn't say it.

I didn't know if I was more relieved or disappointed. Shifting my weight, I said, "I know the police are doing all they can . . ."

"But?"

Feeling foolish, I nonetheless plunged ahead. "Maybe I'm just used to a bigger city and major task force initiatives. The manpower here is staggeringly small and this investigation is crawling."

"And you're intent on helping speed things up."

"If I can," I said knowing how ridiculous that sounded. "That's why I wanted to ask if you remembered anything else about the man you chased. Any details, any impressions?"

His mouth twitched. "Well, city girl, there was one other detail I remembered just this morning. I'm sure it's no big deal, but I figured if I caught up to the police, I'd let them know. Maybe you can tell them for me?"

"Absolutely," I said. "What is it?"

"It dawned on me later that the guy wasn't pumping his arms as he ran. I was behind him for quite some distance and his hands were always in front of his body."

I followed his logic. "He was carrying something?"

"I think so."

"And not just the threatening letter," I said, continuing the thought. "He wouldn't have needed two hands for that." Feeling like I'd been given a gift, I thanked him and started back for my office.

"Hey," he said.

I turned.

"I know you want to get involved in this

investigation," he said, "but be careful. There's a very bad person out there."

"I will."

"Good," he said, "because I really don't know you yet either."

He turned away before I could get a read on his meaning. Was he mocking me? Or flirting?

I looked back once before I pulled open the back entrance door, but Jack had already disappeared into the gardens.

Chapter 15

"IT'S ABOUT TIME," BRUCE SAID WHEN the back screen door slammed behind me. "We almost gave up on you." Standing in the middle of the kitchen wearing a green-striped apron, he held a steaming pot in one hand and a metal colander in the other. "Turn on the light, will you?"

Hefting the banker's box in my arms to one side, I snapped the wall switch, immediately banishing the shadows from the pink-tiled room. With daylight waning, the overhead light made the area feel particularly welcoming and warm.

"What smells so good?" I asked. Pulling open the oven door, I sniffed the heavenly scent of homemade meat loaf. "Oh."

Bruce drained potatoes at the sink. "I think we all need comfort food tonight."

Closing the oven, I stood. "Uh-oh. What happened?"

He winced, but it wasn't from the steam shooting up around his face. "Dina St. Clair didn't call." Turning his back, he shook the colander to release any remaining water. I watched his shoulders shrug. "She said she would be in touch today if *Grape Living* was interested in doing the feature spread."

"Did you try calling her?"

"Twice," he said, still with his back to me. I wondered if he was trying to avoid letting me see his disappointment. "Once she was in a meeting and said she'd call me back. The second time she didn't answer."

"Did you leave a message?"

"No." He turned and smiled. But I could tell it was for my benefit. "Scott's really disappointed."

"Just because she didn't call today doesn't mean she forgot about you. Maybe she had some personal problem. Maybe *Grape Living* hasn't made a decision yet and she's waiting to hear."

"She's their top feature scout. If she recommends us, we're in."

"I don't understand the problem, then."

Bruce pulled out the hand mixer, butter, and garlic. Comfort food, indeed.

His voice quiet, he chanced a look toward the dining room, as though afraid Scott might hear. "What if she changed her mind? Maybe she doesn't want to bother telling us. She probably assumes we'll just figure it out over time."

"Give her a break. And give yourselves a little credit. What magazine wouldn't want to feature you guys?"

Bruce raised one shoulder.

I placed my hand on his muscled forearm. "It's only one day, right? Try her again tomorrow. I'll bet you'll hear some good news."

Turning his back to me again, Bruce plunged the mixer into the potatoes and started it up. I left him there and headed upstairs to change.

AFTER BRUCE'S WONDERFUL, SOUL-nourishing dinner, I pulled my two roommates over. "My assistant, Frances, is a pain in my behind but she is the most efficient worker on the planet." I'd brought home a box of files and began to spread them out on the dining room table. Part of me hoped they would see something I didn't, the rest of me hoped I could get their minds off *Grape Living*, at least for a little while. "I asked her for these records just this afternoon, and she had them for me in under three hours."

Scott lifted the cover of one of the bound folders and scanned the first page. "What are you looking for?"

I sorted through the box again. "The police believe Abe was killed by an intruder intent on robbery. They think the threatening letters have nothing to do with Abe's death."

Both men exclaimed their disbelief. Bruce practically shouted, "But you said that the new letter today claimed Abe wasn't the target. Doesn't that letter *prove* the killing and the letters are related?"

"You'd think so, wouldn't you?" I asked. "The police aren't totally dismissing the idea of the letter-writer also being the killer, but they said they're skeptical. They brought up the story of that Tylenol guy back in the 1980s."

Scott said, "I don't follow."

Bruce said, "I was just a kid."

I stopped foraging long enough to explain. "You know how that one guy tried to extort money but when he was arrested, claimed he had nothing to do with the actual poisonings?"

"Oh yeah." Scott picked up the thread. "I do remember hearing about that. So the police here in Emberstowne think this extortionist is attempting to exploit Abe's murder in the same way?"

"To make their threat seem more grave, yes," I said. "That's what the police are telling us, at least. What they really suspect is anyone's guess."

"It's smarter for the cops to keep their information close to their vests," Bruce said. "Keeps people from trying to help."

"Not going to stop me," I said and resumed my search.

Bruce rubbed his chin. "But wasn't there something in the news not so long ago about that Tylenol extortionist getting arrested again because now they really believe he is the person who poisoned those victims?"

"Bingo!" I pulled out a thick binder and grinned at Bruce. "That's exactly what I'm thinking. You know, the old 'where there's smoke' adage? Even though the police are claiming that the news coverage of Abe's killing inspired our letter-writer,

I'm convinced that the two are related. And with this . . ." I held up the binder, which weighed more than a bag of sugar, "I intend to prove it."

The two looked at me skeptically. "Exactly how?" Scott asked.

Bruce sat down at the head of the table. "Should you be nosing around like this, Grace? Won't the police get irritated with you?"

Scott jumped in. "And isn't that one of the marks of the guilty party? They try to insert themselves into the investigation?"

I'd used that same argument earlier with regard to Tooney. "This is different," I said. "I'm the acting director of the estate. I'm responsible for everything that goes on. I have a fiduciary responsibility to follow up."

Their skeptical looks didn't budge.

Undaunted, I continued, "And as to how I intend to do this, I plan to follow the money. T. Randall Taft lost everything when Bennett turned him in."

Bruce ran his fingers along file folder edges. "Taft is in jail. And was in jail when Abe was killed."

"That doesn't mean he didn't hire someone."

Scott took the binder from my hands, with a grunt. "You're stretching it, kid." He took a look at the blue cardboard cover. "So what's in here?"

"Taft isn't the only person who lost millions. So did a lot of others. That," I tapped the weight in his hands, "is a list of all Taft's clients, and an accounting—to the best of the attorneys' knowledge—of how much each investor lost."

Scott dropped the binder to the table with a thud. He lifted the cover and fanned through the pages. "Geez, how many people did this guy bilk?"

"He was at it for a long time."

"So it seems." Scott sat in the chair to Bruce's right as he flipped pages. "These are arranged in order of investments. The top losers . . ." he glanced up, "those over five million, that is, take up six pages alone."

I leaned over to look. "I'll never get through all of them."

They both looked at me like I was nuts. "You plan to research every name in this file?" Scott asked.

"Of course not. But I do plan to look into the most suspicious ones."

"Suspicious," Scott repeated. "As in, which investors lost the most money?"

"Exactly." I grimaced at the list. "Thank goodness they're listed in dollar order. Now if only I could have a separate copy in alpha order, too, to help me keep track, I'd be all set."

Scott shrugged. "Ask the lawyers to send you the document as a spreadsheet. Then you can sort the data however you like."

"Duh." I clunked my forehead with my fist. "Why didn't I think of that?"

"Because your brain is overtaxed," Bruce said.

He got up from his chair and made his way back to the kitchen, where I heard clinking glasses and the unmistakable cork-creak and hollow pop of wine being opened. His voice rose as he continued, "You've been on the go since you started working there, and now this horrible tragedy has you tied up in knots. You need to chill out, sweetie. Leave the files for one night. Get in touch with the lawyers tomorrow and get the information in a form that works for you."

I took a look at the thick binder and felt all my energy drain. "You're probably right."

"Of course I'm right," he said, returning to the dining room with two big glasses of garnet red wine. "For you," he said, handing me one.

He gave Scott the other before returning to the kitchen. When he reemerged, he held a chilled plate of chocolate-covered strawberries in one hand and his glass of wine and the bottle in the other.

"The oh-six?" Scott said, aghast.

"It won't wait forever," Bruce said, gesturing us into the parlor. "And there are few bad days that can't be turned around with a good Cabernet and a healthy dose of chocolate."

LATE THAT NIGHT, AS I STARED AT THE ceiling of my room—the same room I'd shared with Liza when we were very little—I thought about the twists and turns of life that had ultimately brought me back to where I'd started. The wine should have made me sleepy, but my mind raced with disconnected thoughts.

This room used to be my mother's when she'd lived here as a child. My grandmother had occupied the master bedroom, which she'd reportedly shared with her husband on those rare occasions he returned home. He came back only for money, food, or other sustenance. I thought of Liza. I guess that tendency ran in our family.

From all accounts, my grandfather Peter Careaux had been a huckster. Quick to talk anybody out of a buck. Quicker even to spend it—as long as it was on himself and not his wife or two young daughters.

I imagined he'd been a lot like Taft—just on a much, much smaller scale.

I probably should have at least started going through those investor files.

With my bedroom window open, I could hear frogs croaking out to one another in the murky night. A cool breeze lifted the sheer curtains and drifted past my wine-warmed skin. I thanked God it wasn't raining. I didn't know how much longer the roof would hold out.

What was it about this house? Why did we all come back? When my grandmother died, my mom and dad moved our family to Chicago, leaving this old Victorian to the whims of renters whose backgrounds they didn't check thoroughly. It wasn't until years later, after my dad had passed away and I had moved to New York, that my mom had insisted on moving back. By then the house had suffered, almost too much. But my mother was a stubborn woman.

Maybe the house was bad luck.

Maybe I should sell and get away from here.

I blinked and turned onto my right side so I could stare out the window at the high branches of the tree just outside. I had no idea what kind of tree it was and I felt oddly sad about that. I'd lived here so many years and yet . . . and yet this hadn't ever really been my home.

I should walk away tomorrow and get a job elsewhere. A person with my experience would be snapped up in a minute. Yeah, right. In this economy? Leaving would allow me to step away from Abe's murder. Abdicate responsibility. I could sell this house, take the money, and make my way in the world the same way Liza did—with absolutely no regard for anyone's happiness but her own.

How easy it sounded.

I swallowed. Was Eric with her?

Shadows moved across my ceiling as cars drove past, their headlights reflected in my neighbors' windows, their glow arcing across my room. I heard the soft *shush* of one making its way slowly down our small street. I heard the bass beat of another, its rhythm quick and syncopated, reminding me that we had teenagers in the neighborhood.

If the house really was cursed, maybe the reason my parents' marriage was good was because they'd moved away. Maybe if I hadn't brought Eric here, he would never have met Liza.

And maybe I should stop dwelling on such things so late at night when the world is dark and life holds little promise.

I closed my eyes and whispered, "Stop!" hoping to change my brain's path by sheer force of will. I told myself to think about my roommates and how lucky I was to have them in my life. I thought about my job, which—despite this week's tragedy—was exactly where I'd always wanted to be.

Inexplicably, my conversation with Jack Embers this afternoon popped into my mind—his warning to be careful, and his parting comment about not knowing me well. What did that mean, exactly? Or did it mean nothing at all?

And on that last lingering thought about Jack, I finally fell asleep.

Chapter 16

"THEY SAID THEY CAN'T."

With my concentration broken by Frances's pronouncement from the doorway, I pressed a finger next to the line I'd been reading to hold my place, then processed her words.

"Who can't what?"

"The Mister's attorneys say they don't have Taft's investor information in spreadsheet form. The files they sent were based off of their hardcopies."

Well, that dashed my hopes. "Darn."

"They also said that the information they sent earlier was only done so because Marshfield Manor is one of their favorite clients. They wanted us to know that our request for the list of investors was highly unusual, but they were willing to help Mr. Marshfield." Frances sniffed. "Like they have anyone bigger than the Mister."

I looked down at the files I'd been poring over, blocks of text so dense they made my eyes wiggle. "In other words, this is as good as it gets."

"Looks like."

I wrinkled my nose then placed a yellow Post-it note where my finger had been, and stood up. "I need a break."

"Would you like some coffee?"

You could have knocked me over with a feather. "Uh, thanks, no. I'm good."

"Have you found out anything?"

I consulted the notes I'd scribbled. "Ever hear of . . . ?" I rattled off a few names.

She shook her head.

"So far, they're some of the biggest losers in the Taft Ponzi scheme," I said. "I don't know what I can find on any of them, but I'll look them up on the Internet. You never know what will pop."

"You want me to contact the agency we sometimes work with?"

"Agency?"

Frances's eyes took on a conspiratorial glow as she moved closer to my desk. "We engage a service every once in a while."

"Like a private detective?"

She nodded.

"Not Ronny Tooney?"

"Fairfax Investigations. This agency is extremely discreet."

"Thanks," I said. "I'll look into it."

"They're real good. They know everything about everybody."

"Even more than you?"

For the first time since I'd met her, Frances laughed. A short, high-pitched bark. "Maybe not that good."

The outer office door slammed and a woman's voice called. "Is anybody here?"

Frances frowned. "Oh no. Not her."

I had no idea who she meant.

Two seconds later, the owner of the voice strode into my office. Wearing a bright pink sleeveless tank with a matching cashmere cardigan draped over her shoulders, pristine white linen pants, and strappy sandals, she looked like an ad for summer in the Hamptons. "Where's my father?" she asked Frances. Then addressing me, she asked, "And who are you?"

"Ms. Singletary," Frances said with deference. "It's nice to see you."

Puzzle pieces dropped into place. Hillary Singletary, Bennett's stepdaughter from his second wife. For her part, Hillary didn't seem to share Frances's sentiment. She ran a French manicured hand through her blond bob, momentarily exposing mousy gray roots. I knew she was in her mid-forties, but except for that flash of gray and a few tiny lines near her eyes, she looked fabulous. Trim, tiny, and well preserved, if I'd passed her on the street I would have tagged her for thirty-five.

Until now I hadn't met the woman, and from all accounts that made me one lucky girl.

Extending my hand, I said, "I'm Grace Wheaton—"

She and I shook. "So you're the new Abe."

179

"Uh," I said, momentarily thrown, "I doubt anyone could replace him—"

"But you intend to try, don't you? Now that he's gone." Her smile fell flat. "I'm here for the wake this afternoon."

Frances gasped.

Hillary Singletary had clearly expected that reaction. "My father told me I had to come," she said, sounding more like a recalcitrant teenager than a woman of the world. "I don't know why. I hate these things."

Regaining her composure, Frances cocked her head. "Your father told you?" she asked, her voice an elongated exaggeration. "Your father? I could have sworn he passed away last year." She affected a confused look. "Whose wake did I go to then?"

I watched their little interplay, realizing much had gone on between these two over the years.

Hillary rolled her eyes. "You know what I meant." Sighing, she continued. "My *stepfather*, Papa Bennett, called me and told me I needed to be here today. And whatever my fath—Papa Bennett asks of me, I do."

Frances made a noise that could have been anything, but sounded to me like a snort. "Yeah, right."

"Excuse me?" Hillary said.

Frances didn't answer. She was out the door in seconds, slamming it behind her.

Hillary turned to me. "Why on earth do they

keep that woman on staff? She's always been a total b—"

"Can I get you something?" I asked before she could get the word out. "Coffee, tea?"

She took a seat without being invited to do so. "How long have you been here?"

"Just a few months."

"Mmm."

I had no idea what that meant, so I changed the subject. "You must have known Abe pretty well. You grew up here, didn't you?"

"More or less." She leaned back in the chair and crossed her legs. All she needed was a diamond-encrusted cigarette holder and her image as an aging spoiled brat would have been complete. Except . . . every movement was too studied, too careful. From her rapid blinks, to her shifting attention, to the way she repeatedly clasped her hands, she was far from relaxed. She should have come off as a woman of power, withering the new girl with a mere glance. But this chick was nervous.

Her discomfort emboldened me. "I understand the memorial will be held at Forest Lawn," I said. The small cemetery was technically on Marshfield property, but its location did not appear on any tourist map, nor was anyone allowed in without proper authority.

"You're not going?" she asked.

"I wasn't invited."

She sat up, interested. "Why on earth not?"

I shrugged, choosing to sidetrack rather than answer. "Do you live in Emberstowne?"

"God, no." She waved a finger northward. "I'm about a hundred miles from here. Still no hotbed of excitement, mind you, but at least I'm not half a day away from the nearest major airport." Pressing her lips together, she seemed to consider me for a moment. "So, are you married?"

"No."

One perfect eyebrow arched. "Kids?"

"No."

Shifting forward, she leaned her elbows on the desk. "Then what in the world are you doing here working with old geezers? You're young, you should be out enjoying life in a big city like New York or Chicago. Someday you'll be sorry you didn't sow your wild oats when you had the chance." She made a clucking sound, then narrowed her eyes. "Unless of course, you're here because of a man. Is that it?"

Hillary Singletary delving into my private affairs made me wholly uncomfortable. Part of me wanted to knock down her assumptions and let her know that I'd spent a good number of years in New York City. And any oats I'd sown were my business. I started to ask if she needed me to arrange a room for her at the hotel this evening, when Bennett walked in.

"Hillary, how nice," he said, his expression

belying his words. "Frances said you'd arrived. Thank you for coming." He crossed the room and took the wing chair next to Hillary's. Turning his attention to me, he smiled. "How are we doing?"

I wanted to ask Bennett about some of the names I'd uncovered during my perusal of the Taft files, but not in front of his stepdaughter. I got the distinct impression that the less I divulged in her presence, the happier we all would be. She had a rapt, eager look to her, as though waiting for some tidbit to snatch up and devour. It was rare I had such an instantaneous negative reaction to someone, but Hillary oozed insincerity.

Answering Bennett, I mentioned a few small housekeeping issues then added, "Other than that, we seem to be doing well today, all things considered."

He reached into his pocket and pulled out a set of keys. "As we discussed," he said, handing them to me. "Have you spoken with the detectives?"

These were, no doubt, the keys to the private residence, but Bennett's expression led me to believe he didn't intend for Hillary to know that. "Not today, not yet," I said. "Has something happened?"

He waved my concerns away but leaned forward in his chair. "I want to know that the manor's interests are not being ignored. You're keeping up on things, aren't you?"

"Of course."

"Good girl."

Hillary watched our interchange with keen interest, much like a spectator at a tennis match. " 'Good girl?' " she echoed, a peculiar smile on her face.

I thought she might be making a comment regarding Bennett's use of the word *girl*. While I might have issues being referred to in that manner by a contemporary, it seemed wrong to impose such politically correct sensibilities on a man of Bennett's age. He'd grown up in an era where *girl* was not only inoffensive, but complimentary. He meant well and that's all that mattered to me. I tended to cut elderly men a little slack. Especially when that older man happened to be my boss.

I was about to deflect what I expected to be Hillary's feminist rant, but she cut me off.

"Good girl," she said again, this time very slowly. "Huh." Her eyes flicked from me to Bennett and back again. "I had no idea."

It took me a split second to understand her meaning. Speechless, the best I could manage was, "Excuse me?"

Hillary eased forward on her chair. "I understand now," she said, her voice dripping with derision. "Of course. Now it all makes sense." She licked her lips and stood. "I'll leave you two alone to discuss Marshfield . . . affairs."

She was about to give Bennett's arm a

condescending pat, but he grabbed her wrist and twisted her back to face him. "Stop it, Hillary."

When she tugged away, he immediately loosened his grip though he clearly kept hold of his anger. "I'm tired of your insinuations. It's bad enough you constantly badger me, but I will not have you attacking members of my staff. Is that understood?"

If I'd expected Hillary to rise to the argument and challenge Bennett, I was mistaken. She rubbed her wrist, despite the fact that her stepfather's quick grasp could not possibly have hurt. "I was just making a joke."

Bennett worked his jaw. "One of these days you may finally realize that jokes at the expense of others are not humorous."

Squaring her shoulders, she made a moue of distaste. "What time does this memorial thing start?"

Bennett rose. "Noon." He took Hillary's elbow in a more fatherly way and started leading her out of the room. "But I have some preparations to see to beforehand. You can help me." At the door, he turned back. "Will you have any time tomorrow?" he asked me. "There are several items we need to discuss."

"Absolutely," I said even though I hadn't planned to come in on Saturday. "I can be here whenever you like."

He blinked a couple of times, realization

dawning. "Ah, the weekend. I'd forgotten. Don't worry. This will keep until Monday."

Although the manor was open for tourists every day of the week, and my workdays were only Monday through Friday, I was on call 24/7. "Are you sure? I'd be happy . . ."

He held his free hand up, halting me mid-sentence. "You're young. Go out and enjoy yourself. Go . . . dancing." And with that, he and Hillary left.

Dancing? I thought about what sort of dancing Bennett might have in mind and smiled, picturing men in bow ties and tails and women wearing chiffon dresses that swirled when they spun. Fred Astaire and Ginger Rogers. A happy thought.

I was at a wedding the last time I'd danced, and it had been in a circle with my girlfriends including the bride. I'd been elated, joyful, carefree. Until I'd spied Eric checking his watch again. Although he had agreed to accompany me to the event, he'd hated every moment of my friend's celebration. And he'd refused to get up on the dance floor, preferring to glower at me from the table where he sipped his soda water and counted the minutes until it was time to go home. Eric didn't drink, which, at the time, I thought was quite charming. I'd also thought it quaint that he was so frugal, especially when he told me he was saving up for our future together.

My beer-swilling sister had derided Eric as

boring and uptight. "A teetotaler?" she'd said when I'd mentioned him to her. And then she'd laughed. "Only you would latch onto a stiff like that. Somebody needs to loosen him up."

I swallowed over the knot in my throat. Had Liza done just that?

Too painful to dwell on, I dealt with the fear that my sister might have taken up with my fiancé the same way I had since the day she'd left. Channeling my inner Scarlett O'Hara, I decided to think about it another day.

THE PERSONNEL FILES I'D REQUESTED from Frances turned up nothing suspicious. She'd been asked to provide them all to the police. They'd finished with the files, but before returning them to their proper place in the drawers, I'd decided to take a look at them myself.

Keeping alert for any mention of employees who might have cause to be disgruntled or others who might have some personal vendetta against Bennett, I studied them. Truthfully, I skimmed. Most of the files held little more than the employee's original application and a record of scheduled pay increases. I was appalled to find out there was no set procedure for annual reviews, and I tacked another big job onto my to-do list.

By the time I was done, I knew that Earl Bloomquist, the gardener, had taken time off two years ago for a triple bypass; housekeeper Yvonne Morton ran a home-based jewelry business on the side and had agreed not to sell products to guests; Twyla Lowell, the hotel manager, had a gambling problem and required time off to attend support meetings every week; Melissa Delling's husband, Samuel Jepson, was still covered on her health insurance despite Frances's assertions that he was out of her life; and on and on. All in all not much, but I appreciated the chance to get to know a little background on my employees.

Packing up the files, I returned them to her desk and went back to my quest to find unhappy investors in the Taft files. I was eyeball deep in them when a noise in front of my desk caused me to look up. "Jack," I said, surprised, instinctively glancing toward the outer office.

"Frances must have stepped out," he said, answering my unasked question. "Did you need her to announce me or something?"

"No." Remembering my manners, I stood to greet him properly. "Sorry. I was just so deep in concentration that I didn't hear you come in. You're . . ." I was about to say he was a sight for sore eyes but a half second before the words escaped I realized how forward that would sound. Improvising, I smiled. "You're here at the perfect time. I need a break. What can I do for you? Please sit."

He hesitated, then lowered himself into the chair

across from mine. I settled myself and wondered what was up.

The last time I'd spoken with Jack, he'd been sweaty and sprinkled with dirt. He obviously hadn't yet begun any outdoor projects today because his forest green T-shirt and khaki pants were crisp and clean. His hands, relaxed on his knees, were pink, the nails tidy and even.

I waited until his eyes met mine. What lurked in those dark depths?

"I know you have your hands full," he began, "but I had an agreement with Abe about my contract."

I knew nothing about this. Heck, I hadn't even known we kept a landscape architect on retainer until Earl told me. "Go on."

Jack shifted in his seat. "We had a handshake agreement, and it served us well for the past couple of years, but now . . ."

He let the thought hang as though expecting me to pick it up. I didn't know where this was going. "But now?" I repeated.

"Listen, I'm sure if I kept billing you at the rate I have been, nobody would even notice. But I don't think it's right to expect you to honor an agreement you didn't make. I've sent reports up to this office—you probably haven't seen them yet. What I'd like to propose is that we come up with something permanent in writing. A contract protects you and it protects me. If tomorrow you decide you no longer need my services here, I'm out. But if we have an agreement, we could stipulate that either party needs to give thirty days' notice." He shrugged as though it was nothing, but his words were well rehearsed. "That sort of agreement."

"I understand," I said, buying time to consider what all this meant. The message was clear: He didn't trust me at the same level he trusted Abe. Who could blame him? I was an unknown variable in this equation. "Out of curiosity," I said, "how much of your business does Marshfield account for?"

He looked taken aback by the question. Now it was his turn to buy time. "What do you mean?"

"You have X number of clients who require your services," I said. "What percentage of your business comes from us?"

He opened his mouth and took a breath. The apples of his cheeks pinkened. "Well," he said, staring upward as though making calculations. "I'd have to guess . . ." He faced me again. "Hard to say."

I leaned forward. "Are we your only client?"

He sucked in a deep breath through his nose, looking annoyed. "No," he said, adding ruefully, "but you might as well be. I have one other client. Unfortunately, all my work there is pro bono. I just charge them for material—stuff I have to pay for myself."

"Who's this other client?"

He named a local charitable organization.

"That's nice," I said.

"It feels good to help out." Standing up, he started for the door. "I'll have a preliminary contract to you by next week."

Chapter 17

FRANCES RETURNED WEARING HER funeral clothes. Her black sleeveless shift was piped with gray, and she carried a matching jacket over her arm. The dress fit her like a tent. "I'll be off for the rest of the day," she said, gesturing in the direction of the cemetery with her eyes. "The memorial, remember?"

"Before you go, would you give me the number of that agency that we sometimes hire for discreet investigations?"

Her eyes lit up. "Sure," she said with more glee than someone so solemnly dressed should exhibit. "Who did you come up with?"

I showed her the list of ten names. "This is just a start."

Shoving her reading glasses up her nose, she went over the list slowly. "Hmm," she said.

"You know any of them?"

"This one." She pointed to the name Jeremy Litric at the top. "His family runs that big furniture business just a little downstate. Heard they're in trouble these days."

"Trouble?"

"Financial," she said with a meaningful glance. Handing the list back to me she said, "If you want, I'll call and get the investigation started Monday."

"I don't want to wait."

"That's fine," she said absentmindedly and I followed her to her office. Within seconds, she'd unearthed the information from her cavernous files and scribbled names and numbers on a piece of paper. Handing it to me, she stared, turning in a slow circle, taking in the office as though to make sure everything was in place. Her desktop was clear again, her eyes bright. "Is there anything else you need before I take off?"

"No . . . er . . . yes." Shaking my head, I waved her off. "No, it'll wait."

"What is it?"

"Jack Embers told me that he sent reports up here for Abe, but I haven't seen them."

Frances got a gleam in her eyes, prepared to dive into one of the far cabinets, but I stopped her. "This can wait until Monday. I just was curious."

Frances made a noise of disapproval. "That Embers kid. I don't trust him."

"Why do you say that?"

"Something about that boy . . ." She made a *tsk*ing noise. "He's trouble. Always has been, always will be."

Boy? Jack was at least two years older than I was. I wondered what cheerful musings Frances held about me. Maybe it was better I didn't know.

She was inching toward the door. I knew the

memorial would begin soon and I didn't want to hold her up. But I wanted to know more about Jack. "What kind of trouble?"

"Just stuff I've heard." Frances arched her brows. "Word to the wise: Don't get too close to him. He's a bad seed."

The moment she was gone, I went back to studying the list of investors. The information, as presented in dense, eye-numbing format, did not lend itself to careful analysis. And yet, here I was, trying to find a killer in a haystack of possible suspects. I wondered if Rodriguez and Flynn were following up on this angle. I wondered if they were following up on anything at all. As their liaison to all of Marshfield Manor, I expected them to be in more frequent contact. As their point man, shouldn't I be more involved than this? Of course, I'd never been this close to a murder investigation before, so maybe events were unfolding exactly as they should.

While I was intensely curious, I didn't want to hamper their investigation by constantly badgering them for updates. I placed my Post-it note on the line I'd been reading and picked up my walkie-talkie.

"Terrence," I said, when our head of security responded. "Have you heard anything about how the investigation is progressing?"

He muttered something unintelligible, but was clearly displeased. "Nothing new. I'm overdue for

an update. I'll get back to you if I hear anything."
Again he grumbled, but this time I made out the
word *idiots* before he clicked off.

Great.

I sat back, making my leather chair squeak.
Alone in the office, I stared out the window and
wondered, not for the first time, why everything
about this investigation felt so haphazard. Was it
because those in charge were inexperienced? The
local police had assured us that they'd assigned
their best detectives to the case. I had come to
understand they were the *only* ones on staff.

I thought about the bank robbery two hundred
miles away from us. I understood why so much
manpower had been diverted to that crime, but that
didn't make Abe's death any less important. The
trail was getting colder by the moment. While I
never considered myself an expert, even I knew
that the first twenty-four hours after a murder were
the most crucial. We were well past that time frame
now.

Consulting my to-do list, I realized I still hadn't
been able to reach Geraldine Stajklorski, our guest
from hell. I dialed her again, and again got her
voicemail. Rather than leave a message this time, I
opted to hang up.

The enormous list of those who had lost money
with Taft sat on my desk like an unpleasant lump.
I thumbed through the pages of the printout and
realized, for the first time, how hopeless it was for

me—one person—to sort through this information on my own. Fanning it again and again, feeling the soft flow of air as the pages flipped by, I wondered if Scott and Bruce would be willing to help out this weekend. Of course, weekends were their busiest times, but maybe if I offered to bring in one of our favorite dinners . . .

Standing up, I sighed. Even three people working twenty-four-hour days couldn't effectively analyze this pile in a week. We needed help.

Frances? Maybe. She seemed to thrive when presented with challenging tasks.

I rubbed my forehead. I needed to do something, not just sit here and feel useless.

Flynn had sent me a memo late last night informing me that Bennett's private rooms had been cleared for use again. Which meant I had a window of opportunity to poke around a little bit on my own. Time to finally do something real. I decided to alert the housekeeping staff first.

To my surprise, Rosa answered the phone. "Ya?"

"How are you doing, Rosa?"

She made a so-so noise. "I not complain. What you need?"

"The police have cleared out of Mr. Marshfield's rooms," I began.

"We go in there now? Clean out?"

"Yes."

"Good." She shouted to someone nearby. To me,

Rosa said, "We have it done before the Mister come back from funeral."

It dawned on me that Rosa had been in Marshfield's employ about as long as Abe had. "You aren't attending the memorial service?"

Another noise, this one an unmistakable sound of fear. "Funeral no help him now."

I didn't quite know how to respond to that. Fortunately, she didn't seem to need prompting.

"We clean. Maybe two hours. Okay?"

I said that would be fine and Rosa hung up. I grabbed the keys and trotted up the back stairs.

At the topmost door, I shivered with an unexpected thrill of fear. As acting curator/director of Marshfield Manor, I had the right—the responsibility, in fact—to inspect every inch of the mansion. But entering Bennett's private sanctuary like this felt strange, yet more than a little exhilarating. Just like the time I'd snuck into my parents' room looking for a treasure map.

The day before, my parents had been arguing in the basement, presumably to hide their fight from Liza and me. Whenever they had words, I panicked. And since my dad lost his job, they'd had words often. This time, I was only about eleven years old and I hadn't understood the nature of their argument—I just knew it had something to do with money and our house. My dad, after many months, had finally lined up a job in Chicago. My mom was insisting we keep the Emberstowne house despite the expense of doing so. "We need that money to live," my dad said. "Think about the girls."

I heard discussion about renting it out, but Liza was downstairs with them, whining. Loudly. The discordant cacophony of their angry conversation coupled with my sister's cries served to drown out a good portion of their words. But I clearly heard my mother say, "I showed it to you."

To which my father answered. "You treat it like some sort of treasure map. It's nothing, Amelia, nothing. It's worthless."

Words like *treasure map* are magic to an eleven-year-old, and two days later I discovered where it was hidden. Late at night I was supposed to be sleeping but I'd had a bad dream. Dad was out and Mom was in their room next to her oak dresser. She'd pulled the lowest drawer out all the way and set it on the floor next to her.

I'd been about to speak to her, but the strangeness of her movements stopped me. I watched her lovingly caress some old pieces of paper before stashing them into the hollow bottom of the furniture. As she eased the drawer back into place I backed away. She never knew I'd seen her.

The next morning, I couldn't wait to have a look. As soon as I thought I could get away with it, I snuck into their bedroom and headed straight for my mom's dresser. My parents were in the backyard discussing the move with one of the neighbors. I quietly and stealthily pulled Mom's bottom drawer out all the way.

Crouched in front of the gaping rectangular hole where the drawer had been, I reached my little hands down deep into its dark emptiness and felt around until my fingers skimmed the edges of folded papers. They crackled a little as I pulled them up into the light and I sensed, even at that tender age, that these were papers of importance. I'd found my treasure map.

My heart pounded as I lifted the edge of the first page. I started to read. I got as far as the words "My dearest Sophie."

"Grace Louise!"

I jumped ten feet.

My mother stood in the doorway, Liza clinging to her leg. She stuck her tongue out at me before launching into her sing-song pronouncement, "Told you, Mommy. Gracie was sneaking into your stuff."

All I remember next was a flurry of activity as my mother grabbed the pages from my hands and slammed the drawer back into place, all the while lecturing me on privacy. She quizzed me repeatedly about what I'd read. Despite the fact that I assured her I hadn't seen anything, she was unappeased.

"Have to find a new place to keep these now," she said half to herself, half to me.

"I won't do it again," I promised.

Maybe it was the plea in my voice begging for forgiveness, but at that moment she turned to me and her expression softened. "Someday," she said, tapping the sheaf still in her hand, "I'll show this to you. But you're too young now. And these papers are too important for me to leave out. Do you understand?"

I didn't, but nodded vigorously.

When my mom had fallen ill, it had occurred to me to ask her about the papers, but the cancer had taken her so quickly I didn't have the heart to do anything but focus on her comfort. At the very end she said something to me, grabbing my hand and whispering about papers, but by then it was too late for her to form coherent sentences, and the moment was lost.

After she died and Liza took off, I was in charge of going through my mom's effects—to clean out and get rid of stuff. I'd kept an eye out for the papers but they appeared to be long gone. I hadn't had time to search through the dozens of boxes my mom had stored in the attic but those were things she'd kept since my grandmother died, and I doubted the papers were in there.

Now, with that bitter memory suddenly blasting through my mind, I hesitated before unlocking the door to Bennett's apartments. But the knowledge that I wouldn't have another opportunity to look around the crime scene spurred me forward. The key turned with a soft *click* and as I pulled open the door, I stepped firmly out of my comfort zone.

A vague, unpleasant odor met me as I made my way to the study. Stale and musty smells mingled with a sick metallic tang. I had heard that Bennett hadn't entered this part of the corridor since Abe's death. I understood why.

While today's weather promised sun and mild temperatures—consistent with spring in this part of the country—these rooms remained lifeless and dim. The wood-grain walls, rather than provide a warm welcome, were dark and cold. Reaching down, I flicked the switch of the nearest floor lamp, practically sighing with relief when warm, yellow light flooded the immediate area.

My heart was skip-beating, my face flushing with excitement, and I was annoyed by these reactions. I had every right to be up here and every good reason as well. It wasn't just morbid curiosity that impelled me, it was the very rational belief that the police's involvement seemed pretty lackluster thus far. Had Abe's murder received the task force assistance we'd expected, I probably wouldn't have any need to go exploring on my own. But I loathed incompetence. While I believed Rodriguez and Flynn were doing the best job they could, I also believed that the two detectives were in over their heads.

At the study door, I stopped, suddenly less sure of myself. What exactly did I expect to find here that the police had overlooked? What possible insight could I offer that veteran staff members could not? I bit my lip and almost turned back.

My fingers tightened around the set of keys in my hand and I drew in a deep breath, immediately sorry because the smell in this room was far worse than it had been in the hall. That, however, was what decided me. "We need windows open in here," I said aloud, partly to dispel any further hesitation, partly to announce my presence. But to whom?

The room's area rug was pulled back on itself, exposing the wood floor, a dark stain reminding me where Abe had lain. I tiptoed around it, making my way across the room to the windows, pushing the heavy curtains back in order to reach the crank to open them. The first one wouldn't budge. Neither did the second, nor any one of the four windows that should have opened easily. I took a closer look and realized these sections were permanently sealed. That proved, at least, that the killer didn't come in through the window.

So where *had* he come from?

Nobody seemed to have a theory about that. At least not one they cared to share.

I heard a scuffling noise and stepped out of the room again. "Hello?" I called.

No answer. It might have been one of Bennett's cats. Although they were generally free to roam the mansion as they pleased, they had been confined to the lower levels while the crime scene remained live. I was certain that if Bennett knew we'd received the all-clear, he'd have released them at once.

I returned to the study and crossed the room to stand with my back to the windows. This must have been where the killer stood. I let my gaze wander around the room's perimeter, though it was difficult to keep my eyes from the stain on the floor. I listened for some sound—hoping for one, actually—of other people up here with me. But everything was silent. Like a tomb.

The study was aptly named and if it hadn't been the scene of a murder, I would have liked this room very much. Bookshelves lined three walls and there was an intricately carved panel inset into the oak shelves on the east wall. A low persimmon sofa sat in the room's center, just behind where Abe had fallen. One wing chair in a coordinating paisley sat perpendicular to the couch, a small table with crystal goblets between them. Dust covered everything. Although I knew there were state-of-the-art technologies available for fingerprinting, I saw that the police had left black powder on just about every surface in the room, save the books.

I wondered about that. Was it that the cops didn't expect that the killer bothered with the tomes, or was it just impossible to lift prints from leather bindings?

The aggravation of not knowing such things—of

not even knowing what might be missing from this room—made me feel utterly helpless. Jack's description of the runaway man carrying something made me believe an item had been stolen from this room. But what? Until Abe's death, I'd never been up here so I had no idea of what might be missing. That's where Rosa's expertise would come in. She would probably spot any absence right away.

The floors creaked as I walked slowly around the room, still not entirely certain of what I was looking for but so desperate to do *something* that I refused to give up.

Unfamiliar as I was with the layout on this level, I thought that the inset panel, while lovely, seemed to take up space that should have been used for more bookshelves. I knocked on the carved oak, keeping my ear close. It didn't sound hollow. It sounded like any wall would sound when knocked upon. Like knuckles on wood.

Okay, fine.

Undeterred, I returned to the hallway and turned right. I decided there must be a room next to the study but I couldn't figure out how to access it. I walked along the long corridor wall, looking for a door. None. The paneled wall extended down to the cross hall where it turned, then ended at a window. It was as if there were a mystery room just beyond. But with no way to get inside.

I returned to the study and crossed to the

windows. Fat swaths of sage green fabric bookended the bright expanse, rising nearly ten feet to the rod near the ceiling. I fingered the heavy draperies, pulling the fabric out wide to examine it. Could a man hide within these folds? Only one way to find out. I stepped into the mass of cloth and tucked myself tight against the wall. Standing absolutely still, I tried to imagine how a killer might have secreted himself here, lying in wait for Bennett, and stepping out long enough to kill Abe instead.

Too bad there was no way to know how well hidden I actually was. Maybe I could convince Terrence, or even Frances to accompany . . .

I heard the unmistakable *click* of a lock turning, close enough that it had to have come from inside the study itself. I was about to step out from the protection of the draperies but some innate instinct froze me where I stood.

Field-testing my cover under these circumstances was not the plan I'd had in mind. But trying to convince my gut that it would be smarter to make my presence known wasn't working either. Rigid with panic, I tried forcing myself to step out from the shadows, but in the two seconds it took for a nearby door to open and someone to enter the room, I knew I couldn't do it.

Every breath I took suddenly sounded ridiculously loud. At the same time, adrenaline coursed through my body, forcing me to breathe harder, faster. I opened my mouth to keep the noise down, dreading the need to swallow or sneeze. Trying not to think about either.

I stared up at the drapery hooks, hoping the focus would help me keep still. As much as I wanted to know who had come in, there was no way to peer around the curtain without rustling the fabric and giving away my position. And how would I explain my reasons for hiding in the curtains in the murder room? This was not how the director of the estate should behave. I could just hear Frances gossiping about it now. It might be years before I regained my credibility—if ever. The potential for embarrassment sealed me to the spot.

Whoever had come in apparently didn't want to be noticed either. The door was closed shut with the quietest of movements.

Realization stopped me cold. What if the murderer had returned to the scene of the crime? Trite as it sounded, it wasn't out of the realm of possibility. I listened as the intruder tiptoed around the room, apparently searching for something. Items were moved about, glassware clinked softly, and books were slid out and replaced.

The knowledge that the killer might be back looking for something he left—or neglected to acquire—on his last visit, shot cold sweat out of every pore of my body. My knees quivered and I panicked that my struggles to remain standing would give me away. Embarrassment evaporated. Survival instinct kicked in.

I could make a run for it—the element of surprise would give me a good head start—but the sudden weakening in my legs made me doubt I'd get far enough fast enough.

The tiptoed steps moved closer to the window—the intruder was now to my right, near the room's eastern corner. If I was going to make a move, it would have to be now. I just needed to make certain I bolted when the person wasn't looking my way. Blowing out a quiet breath of decision, I reasoned that I could race around the sofa and make it to the door by the time the killer raised his gun. With any luck, I'd be out the door by the time he pulled the trigger.

My heart pounded in my throat as I inched closer to the drapery's edge and, with great trepidation, peered around it into the room.

In an instant, my brain shifted gears, and I stepped out from behind the fabric. "What are you doing here?" I asked.

Hillary Singletary's flushed face went through about a dozen expressions in the two seconds it took for her to reply. She pointed to the window and mustered an accusatory tone. "Why were you hiding in the curtains?"

I sensed I had the upper hand here, and pushed it. "When I heard you sneaking in, I thought the killer might have returned, so I took cover." It sounded perfectly reasonable. I took a step closer to her. "Where did you come from? Why aren't you at the memorial?"

She shook her head, and for the first time I noticed tiny flecks of dust in her hair. "All that crying . . . I couldn't stand it another minute." Clearly flustered, she glanced at the room's carved panel, then back at me. Brushing dust off her clothing—to buy time, I assumed—she made a point of looking at the mantel clock.

Having not been wound for several days, the clock had stopped. Right now it read eight-twenty. Whether morning or evening, the time was way off.

In her hurry to get away from me, however, Hillary apparently didn't notice. "It's late," she said with a sigh. "I should head out."

I stepped into her path, preventing her escape. I wanted to ask her what she was looking for and why she'd been tiptoeing, but the topmost burning question popped out of my mouth first. "What's in that room?" I asked, pointing to the carved panel. "I couldn't find a way in."

Her face flushed again, more deeply this time. "Just storage."

"Uh-huh." The fact that she was still standing here reluctantly answering questions from an employee, instead of ordering me to mind my own business, spoke volumes. I wanted—no, I *needed*—to know what was in there. "How did you get in? Do you have a key?" I asked.

She opened her mouth, but shut it again before answering me. "Just leave it alone, okay? Just forget you saw me."

"Not a chance." I crossed my arms. "What exactly were you looking for anyway?"

She started to deny it, but I interrupted.

"Hillary," I said. "You were creeping around here, looking for something specific. It's just your very bad luck that I happened to be here at the same time. When Bennett finds out . . ."

"No!" she nearly shouted. "You can't tell him about this. You can't."

My loyalty was to Bennett, not Hillary. But no need to remind her of that fact right now, if keeping quiet encouraged her to spill. "Why not?"

Hillary rolled her eyes, visibly frustrated. "I told him I was feeling sick, okay? I did it to get away from all the grieving and . . ." she waved her hands in the air, grimacing, ". . . funeral business. I really hate that stuff." She shuddered again and I saw a flash of real pain in her expression. "If he hears that I was up here, he's not going to be happy with me."

"I'll bet."

She placed both hands on my forearm. "I wasn't doing anything wrong. And besides," she added, letting go and standing straighter, "this is my father's house. I have every right to be here."

"Of course you do. Which is why it will be no big deal for me to mention this little conversation to Bennett." I stepped back to allow her to pass me. "Have a nice day."

She didn't budge. "What's it going to take?"

I feigned ignorance. "For what?"

"Listen," she said, her tone conspiratorial. "I'll show you what's in the room, okay? And then you'll understand. I'm not supposed to show anybody, but I trust you."

She shouldn't trust me. At least not if her revelation compromised the security of the mansion. If she was up to something that threatened Marshfield, I would be sure to tell Terrence and Bennett about it. I decided not to share that particular insight with Hillary, however, until after I saw what was behind the inset door.

"I can't find a keyhole," I said.

She shrugged. "There isn't one." With that, she ran her fingers along the panel's wide oak molding, near the top left corner. I heard a faint *click*.

Nodding to herself, Hillary then laid her hand against the door's upper left-hand panel. The pads of her fingers rested against the intricate carvings and she felt around for a moment until a second *click* sounded. "There," she said. "Now remember, this is a secret."

Chapter 18

THE ROOM WAS CAVERNOUS AND DARK, with sliver-thin windows providing scant illumination. I would bet these skinny openings wouldn't even be visible on the outside. Not this high on the fourth floor, at least.

My eyes didn't immediately adjust to the dimness and I appreciated the faint spill of light from the study doorway. At first I thought Hillary might have originally been telling the truth about the room being used for storage. Boxes piled two corners, and the room was devoid of decoration. Whereas every other room in Marshfield Manor boasted paintings and sculpture, tapestries, and handcrafted furniture, this room was barren and bland. Its sole claim to ornamentation was an enormous painting of a female I didn't recognize. Hillary stepped in ahead of me and made her way through the shadows to stand in front of the painting.

"Who is it?" I asked.

"Some great-aunt, I think. Don't remember her name."

Dust tickled my nose. The room was not only dirty, but stuffy and warm. I couldn't imagine Hillary hiding out in here. No way.

"You were . . . what?" I asked. "Just sitting here? For how long?"

Instead of answering she shook her head and wiggled a finger indicating I should come closer. "*This* is the secret part." With that, she lifted a panel next to the lower corner of the painting's frame and turned a latch.

I held my breath, more than half-expecting the painting to swing open to expose a secret passage, the way such things do in tales of fantasy. I was disappointed when nothing happened. "So?" I said, a little agitated.

Hillary moved to the southeast corner of the room where she revealed a pocket door that hadn't been there before. "That's just how you get it to open," she said pointing toward the painting. "This," she slid open the door, "is where it goes."

I peered inside to see a narrow set of stairs leading downward. Again, the only light came from slits in the outside wall, and I suddenly recalled the decorations outside that obscured the windows. Genius. "Where does this go?"

"It leads all the way to the basement. You know, where the employee parking lot is," she said very matter-of-factly, "with a couple of extra openings along the way. I used to use it to sneak out of the house when I was a kid." She started in. "Want to see?"

"And you don't think this is a security risk?" My voice trembled. "You don't think maybe this is how the killer got in? Do the police know about this?"

"I doubt it. Not unless Papa Bennett told them. This was never to be shared with the staff—just a family secret." Shrugging, she added, "But Abe knew about it, so I guess it's okay I told you."

My mind was spinning. I wasn't about to take the trek downstairs at this moment and compromise any evidence. "Don't you understand, Hillary? This *has* to be the way the murderer got up to the study with nobody seeing him."

She was vehemently shaking her head even before I finished talking. "Couldn't be. Nobody knows about this except me and Bennett."

I was convinced she was wrong. "We have to tell the police about this."

"You can't. Then Papa Bennett will know I didn't go straight home." Her voice wavered. "He'll be really angry with me."

For a moment, I felt as though I was arguing with a stubborn toddler rather than a woman ten years my senior. "Hillary, this is very important. This could make the difference between catching the killer and letting him go free. There might be evidence in there."

"There isn't. I swear. I would've seen something, right?"

My patience snapped. "You wouldn't know a clue if it came up and bit you."

Stunned by my tone, Hillary sucked in her

cheeks. I watched her swallow back frustration as tears welled in her eyes. "Please," she said. "Can't we just keep this between us?"

I moved out of the doorway and crossed the dark storage area, to return to the study where daylight made everything seem sane again. The less we messed with what could possibly be part of the crime scene, the better. Hillary trotted after me, her voice whiny and thin. "Please. You don't understand."

I turned. "Then enlighten me. What was so important that you had to sneak in to look for it?"

"Honestly, all I wanted was to get away from the funeral."

"We're going to get along much better if you tell me the truth."

She looked away, then back at me. "Okay," she said slowly. "Let's sit down."

I'd been up here for nearly an hour already. Rosa and her cleaning team would arrive soon and I hadn't had any chance at all to do the exploring I'd hoped for. "When do you think your stepfather will be back?"

Her eyes widened and she seemed genuinely distressed by the thought.

"Maybe you should talk quickly if you don't want to run into him," I said.

"Okay," she said, her voice cracking. She took a deep breath, then let it out. "I was here. The day Abe was killed."

"What?" A thousand thoughts ran through my mind at once. "No one told the police you were here that day."

"*Shh,*" she said, although no one was anywhere near. "That's because nobody knew."

My hands clenched in frustration. "Tell me," I said.

We were standing behind the persimmon sofa. Hillary reached out her right hand to grip its back, steadying herself. I couldn't believe no one had noticed her on the grounds Tuesday. Hillary stood out.

As though answering my question she said, "I didn't come in the regular way, okay? I drove in through the tourist entrance. I even paid a one-day fee. And I was . . . wearing a hat."

I cocked an eyebrow. "You were in disguise?"

"Listen," she said, talking excitedly. "You have to swear you won't say a word about this to anyone."

I didn't swear, but she didn't notice.

"I came in like a tourist, but I know all the back doors and empty hallways. Hell, I was teenager here. I know all the place's secrets. I had to get up to this room because I needed to put something back without anyone knowing."

"You'd stolen something?"

"Not exactly," she said. "It belonged to me. I thought it did, at least." She frowned. "Don't ask me that. It wasn't like that."

I was shaking my head, but she continued so emphatically, the phrase *confession being good for the soul* came to mind.

"Mom had a very special music box my stepdad gave her when they were first married. I used to play with the music box when no one was looking. My mom caught me a couple of times and made me promise to be careful. I was, too."

As she explained how much she enjoyed listening to the music and how there were little drawers that opened and closed, I groaned inwardly. This was getting me nowhere. I wanted to suggest she cut to the chase, but she seemed determined to tell the whole story.

My attention perked up when she said, "After my mom died, I asked Bennett about the music box, and he said that he'd put it away with her things. I told him that I would really like to have it, but he refused. Said that it held too many memories." She gave a one-shoulder shrug. "I kept asking him about it, but eventually he got mad so I gave up. Then last time I was here, in this room, I saw it again. Bennett had put it back on display."

"And you took it."

She started a denial, stopped, then admitted, "I took it."

"When was that?"

"Papa Bennett invited me over about three months ago. But at the last minute, he didn't show. While I waited, I noticed the music box right there." She pointed. "When Abe left the room, I picked it up and took off." Hearing herself, she tried desperately to make me understand. "It was my mother's. I expected it to come to me when she died."

"I'm sure your mother had a will."

Hillary bit the insides of her mouth again. "Yeah."

I guessed: "The music box wasn't part of her estate."

"No."

"Explain to me why you decided to bring it back the day Abe died."

"Well I certainly didn't plan it that way. I didn't *know* somebody was going to kill Abe, for crying out loud." She sighed with exasperation. "I decided to put it back because Bennett stopped talking to me." Her mouth turned down so tightly, I thought she might cry. "It dawned on me—too late—that he put the music box there to test me." She swallowed. "And I failed the test."

"So why not just give it back to him?"

She blinked. "Then he would know I took it."

I was confused. "He already knew."

"No, you see, if I put it back in the study where I found it, then it would look like it had just been misplaced for a little while."

Her childlike logic took me by surprise. Did she really believe that bringing the music box back would make everything right again? That it would negate the fact that she'd taken it in the first place?

That Bennett would pretend nothing had happened? From what I knew of the man, this double deceit would only make a bad situation worse. "You should have just admitted what you'd done," I said. I looked around the room. "I don't see the music box here anywhere."

She followed my gaze. Miserably, she nodded. "I know."

Jack had seen a man running from the house carrying something. At least now we could assume what that something was. I had so much to share with the detectives. "Describe it for me. What does the music box look like?"

"Just a music box," she said. "Nothing special."

"Hillary." My voice was stern. "Unless I know what it looks like, there will be absolutely no chance of getting it back."

"Okay," she said, making a face. "It was round, about so big." Her hands worked an invisible ball, about eight inches in diameter. "The top opened on a hinge. When I was little I used to call it my mom's Pac-Man, because it looked like one with its mouth open. Inside was black velvet and it played three different songs."

"What were the songs?"

"I don't know."

That struck me as odd. If she were so enamored of this trinket, why wouldn't she have known the songs it played? "What about the outside, what did it look like?"

"Well," she said slowly, "it was mostly gold."

"Real gold?"

She nodded. "It was like a lot of gold string that had been solidified into a ball. With a few diamonds and some other, you know, gems."

The light began to dawn. "Diamonds," I repeated. "And other gems."

She didn't meet my eyes.

"How much is it worth?" Before Hillary could feign ignorance, I added, "You had it appraised, didn't you? That's why it took you three months to find your conscience."

She sighed again, more exasperated than ever. "It would probably go for three hundred thousand at auction," she said. I was stunned by the figure, but even more so by her next pronouncement. "But without proof of ownership, I couldn't get more than ten for it."

"It appears to be gone, now. We have to assume the killer took it with him."

She came around the paisley chair and dropped into it, belatedly noticing the bloodstain in front of her. She tucked her feet close and sighed. "Now Bennett will always think that I stole the music box."

I wanted to remind her that she had, indeed, stolen it, but from the look of abject despair on her face and the clear conviction that she was the wronged individual in this situation, the message would be lost.

"So now you know," she said finally. "And I told you the truth."

"I appreciate that."

"There's no reason to tell Bennett, is there? I mean, you see that none of this has anything to do with Abe's death."

I leaned forward. "What time were you up here that day?"

"The morning. Maybe ten, ten-thirty."

Too early. But I didn't like to leave any loose threads. "Did you see anything suspicious?"

"Like what?"

"I don't know. Anything wrong. Out of place. Different."

"Everything seemed normal to me."

I didn't know what I expected, or hoped for, but I wouldn't get any further with Hillary. "Maybe you'd better get going," I said. "Before Bennett gets back and catches you here."

"You're not going to tell him?"

I was spared answering by the arrival of two maids, Melissa Delling and a young woman named Beth. "Where's Rosa?" I asked.

The two women exchanged a glance. "Rosa thinks that Abe's ghost is up here looking for revenge." Melissa shot furtive glances around the room as though she expected an apparition to jump out at her. "She sent us up to do the cleaning because she's afraid to."

Taken aback, I didn't know what to say.

Beth added, "Rosa thinks we ought to send for a priest to chase the ghost away."

I rubbed my temples. "She's serious?"

"Dead serious," Beth grimaced. "Sorry, didn't mean it that way."

I looked at the two of them. "What about you? Are you okay being up here alone?"

Melissa bit her lip.

"Do you want me to call someone?"

Before Melissa could answer, Beth said, "Would you?"

I pulled up my walkie-talkie and asked Terrence to send two security guards up as soon as possible. He said he would.

"Great," I answered him. "I'll stick around until they get here."

Melissa and Beth set to work, apparently relieved not to be left up here alone.

"Two?" Hillary asked when I terminated the connection.

"One to keep our staff company," I said, "and the other to escort you back to your car."

ONCE HILLARY WAS GONE AND THE maids were safe, I decided to visit Terrence. "There's what?" he said when I told him about the secret room and staircase. "You'd think they would tell the security staff something like this, wouldn't you? I have floor plans from Bennett, but there was no indication . . ." Shaking his head, he started walking away, then stopped and turned. "Thanks, Grace. I'll look into it right away."

When I got back to my office, I found a message from Rodriguez. "Just the man I wanted to talk to," I said when he answered my return call.

"My partner and I need to speak with you," the detective said. "May we stop by for a few minutes to chat?"

The careful, yet oh-so-casual tone of his voice put me on edge. "Of course," I said, injecting warmth into my words. "I'll be here the rest of the afternoon." I glanced at the clock. It was almost four.

"Good. Don't leave."

He hung up before I could reply. Temple rubbing was becoming a new habit of mine. What a day. I hoped whatever the good detectives had to say wouldn't take a lot of time. I hoped to share my new insights with him and hear their thoughts. Most of all, I longed to put an end to this terrible week.

Chapter 19

WHILE I WAITED FOR THE DETECTIVES, I decided to call our "discreet" investigation agency and give them the names of the investors who had lost a lot with Taft and who might blame Bennett for their demise. Ten minutes later I'd identified myself to Fairfax Investigations, explained my needs, and provided all the information I had on file. The woman on the other end of the phone promised me results by Monday morning.

"That's pretty quick."

"We're the best," she said simply. "Will there be anything else at this time?"

I told her no and we hung up. With the receiver still in my hand, I decided to try Geraldine Stajklorski again. This time if she didn't answer, I'd leave a message and suggest she call me Monday morning to work out some compromise with regard to her complaint.

Her phone had rung only twice when my office door opened and Rodriguez came in. He lifted his chin in greeting. "Ms. Wheaton," he said. Too formal.

Flynn stepped in right behind him, staring at me with menace.

I hung up. Stood up.

"Good afternoon, gentlemen," I said, gesturin[g] them both to sit. "I have something important t[o] discuss with you."

"Oh?" Rodriguez's sly tone bugged me.

Flynn made a noise that sounded like, *"Pfff."*

I looked from Rodriguez to Flynn and bac[k] again. All the excitement of sharing news about th[e] secret room flew out the window. These two ha[d] something on their minds and from the look of i[t] it wasn't good. "What?" I asked uneasily.

Rodriguez slid into his chair. "Did you forget t[o] tell us something?" he asked.

I waited.

Flynn looked ready to pounce. "We talked t[o] Frank Cassano."

Frank Cassano. Marshfield Manor's unhapp[y] neighbor. "Let me guess," I said. "He told you tha[t] if he'd known that we planned to build anothe[r] hotel he would never have sold his property to u[s] right?"

"No," Rodriguez said slowly. "He claims that . . ." the older detective made a show of consulting hi[s] notes, ". . . you told him that Mr. Vargas wasn'[t] going to be in charge any longer. That you wer[e] taking over."

"I took over the Cassano problem," I said, n[ot] understanding.

Flynn fidgeted with eagerness. "Cassano seem[s] to think you knew that the victim was going to b[e] killed—before it happened."

Too flabbergasted to form a reply, I could only manage, "What?"

Rodriguez tugged at his tie and sat forward. His dark eyes didn't waver. "Frank Cassano claims that last Wednesday afternoon, you and him had a discussion." He waited for my acknowledgment.

"Sure," I said. "Probably. He calls here pretty often."

"In that conversation, according to Mr. Cassano, you indicated that Mr. Vargas would no longer be running Marshfield and that from now on you were to be considered in charge."

I was shaking my head before he finished. "No. What I said was that I had the authority to handle his complaint. He wanted to talk to Abe, but Abe didn't want to talk to him. I was told to handle it. I handled it."

The two detectives looked at each other, then at me. Flynn took up where Rodriguez had left off. "You always wanted the position of head curator of Marshfield Manor, didn't you?"

No sense in denying it. I squared my shoulders. "Yes. I still do."

Rodriguez made a *tsk*ing sound. "With Mr. Vargas out of the way, that . . . sorta . . . clears the path for you to move into the top job, doesn't it?"

I wagged a finger. "Don't even go there."

"We've been talking to some of your acquaintances."

"Give me a break," I said with vehemence. "I've

225

been trying my darndest to find out information to help you guys and you've been wasting your time investigating me?" I laughed, despite the sick realization that these guys weren't kidding. "Did you forget that I was in the Birdcage room when the shooting took place?"

"No," Flynn said with such arrogance that I wanted to slap him. "We have no doubt Mr. Vargas was shot by a man. But . . ." he gave me a wicked smile, "that doesn't mean you weren't involved."

I opened my mouth to answer, but just then the phone rang. The caller ID number was familiar, but there was no name and I couldn't make the connection.

Rubbing my temples, I said, "I'll let that go to voicemail."

"No," Rodriguez said between phone chirps, "go ahead. Take it."

I was too angry and frustrated to do more than deal with the dunderheads sitting at my desk. "Not now."

He smiled and, without asking permission, lifted the receiver. "Ms. Wheaton's office," he said falsetto. "Can I help you?" He listened, scowled, then held the receiver away from his ear. I could hear a woman's shrill voice. "Uh-huh, sure. Just a minute." From the look on his face, Rodriguez was surprised and disappointed to discover it wasn't the killer calling me to arrange a clandestine rendezvous. He held the phone out. "A Geraldine something-or-other wants to talk to you about compensation for her pain and suffering."

"Great," I said a mite too loudly and grabbed the receiver.

"That's a rather rude way to answer the phone," she said by way of greeting. I winced. Her high-pitched voice would have sent me screaming from the room if I thought the detectives would allow me out of their sight.

"I'm sorry, Ms. Stajklorski," I began, "I didn't mean you. This is a bad time right now. Can I call you back later?"

"Didn't you just call me? There's a missed call on my cell. It comes back to this number. And I've been trying to reach you for days. Have you been avoiding me?" Her anger bubbled over, two octaves too high. Now it was my turn to hold the phone away and wince. "Or are you just unwilling to keep your guests happy after you've put them out and ruined their vacations?"

"I did call you and of course we want to keep all our guests happy. It's just that—"

"I expect at least a week's stay."

Was she kidding? "You were with us only one night."

"I checked out early. My vacation was ruined by your people. And now, do you see the runaround you're putting me through? I was so upset about the murder—murder!—at your hotel that I couldn't even consider coming back that day. I had business that couldn't wait and was forced to stay at one of those shoddy little places on Walnut Street."

Most of Walnut Street was gorgeous. I couldn't imagine what she was referring to. "Business? I thought you said this was your vacation—"

She shrieked. No other word for it. "It's the little peons like you who waste my time. Does it really matter what I was in town for? Does it? All that matters is that I paid good money to stay in your hotel and I had a perfectly horrible time."

The two detectives were watching me. I had no doubt they could hear both sides of the conversation. "I'm sorry you had a bad experience—"

"I'll tell you what," she said, her voice dropping from dolphin-pitch to calculating cackle, "I have to be back in Emberstowne next week . . ."

"What do you want?" I asked, ready to give her anything to just get her off the phone.

"I want a luxury suite on your concierge level next Monday through Friday. Give me those nights gratis, along with a voucher for dinner in your restaurants each evening I'm there. Five nights total. Then I'll be out of your hair."

"Five? To compensate you for one night?"

"You had a murder there, you know."

"I'm well aware," I said. "I can offer you two nights."

She made a noise before countering. "Three."

Rodriguez tapped his fingers on my desk and stared at me. Loath to allow this conversation to continue, I gave up. "Done. I will notify the hotel regarding our agreement," I said, keeping my tone as businesslike as possible. "Just, please, give us twenty-four hours' notice before you arrive. We do get busy and I wouldn't want there to be any problems this time."

"Oh, of course," she said with a giggle. Her voice returned to normal, which is to say—grating. "Thank you so much. I knew I could count on you."

I hung up, depleted. "What kind of people are there in this world?" I asked rhetorically.

"I dunno," Rodriguez said. "Why don't you tell us?"

"Listen," I began.

"No, you listen," Flynn said, inching forward. His finger came up and he pointed. "You're the one in the hot seat. We don't have a lot on you yet, but we're not finished looking. You're the one who ought to be worried."

"Do I look like a picture of serenity?" I asked, my voice rising. "I don't think so. Now, before this goes any further, I'm going to tell you everything I think you ought to know. Take as many notes as you want. Try to figure out why I'd be telling you this if I had anything to do with Abe's death." Pausing long enough to catch my breath, I also took a moment to realize what they were accusing me of. "Do you think I would really kill a person? For a job?"

Rodriguez blinked slowly. "People have done so for less."

"I haven't," I said. "And unless this is an official interrogation, which it isn't, I'd rather we talk about some important information that just came my way."

Had they been bluffing? What was their angle? Were they so in the dark that they were throwing darts, desperately hoping one would pop the winning balloon? Whatever their story, the two men quieted. While I wouldn't have termed them as an eager audience, they apparently would at least let me have my say.

"Did you examine the room next to the study?" I asked. "The room accessed through that secret panel in the bookcase?"

Flynn looked dumbfounded.

Rodriguez took the bait. "What secret panel?"

"The one where you have to use a hidden mechanism to open. It leads to the room right next door."

Rodriguez's jaw slacked slightly and Flynn sent a furtive glance his partner's way. Aha! Got 'em.

Rodriguez scribbled. "And how do you happen to know this?"

"You know Hillary Singletary?"

"Mr. Marshfield's stepdaughter?"

I nodded. I told them that she and I had been

upstairs earlier and that she had shown me the trick to opening the inset door.

"You entered the adjacent room?" Rodriguez asked.

"And I saw the hidden stairway, too. It leads to the basement."

"Where in the basement?"

I shook my head. "I decided not to find out on this trip. I didn't want to disturb anything. But I suggest you take a look. If the killer knew about this secret access that may be how he got in and out of the study without being seen."

Flynn's eyes narrowed. "Of course now if we find your fingerprints all over this room and this stairway, you have an excuse as to how they got there."

"If I were guilty, why would I tell you about the secret staircase at all?" There was no disguising my exasperation any longer. And I had them there.

Rodriguez stood.

"There's one more thing," I said. "The killer may have stolen a valuable music box."

Flynn had gotten to his feet, too. He edged closer to my desk. "How come we didn't hear about this before?"

"Because nobody knew it was missing until today. Hillary told me. She . . . left it there." No need to explain her original theft, nor her attempt to absolve herself by returning it, but I did think the missing item offered a valuable clue.

When the two exchanged a look this time, their intent was unmistakable. I had successfully deflected their interest in me—for the moment. But now Hillary was right in their sights. I almost felt sorry for her.

Chapter 20

SCOTT MET ME AT THE DOOR. "WE'RE celebrating," he said, shooing me past him. "Get upstairs, put on something fabulous, and let's go."

I turned. "What are we celebrating? Did you get the feature?"

Bruce joined us in the kitchen, smiling so hard his face had to hurt. "It's not a sure thing, yet," he said, the glee in his voice making me smile, too. "But Dina said that *Grape Living* has agreed to review our samples."

"I thought they did that already."

Scott shook his head. "They originally agreed to take a look at us and to read Dina's write-up about our store. That was just the first hurdle. Now they want samples of what we carry so as to make a final decision."

Bruce added. "This is it. This is the make-or-break. If they like our wines and the specialties we offer in the shop, they'll send out a team for a photo spread."

"Excellent!" I said. "That's the best thing I've heard all day. Will this Dina write the article, too?"

"No, Dina is just the scout for new stories. One of the regular contributors will come out to interview us." Scott made the shooing motion again to hurry me along. "We know we can't count on anything but Dina says it looks really good. So let's celebrate while we can, okay? Days like this don't come around too often."

He was right about that.

Upstairs, I slipped into a comfortable-yet-classy jersey dress, a bit worried for my friends. They were so excited—but what if the magazine took a pass on them? They would be crushed. I knew they'd sent some of their best merchandise, at their own expense. Shouldn't the magazine have at least offered to pay? Magazines had deep pockets and my roommates couldn't afford things like health insurance. But a feature in *Grape Living* would bring in enough tourist trade to make the investment worth it. I whispered a prayer of sorts, that everything would work out for them in the best way possible. And then I shook off my worries, realizing it was probably just my mood carrying over from all that had happened at the mansion. Tonight I would let go of all that. Tonight we would celebrate.

An hour later, the three of us were seated at a high-top table for four at Hugo's, one of Emberstowne's finest restaurants and only about a six-block walk from the house. Reminiscent of a swanky 1940s dinner club, the place boasted burled-wood walls, linen tablecloths, and shiny trim. Just sitting here with the heavy leather menu in my hands made me feel like a star. Of course, even though we were celebrating, we still couldn't afford the restaurant's pricey steaks or seafood. What we could afford were meals from the bar menu and a cocktail or two.

We apparently weren't the only ones in this predicament. The restaurant was half empty, but the bar area was getting busier by the moment. We'd been lucky to get a table and I mentioned as much to my companions as more and more people streamed in. Any minute now, I knew someone would ask to use our empty chair.

"You can tell it's Friday," Scott said. "Nice to see so many people getting out again."

"Especially us," I said.

Bruce watched a keyboardist set up in the small space next to us. "It's been a while, that's for sure. And look, entertainment tonight, too. It's our lucky day."

"Not to put a damper on things," I began, "but the roof's getting worse by the day. Do you two know anyone in the business? Somebody who will do a great job and not cost a lot of money?"

They both shook their heads. "We'll keep our ears open," Scott said. "We've got that neighborhood announcement board up near the door. I'll see if anything looks promising."

Our drinks arrived. I'd ordered a raspberry lemon drop—a wonderful beverage for celebrating if there ever was one—while Scott had a daiquiri and Bruce a mojito. After taking our food order, the waiter left again, wending his way through the ever-deepening crowd.

"So tell me more about this Dina St. Clair," I said.

The two exchanged a look then simultaneously answered: "Cougar."

I sat back. "Seriously?"

They laughed. "Definitely," Scott said. "But that's why I feel good about our chances. She's clearly on the make, though obviously not with either of us. She's a little powerhouse, that one. If she's on our side, *Grape Living* doesn't stand a chance."

We were each only about three sips into our drinks and giggling already. Yep, it had definitely been too long since we'd been out on the town.

Next to us, in a space that looked far too small to accommodate one person, let alone three, a drummer set himself up next to the keyboardist. They were joined by a cello player and a female vocalist. "Interesting combination," I said. "Think we're going to be too close to actually enjoy it?"

Scott lifted his daiquiri. "I'm already enjoying myself and nothing's going to change that."

Just as he said that, he was jostled from behind, causing him to spill. The man behind apologized, keeping his face averted but I recognized him immediately. "Ronny Tooney," I said with a gasp.

Before my friends could react, Tooney was at my side. "Can I buy you a drink?"

"What the hell is wrong with you?" I asked.

"Can I at least talk with you?"

To my left, the band tested out a chord—loudly. "Sorry," I said, pantomiming that I couldn't hear. "Now go away."

"Don't you want to talk with—?"

The band played a little more warm-up and I missed the end of his sentence. "Who?"

"Percy," he shouted. "The kid who caused the disturbance in the Birdcage room the day Abe died."

"He's here?"

Tooney placed both hands on the back of our empty chair. I hoped he wasn't planning to join us. "I know how to reach him."

"Good for you."

With a look of disappointment I couldn't parse, Tooney reached into his pants pocket and pulled out a card. "Call me, okay? I promise no more—"

Whatever he said next was lost as the band broke out into their first song. Right next to my ear. I flinched, and hoped the musicians didn't notice. What the heck were they playing?

Bruce made a little finger-walking motion in the air. "Why don't you scurry off," he said loudly. "Grace is here to relax."

I finally recognized the song being played. A frighteningly bad version of "Kung Fu Fighting." At a place like Hugo's, I would have expected Sinatra.

Tooney put both hands up, much like a victim in a robbery. He smiled warily. "Not trying to cause trouble here," he yelled over the din. "But can we talk, maybe?" His voice strained with desperation, and he reached back down to grab the empty chair again. "I'll only take a minute."

A hand grabbed the back of the empty chair, but it wasn't Tooney's. Jack Embers pulled the seat away from the would-be private investigator and placed his beer bottle on our table. The look on his face was murderous. He didn't shout, so I had to lean in to hear him say, "If I ever catch you trespassing on Marshfield Manor property again, they'll have to carry you off on a stretcher."

Tooney backed away. Almost into the lead singer's microphone. "No need to threaten me, okay? I don't want any trouble. I'm just here trying to enjoy my Friday night."

Jack gestured toward the door. "Why don't you enjoy yourself somewhere else?"

"There's no law preventing me from talking to a pretty girl."

Jack looked over to me, clearly surprised. I hoped it was the shock of recognition and not my being referred to as a pretty girl.

I turned to Tooney. "You'd better leave now."

Tooney shrugged as if to say it had been worth a shot. He got about two steps away before turning around. Looking at me, he held his thumb and pinkie near his face mimicking a telephone receiver. "Call me," he mouthed.

The band's song ended just then, and their next choice was an acid-rock rendition of Elton John's "Daniel." These guys were bad. But at least they'd turned down their amps.

"I'm sorry to have intruded," Jack said, picking up his beer bottle and looking awfully sheepish for a man who'd just chased someone away. "I didn't know it was you he was talking to until I started in on him." Humor spread across his features. "You weren't giving him your number, were you?"

I laughed, and realized how fresh it felt to do so. "Not a chance," I said. Then, remembering my manners, I introduced Bruce and Scott.

"Roommates? Where do you live?"

I told him.

"The old Careaux place?"

"You know it?"

Jack took another drink of his beer. "Everybody in Emberstowne knows all the painted ladies. How did the three of you wind up there? Are you renting?"

Apparently Earl hadn't shared my history. "No," I said. "Long story." I looked back into the sea of happy, partying people and asked, "Are we keeping you from your friends?"

His raised an eyebrow. "Trying to get rid of me?"

"No, no," I said too eagerly.

Bruce piped in. "Have a seat. We ordered a few appetizers to share. You're welcome to join us."

Jack looked to me, as though asking permission. "We ordered southwestern egg rolls," I said, doing my version of a tempting voice. "You wouldn't want to pass those up, would you?"

At that moment, our food arrived. In addition to the egg rolls, we'd ordered lobster-stuffed potato skins and crab cakes. The smell of the warm delights was heady. The waiter, smart man, brought out four plates instead of three. That earned him a bump in tip from me.

"No," Jack said as he took the seat, "I definitely don't want to pass this up."

Bruce asked the waiter for another round of drinks, and requested a respite from the energetic, if not quality, music. To our surprise, less than five minutes later the band took a break. Quiet music, more in keeping with the restaurant's 1940s ambience piped in from the speakers above, soothing our frazzled senses. A moment later the restaurant manager came over and introduced himself, draping his arms over the backs of Bruce's and Jack's chairs. "Sorry about the music, guys. We were trying out a new band today. I just told them to take a fifteen-minute break." Wryly, he added: "For the rest of the night." Lifting his chin toward the bar area, he continued. "A half hour ago this place was packed. The music started and . . . look."

We did. He was right. The crowd had thinned down to less than one-third its size.

The waiter arrived with our drinks. "This round's on me," the manager said. "Thanks for sticking it out."

After expressing our thanks, we returned to our conversation. Jack asked again about "the Careaux" house, and over our flavorful treats and fresh drinks, I gave him a quick history of my family in Emberstowne. Just like Earl, Jack was surprised to find out I'd not only been born here, but that I'd spent some of my childhood here as well. "Really? How old are you?" he asked.

Bruce and Scott nearly spit out their food. "You don't ask a woman that question," Bruce said.

Even in the dim light I could see Jack's cheeks color. "Sorry," he said. "I wasn't thinking. Just wondered if we might have gone to grammar school together."

I waved a hand at my roommates. "Makes sense," I said, then told Jack my age.

He made a *tsk*ing sound, but smiled as he did so. "Nope, that makes you two years younger than me. I wouldn't have even noticed a little girl like you."

"You're noticing now," Bruce said. "So, make up for lost time."

"Bruce!" I said. "You sure you need that next mojito? Seems to me like you might have had enough already."

He picked up his glass and grinned at me. "I'm just sayin'."

Jack politely pretended not to notice our interchange. He and Scott started talking about gardening while I fumed. Bruce might have good intentions, but his methods left a lot to be desired. I watched Jack as he discussed pink peonies. He wore a collared polo shirt and black pants—not quite formal dress, but a far cry from his usual T-shirt and khaki shorts. He nodded thoughtfully at Scott, then turned to me. "What do you think?"

Caught daydreaming, I had no idea what the question had been. I opened my mouth, but Bruce interrupted, saving me from having to admit I wasn't paying attention. "Grace would love it. She's been talking about what a mess the garden is." He met my eyes. An outsider would never have caught the sparkle there, but I saw it for what it was. Bruce was in high matchmaking mode. "I know she would really appreciate you coming by to take a look. We could sure use a professional opinion."

Jack looked pleased. "Great," he said. "How about Sunday? Will you have time around, say, two in the afternoon?"

"Could we make it later?" Scott asked. "Bruce and I have to keep the store open until five." I felt a rush of air beneath the table as Bruce's foot smacked Scott in the leg.

"Yeah, sure," Jack said. "What's good for you? Six?"

"That would be great." Scott said, shooting a glare at Bruce. "You'll be home, too, won't you, Grace?"

I tried not to smile at Bruce's exaggerated eye roll. "I'll be there," I said. Then to Jack, "I'm looking forward to it."

"Jack!" a male voice called to him from the front of the bar. A heavyset man held his empty glass aloft, and waved it. "You ready to lose, or what?"

Jack lifted his beer to his lips and drained it. "I better take off," he said. "Couple of friends have a card game going tonight. I said I'd stop by." He eased off his chair, and pointed north. "Fortunately, it's walking distance and after three beers, I can use the exercise."

"Do you live nearby?" I asked.

This time he pointed east. "Half a mile or so."

I mentally calculated. That put him just over a mile away from me.

The guy at the front of the bar waved to us, then pointed at his friend. "Time's a wasting."

"Coming," Jack said. Then to me, "See you Sunday."

"Yeah, Sunday," was all I could manage. And then he was gone.

After enduring jibes from my roommates about not having told them about my "studly colleague," the three of us settled up and headed home, cheery for the first time in days.

Chapter 21

I SPENT ALL DAY SATURDAY TRANS-
ferring boxes from the leaky attic to the main
floor. My intent was to sort through all my mom's
stuff once and for all, then relocate the rescued
"keepers" to the basement. By noon I'd managed
to lug about half of the collection to the parlor, and
after a quick break for lunch, I returned to the attic
to get the rest.

Exhausted, both from the multiple trips up and
down two flights of stairs, and the enormity of the
task I faced, I stood in one of the few empty spots
in the parlor and stared at the boxes of various
sizes and shapes that stared back at me. Some had
already suffered rain damage from the leaky roof
and I decided to attack those first.

"My own personal treasure hunt," I said aloud,
thinking about my parent's conversation from oh-
so-many years ago. Would I finally find the papers
my mother had so carefully secreted from me? And
would I ever understand why she had? Grabbing a
glass of lemonade from the fridge, I settled myself
on the sofa and dug in.

An hour later, I had an enormous garbage pile
of phone bills, water bills, and heating bills from
the house when my grandparents owned it, but

had not come across one single item of interest.

Three boxes later, after more of the same, I headed to the kitchen to refresh my lemonade and grab a ham and pickle sandwich—lots of mayo—on rye. My favorite. I stood over the sink to eat, lamenting the colossal job ahead of me, and envisioning Bruce's and Scott's reactions when they returned. Saturdays were their busiest days at the shop, and it was also one of the days they stayed open late.

Finishing my sandwich, I sighed. The house was too quiet. The job was too big. Exhaustion, boredom, and a full tummy combined to make me want to sleep. Which meant that I needed to move or risk losing momentum.

The moment I stepped out the back door and into the cool, fresh air, I felt my spirits lift. I strolled past the big tree next to the garage, and walked down the driveway to the sidewalk, enjoying the fleeting warmth of the setting sun whenever I passed through a break in the shadows. I walked down to the corner, around the block, and back, feeling energized and rejuvenated on my return.

Back in the parlor, I set to work once again, using one edge of a pair of scissors to slice open the next sealed box. I hadn't even pulled up the lid when I heard a car in the driveway. Expecting it to be Scott and Bruce coming home, I scrambled to my feet and headed to the back door, only to twist around in surprise when the front bell rang.

I swung open the door and Ronny Tooney held his hands up as if to stave off my fury. "You dropped this."

He held out a black permanent marker just like the one I'd been using in my box-inventory project. My hand reached for my back pocket, where I'd jammed it, but the marker was no longer there. I whipped the writing instrument from his hand, instinctively positioning myself tight inside the door so he would have to bowl me over if he tried to get in. "You followed me?"

His words came out in a rush. "I swear I'm not stalking you. I just need three minutes of your time. Three. That's it. I didn't bother you on your walk because I thought it might creep you out."

Having him here on my doorstep, admitting he'd followed me was creeping me out plenty. Give him credit for stealth. I hadn't even noticed anyone nearby.

"Three minutes and then I promise, if you want, I'll leave you and Marshfield Manor alone for good."

That was an offer too good to pass up. But I was alone in the house and not willing to let this oddball know it. The brief delay it took for me to process this ignited a spark in Tooney's eyes. His hands at his sides again, he took a step forward, "I swear this won't take long. Can I come in and—"

I didn't budge from my sentry position. "How is

it that you haven't been locked up for impersonating a police officer?"

"I never did," he said. "You and a few other people assumed I was with the police, but I never identified myself as such."

"Really? Just like you never 'identified' yourself as a Marshfield employee when I caught you roaming the halls the other day? What, did you just happen to find a uniform jacket in your size at the local department store?"

He held a finger up. He had green eyes, big and bloodshot. You could see white all the way around his irises. "That's another thing I can help you with."

I was lost. "You want to help me order uniforms?"

"Of course not," he said, annoyance tincturing his tone. "Tell me: What happens when an employee quits, or is fired? What happens when a uniform wears out?"

I took a breath. "Time's up, Mr. Tooney. I have work to do."

Frustration twisted his features, widening his already bulging eyes, and reddening his cheeks. "I'm trying to help you. I can get you in touch with Percy."

"I have no interest in 'getting in touch' with him."

"The police have released him."

I started to shut the door.

"He knows more than he's telling."

You know how people say your life rushes before your eyes just before you die? Well, I think sometimes the future rushes before your eyes, right before you make a decision. I could see Tooney following me around, pestering me with his suggestions until Abe's murder was solved. Considering the progress the detectives were making, that could be a very long time. Better to let the man have his say and be done with it.

"Fine." I stepped out onto the porch. "Talk. And when you're done, you will not contact me again unless I ask you to. Do we have a deal?"

He looked ready to offer a counterproposal, but thought better of it. "Yeah. I swear."

"You swear a lot," I said, wrapping my arms around myself. This late in the day, the shadows were heavy as the sun sank low in the west. A cool breeze snaked around us, causing me to shiver.

"I'd be happy to come in," Tooney said.

"We're fine right here."

"Yeah, yeah." As if to assuage my discomfort, he took a small step back.

"Three minutes," I repeated.

"Percy acts stupid but the kid is really pretty shrewd. He's got a rap sheet a mile long. It's all misdemeanor stuff, but he's been in and out of the Emberstowne police station so many times, I wouldn't be surprised if they assigned him a locker."

"So why did the detectives let him go?"

"It's *because* they know him. He may be prone to disorderly conduct. Maybe even petty theft, but he wouldn't be involved with murder. Not intentionally, that is."

"Cut to the chase, Tooney," I said.

His big green eyes clouded. "Call me Ron?"

"You're down to two minutes."

"Okay, okay." His hands came up again, as if to keep me in place. "Percy is willing to talk to you about the guy who hired him. He said he might be able to remember a few more details."

"He should share those details with the police."

"Percy says he trusts you."

"Aren't you a piece of work?" I said rhetorically. "Both of you. What you really mean is that Percy thinks I might be able to benefit him in some way, isn't that it? What is he looking for? Cash? A place to stay? A month of free meals?"

Before Tooney could answer, I continued, "And you . . . you're looking for me to 'hire' you as facilitator of this little tête-à-tête, aren't you? Being hired by Marshfield in such a role would be quite a coup for your private-eye-wannabe resume, wouldn't it?" I closed in on him, lowering my voice. "Isn't that what you're *really* doing here?"

He looked down at the porch floor then back up at me. I read determination in those watery green orbs. "Employees don't turn in their uniforms."

The non sequitur stopped me. "What?"

"I was trying to tell you before. It's ridiculously easy to get one of those blazers. When an employee quits, or is fired, no one makes them turn in their uniform. In fact, the old vintage shop on Main buys them up and sells them as souvenirs."

"You're kidding me." I thought of all the upgrades and precautions Terrence Carr was striving to put into place. Here was one neither of us had considered.

"Told you." Tooney wagged his head. "I can help. I know all sorts of things like that. I'm an expert on Marshfield."

He looked ready to launch into a lecture. I stopped him. "Back to Percy," I said. "Tell him to talk to the police. I don't want to get involved in this."

"You're already involved, whether you want to admit it or not."

There was no evidence of threat in Tooney's tone. Rather, he looked sad.

"Percy's a messed-up kid," he said. "I don't know what the official spiel is, but he doesn't connect with people. Not many, at least. He wants to be liked, but doesn't have social skills. He's an outcast. In that way, I understand him."

That much I believed.

"Whatever you said to Percy that day in the Birdcage room," Tooney continued, "struck a chord with the kid. He wants to talk to you, but he's not allowed on Marshfield property and I opted not to let him know where you lived."

"Thanks for that, at least."

"Look, just meet with him. And you're wrong about having to 'hire' me. I know I have to prove myself before Marshfield respects my talents. Call this one a freebie, okay? If it works out, maybe it will be my foot in the door."

"Don't count on it."

Tooney shrugged. "We all have to trust sometime. Percy trusts you. I do, too." He smiled then, a move that immediately changed his face from lumpy and plain to friendly, and almost attractive. The transformation took me aback. "I think you should meet with Percy. Really."

The tide of indecision was pulling me toward a destination I hadn't counted on. I knew I could fight it, but I wasn't sure I wanted to. I recalled Percy apologizing for bumping one woman's chair, and for congratulating the old lady on her good aim when she smacked him with a teacup. There was good in everyone. I firmly believed that. Still . . . "I don't know," I said. "This seems wrong. If you have information of substance, you should take it to the police."

"Trust me," Tooney said.

"I don't."

"I'll be in touch, and then you'll see. And I think it would be best if we kept Marshfield out of this for now. I'll contact you on your cell."

"I don't plan to give you that number."

"Don't worry. I've got it."

"How—"

"I'm good," he said with a wink. "I keep telling you that. Maybe soon you'll start believing me."

"SHOULDN'T WE GET RID OF SOME OF THE weeds before he gets here?" I asked my roommates.

They sat at our kitchen table, each with a glass of iced tea in one hand, and a section of the newspaper in the other. Crusts from what was left of their portobello mushroom panini sandwiches sat on discarded plates nearby. Bruce glanced up at the plastic sunflower clock over the sink. "You think of this now?" he said. "Your handsome suitor is due here in fifteen minutes." He made a show of standing up and looking out the back screen door. "That's not enough time to make a dent."

Scott put the paper down. "What's this Jack's last name? I didn't hear what you said at the bar."

"Embers."

Both of them raised eyebrows. "As in Emberstowne?" Bruce asked. "Like the local royalty?"

I laughed. "The Marshfields are the local royalty."

"True that." Bruce nodded. "He's not really coming over to look at the landscaping, Grace. You know that."

"I think he's really coming here to give us gardening advice," I said. "He's always so serious about his work."

"Is he married?"

I shrugged.

"Don't worry," Scott said. "We'll find out for you."

"Yeah, right, Mr. Suave," Bruce chided, then mimicked him, falsetto, " 'Can we make it closer to six? Bruce and I won't be home until then.' " He shook his head. "You're right on top of things."

"All I want is to shut our neighbors up," Scott said as he waved away the tease. "I think it's about time we got a professional opinion on the landscaping."

A voice from the open doorway: "Then it's a good thing I'm not late."

I greeted Jack, hoping he hadn't overheard much more than he obviously had, and invited him in as Bruce and Scott cleared the table. "Can I get you something to drink?" I asked.

"No thanks," he said then glanced around appraisingly. "This is a great old house." He turned, his attention apparently caught by something in the hallway. "You're not moving, are you?"

I followed his gaze. "No," I said. "Just in the middle of a cleaning project—sorting through all my parents' and grandparents' junk before it gets ruined in the attic."

He looked at me quizzically.

"The roof leaks."

"Better get that fixed quick," he said. "Nothing good can come of waiting."

I couldn't get it fixed until I had the funds to do so, but I didn't want to come across as a Debbie Downer in the first five minutes of our conversation. There was always hope of things working out.

"Yep, that's what we're doing," I said. "We're getting bids."

Ignoring the twin looks of surprise from Bruce and Scott, I led our little party outside.

An hour later, scratched and bitten from wandering through my yard's overgrowth, I was ready to call the concrete mixers to pave the whole property. We'd spent the entire time walking through mangled shrubbery and weeds to get a feel for what the original design had looked like.

"I remember the front of this house," Jack said. "It was always gorgeous. Colorful and bright with blooms." Jack pointed to a grouping of stones. "See these? There was a flower bed here, a good-sized one from the looks of it. And I'm pretty sure this area . . ." he shoved away a thick clump of branches, ". . . used to be a vegetable garden. With a little hard work, and some cleanup, this property could be a showplace again."

Hands on hips, I surveyed the area as the three men discussed plans for its renewal. How they could get so excited over grass, mulch, and dirt, I didn't understand. My mother and grandmother had always grown flowers and vegetables. I remembered that. I'd apparently inherited a brown thumb rather than a green one. To my mind, herbs, veggies, and fresh-cut blooms were best harvested from a local store. Bruce and Scott took notes, chatting amiably with Jack about peonies and ground cover, while I dreamed of cement.

Jack's cell phone rang. He excused himself to take the call out of earshot.

Bruce nudged me. "He's a keeper."

"Give me a break," I whispered. "He came for the gardens. That's it."

"Uh-huh, right," Scott said.

"You sure I can't get you anything?" I asked Jack when he returned. "Iced tea?"

"Nah, I need to get going, actually," he said. "Hope I was of some help."

"Definitely," I said, disappointed. Maybe he really *had* only stopped by to talk shop. "Thanks for all your ideas."

"No problem."

Bruce poked me in the back, prodding me to walk Jack out front. I really had nothing more to say and the awkward silence when we got to the end of the driveway made us both uncomfortable. "Well, thanks again," I said. "Hope you have something fun planned this evening."

"You, too." He gave a little wave, and started walking toward town. "See you around the manor."

"Yeah," I said.

Bruce met me on my way back. "Did he suggest dinner? Drinks?"

"No."

"Why not?"

I gave my matchmaking roommate a scathing look. "Maybe he was more interested in the two of you than he was in me. Did you ever think of that?"

Scott joined us. "Nope. No way. Jack's hetero. Definitely."

"Maybe he's married, after all," I said. "You didn't find out, did you?"

"Never got a good opening. Would have been clumsy." Bruce patted me on the shoulder as we headed back in. "But I had the most brilliant idea. You have access to all personnel records. Why not do a little . . ." Bruce winked, ". . . snooping?"

"Sorry. He's a consultant. No personnel records on file."

"That's even better," Bruce said. "If he worked for Marshfield, you wouldn't be able to date him because you'd be his boss."

Chapter 22

BRUCE'S SUGGESTION TO SNOOP THROUGH Jack's records—however inappropriate—did remind me of another plan I had.

Monday morning, I asked Frances, "Do we keep old personnel files?"

"We keep everything," Frances said flatly. "What are you looking for?"

"I know it's silly, but my grandmother used to work at the manor. I thought I might take a look at her file."

"Your grandmother? Here? When?"

I told her.

"That was well before my time. Those wouldn't up here any longer," she said. "But we keep old files in storage in the basement. The same room with the floor plans." She'd taken me on a tour of the storage area my first week and I knew exactly where she was talking about. "I'd try there first. You want me to look for you?"

"No thanks." The idea of Frances grabbing a first glimpse at what was, in essence, my family history was totally unacceptable. "Have we heard from Fairfax yet on the names I gave them to check out?"

"Nope, but I'm sure the information will be here soon."

"I'll run down to the basement, if you'll hold down the fort."

"Don't I always?"

While I was in the basement I tried to locate the exit to the study's hidden staircase. No luck. Granted, it was supposed to be hard to find, but I paced out the approximate location based on the information Hillary had shared and tried again. I didn't want to make my inspection obvious, so after about twenty minutes I gave up. The police would figure it out and with any luck, Rodriguez might share that knowledge with me.

My trip to the lower level was not without its reward, however. I headed back, clutching my grandmother's personnel file folder, anticipation springing my every step. My family's love affair with Marshfield Manor had begun when my grandmother Sophie settled in Emberstowne in the late 1930s. She married Peter Careaux, who, according to my mother, was a ne'er-do-well and a barely functioning alcoholic. Unable to depend on her husband to provide for their first child—my aunt Belinda—Gram sought work outside the home and Marshfield was hiring. The moment she started work there, our family tradition of admiring the manor began.

In some ways, I felt as though I was bringing the family tradition full circle by working here. My gram had been a member of the house-keeping staff, and now I was in an administrative position. I liked to think she would be proud of me.

As much as I wanted to read through her file, I couldn't squeeze that in right now. I didn't even have time to get this file back up to my office. Not if I wanted my next plan to work.

I stepped outside the back doors into the early sunshine and made my way to the fleet of golf carts we kept for shuttling personnel back and forth around the grounds. I snagged one of the newer vehicles from the cart manager on duty and bounced my way along the narrow asphalt path that connected the mansion to the hotel. The day was warming up nicely. Puddles on the path, left over from the morning's watering schedule, were just beginning to vanish.

The doorman outside the hotel welcomed me, and a second doorman inside did the same. Both wearing long-sleeved white shirts, black ties, and crisp black slacks, they smiled and wished me a good morning. Shining marble, fresh flowers, and the scent of clean gave the hotel an elegant feel. Any time I walked in here, I felt like a rich person.

My heels clicked brightly along the floor to the cherrywood reception desk. The on-duty representative, Zoe, a young, tiny thing with a red pixie, seemed surprised to see me.

"Has Geraldine Stajklorski checked in yet?" I asked.

"No, but it's still early," Zoe said. "Check-in isn't until three."

"Ms. Stajklorski requested early check-in. I thought it might be good for me to be here when she arrives."

Zoe checked her records. "You're right. I have it all here." Glancing up at the clock, she said, "But she isn't due for another hour."

"I didn't want to chance missing her." Pointing toward the seating area near the window, I held my file aloft. "I've got this to read while I wait. Let me know when she arrives."

I took a seat in an overstuffed chair ready to delve into my grandmother's records, but the moment my backside hit the cushion, a ruckus at the front door grabbed my attention. A shrill voice shouted, "When is this place going to invest in automatic doors?"

Although the doormen had opened a path for her, the woman's oversized wheeled suitcase jammed sideways as she fought to get it through the second set of doors.

"What is wrong with you?" she demanded of the young red-faced bellboy who rushed to help right her luggage. "Can't you see you have to back it up first?"

No doubt this was Geraldine. Not only was her voice unmistakable, her manner—brusque and demanding—gave her away on the spot. She was not at all like I pictured. About five-foot-five, she was attractive, trim, and wore a glittering cluster of diamonds on her right wrist. I'd expected someone older, but Geraldine was only in her late thirties. Dark, shiny hair in a blunt, chin-length cut swung when she whipped her head around.

I made my way toward the angry woman who was still berating the poor bellboy. "Ms. Stajklorski," I said. The bellboy looked up at me, but Geraldine didn't respond. I raised my voice and waited for a lull in her diatribe. "Ms. Stajklorski."

She turned away from the boy and spotted me. Puzzlement battled with entrenched anger for control of her face. Too bad. She would have been pretty if she smiled. Her eyes—pale brown— sparked with energy and intelligence. Nothing at all like I pictured from the voice on the phone. "Are you the manager here?" she asked.

As much as it pained me to be nice to this woman, I extended my hand. "In a matter of speaking. I'm Grace Wheaton. You and I spoke on the phone."

"Oh, sure." She tugged her suitcase closer as she sized me up. "I got the impression you worked in the mansion," she said with a little flick of her head. "Not here."

"That's true. But I knew you were arriving this morning and I wanted to be sure to welcome you personally."

"Oh?" She thought about that for a moment. "You're not changing your mind about my stay here this time? Everything is on the house, right?"

"For three nights, yes," I said before she could finagle anything else out of me.

"I'm on the concierge floor?"

I nodded. "That's right."

"Free dinner, right?"

Again I nodded. "For three nights." I stepped aside, allowing her a clear path to Zoe, who looked poised to kill with kindness. "I'll be happy to accompany you up to your room to ensure it's satisfactory."

Geraldine squinted at me. "No thanks."

"As you wish," I said, handing her a business card. "If you encounter anything amiss during your stay here, be sure to contact me right away so we can correct it promptly."

She took the card, but didn't seem too happy about it. Maybe because it gave her less wiggle room for complaints later.

We chatted briefly as she checked in. I directed her to the elevators and asked again if she needed assistance. With a pointed look she said, "No."

The moment she was gone, I turned to Zoe. "Was it my imagination, or was she in a hurry to get away from me?"

"Like you were an ogre or something."

I raised an eyebrow.

Zoe put her hands up. "You're not. I mean, I just got the sense that Ms. Stajklorski was afraid of you. Isn't that weird?"

It was weird, but it also felt good. Maybe next

time, Geraldine would think twice before demanding ridiculous restitution.

Finally back at the office, I sailed past Frances, who was on the phone. I waved my grandmother's file in the air to let her know I'd found it. Frances gestured animatedly to me and I concluded the investor reports were on my desk.

Just as I sat down, I heard the outer door open. Frances hung up the phone and said, "Good morning," but before I could even guess who she was speaking with, Bennett strode into my office.

"What the devil are you trying to do?"

Instinctively I stood, desperate to decipher his question. "What happened? Is something wrong?"

"I'll say it is," he said. Turning to the doorway where Frances stood, patently curious, he said, "Get out and close the damn door."

Her tadpole eyebrows shot up but she did as requested. The moment I heard the knob click shut, I tried to cut the tension. "Why don't you sit—"

Bennett ignored me. "You told the police about the side room!" His voice rose. "About the staircase!"

Flabbergasted by this unexpected attack, I couldn't find words fast enough.

"That information was private," Bennett continued. One hand gripped the edge of my desk, as he leaned forward, spittle forming in the corners of his mouth. "You had no business sharing that information with anyone outside the family."

I couldn't believe what I was hearing. "Please, Bennett," I said in a calming voice. "Let's talk about this. Why don't you—"

"I will not sit down!" His voice gurgled. "Not until you explain to me why I shouldn't fire you on the spot."

Blood rushed to my face, making my limbs tingle and my throat tight. I knew I'd been right to take that information to the police. I would defend that decision no matter what. But Bennett was so worked up at the moment that any attempt to explain would simply incur further wrath.

I sat.

He stared down at me, eyes bulging.

"You don't want to fire me."

Impossible as it should have been, his eyes widened.

I gestured to the empty seat behind him. "Please sit."

Color returned to his white knuckles as he released the edge of my desk and lowered himself into one of the red wing chairs with an audible *whoosh*. He sat very rigid with his chin up. Waiting. But at least he'd calmed enough to let me speak.

I took a deep breath. "It's only been a week since Abe died, but this office is dealing with hundreds of important issues. Whether it's been coordinating with the detectives, dealing with complaints from guests, approving purchase orders, displaying a new acquisition, or overseeing the authentication of one of the mansion's treasures, we have been very busy in this office." I paused for another breath, crossing my fingers under the desk. While I *had* been handling all of the above to the best of my abilities, I'd been flying by on good guesses and a fair share of luck. "Abe isn't here, and I'm doing the best I can. I'm managing because I have Frances to help me. You take me out of the equation and it will be *you* running the estate. Unless, of course, you believe Frances could handle it on her own."

His bright blue eyes lost some of their steely anger. "Not Frances," he agreed reluctantly.

"I'm not suggesting I'm indispensable," I continued, as though we were just having a pleasant conversation, and not like he'd stormed into my office to yell at me. "But I do think this is a particularly vulnerable time for the estate. I think the less upheaval in the staff right now, the better." His shoulders relaxed—just enough for me to notice—so I pressed on. "I understand that I'm still in my probationary period, but I hope you can understand that although I'm doing my best, I may make a mistake here and there."

"Mistakes I understand." A tiny bit of the fire returned to his eyes. "But an intentional act meant to hurt is altogether different. Hillary is furious. She trusted you and you betrayed her. She says she only showed you the room because you begged to know what was behind the panel. But she said you swore you'd keep the information confidential."

"She said *what*?"

His eyes clouded momentarily, then narrowed. He waited.

From the time I was a little girl and Liza had told our mom that I'd been searching for that "treasure map," I hated snitches. Divulging Hillary's confession to Bennett now, to get myself out of this jam, seemed wrong. But I had no intention of losing my job because Hillary had itchy fingers and a late-to-the-party conscience.

"I went up to the study to look for anything the police might have missed," I began.

Bennett propped his elbows on the arms of the chair and steepled his fingers. I'd known the man long enough to recognize he was striving to maintain calm.

Wanting to give the impression that I was entirely at ease, even though my head pounded with every heartbeat, I sat back a little. "I know it probably sounds silly, but I wondered if the killer might have been hidden in the drapes when Abe came into the room, so . . . I tried it."

Bennett's hands dropped into his lap. "Go on."

"Just then I heard scuffling from the next room—a room I didn't even know existed." I shrugged. "I was up there alone and a little nervous. I thought maybe the killer had come back. I decided to stay hidden."

Bennett blinked. "You didn't ask Hillary to accompany you up to the study to look around?"

I shook my head. "Is that what she told you?"

Taking a deep breath through his nose, Bennett answered slowly. "Not exactly, but that is what I was led to believe." He shifted in his seat. "How, precisely, did you run into Hillary?"

Before I could open my mouth to answer, commotion from the other room made us both jump.

"Where is she?" By the time the words were out of her mouth, Hillary was in my office, red-faced and fuming. Her hands in the air, she yelled at me, "What did you tell those detectives?"

Again, I didn't have time to respond. Bennett had turned to face her, and Hillary took a step back. "Oh," she said dropping her hands to her sides. "I . . . I . . ."

Bennett stood. "Come in, Hillary. Sit down. We were just talking about you."

Her face stayed red, but I caught her nervous swallow as she crossed the room and took the seat next to Bennett's.

"So," he began. "Why don't you tell me, truthfully this time, what went on in the study Friday afternoon."

Hillary shot me a vicious look. "Why should I? She already gave you her side of the story. You're going to believe her. You've always believed everyone except me. Even when I was little."

Softly, Bennett said, "That's because you always lied."

I was like a fly on the wall during this family meeting and I wanted no part of it. Switching to a more pressing topic, I said, "Maybe we should discuss the possibility that the killer used the secret room and staircase."

Bennett frowned. "Impossible. No one knows about that room."

I wanted to suggest that Hillary wasn't exactly the most trustworthy individual, and that there might be lots more folks who knew that secret, but I couldn't come up with a diplomatic way to put it fast enough.

Hillary, however, was quick. "Now *everybody* knows about it. Because of her." Pointing an accusing finger, her voice rose. "She told the police and they came to interrogate me. They consider me a suspect. Can you believe it? I'm appalled. I was mortified." Still pointing, she stood, growing more animated by the second. "I insist you fire her on the spot, Daddy. She's out to ruin me."

Frances was getting an earful, that was for sure. She didn't even need to skulk by the doorway—Hillary's voice probably carried down the hall to every other department on the floor.

Still seated, Bennett stared up at his stepdaughter. "Sit down, Hillary. You're making a fool of yourself."

Her pretty face went redder still, and her mouth twisted downward. I thought she might cry. "She's lying to you, Daddy. Can't you see that? She is trying to make herself look good by sharing secrets—our family secrets—with outsiders."

Through clenched teeth, Bennett repeated, "Sit down, Hillary. And tell me why you went to the study Friday when you were expected to remain at Abe's memorial service."

Swallowing hard, Hillary sat. "Whatever she told you is a lie."

My discomfort peaked. I almost wished Bennett *would* fire me on the spot so I could run screaming from this place and not look back. Why was my dream job turning out to be so very different than I'd expected?

"Hillary," Bennett said, his voice dangerously low, "where is the music box right now?"

His question surprised the heck out of me. Apparently it flabbergasted Hillary as well. Her eyes went wide, tears pooling in her lower lids. "I put it back. I swear I did. I put it back before Abe was killed. But now it's gone." Sending me another scathing look, she started to cry. "Why did you have to tell him that?"

Bennett stood. "She didn't tell me anything. You just did. Now let's leave Grace to do her work." To me, he said, "I'm very sorry about all this. Carry on."

Taking a shaky Hillary by the elbow, he led her out of the room.

Two seconds later, Frances peeked around the doorway. "I thought you were a goner for sure."

"Gee, thanks for the vote of confidence."

Rattled by the squabble, I stood up and stared out the window. A sunny day. About time we had a few nice days in a row. Tourists were navigating the hedge maze while others posed for pictures, and in the distance I saw a group of them on horseback taking the "Backroads" tour. I leaned toward the glass, straining to see who might be working on the grounds this morning. I could have stayed there, staring, but right now I had work to do. I sat at my desk to read the Fairfax investigative reports. Jeremy Litric. Rupesh Chaven. They, along with several others, had been the names on my radar since I'd received the investor reports. But these two had turned up as the most intriguing.

Jeremy Litric, fifty-six years old, was the fourth-generation owner of Litric Furnishings. The company had been in his family since his great-great-grandpa emigrated to the United States in the late 1800s. Started on a shoestring, the little furniture store grew to become a design empire, with each successive son adding his personal stamp. What was once a company that offered basic furniture to new immigrants had become a major player in the world of avant-garde design.

Litric had believed Taft's plan would transform him from millionaire to billionaire by the time he turned fifty-five. Hadn't happened. Instead, trying desperately to recoup unexpected losses, Litric dipped into company funds to invest on additional "sure things" Taft promised. At the same time, economic upheavals in the world sent the sales of luxury goods into a tailspin.

Jeremy Litric's father and grandfather—both still alive—now watched helplessly from the sidelines as the company they'd lovingly grown from seedling to towering oak toppled from Jeremy's dealings with Taft.

I made a few notes. He was definitely worth keeping on the list.

As was Rupesh Chaven. A relatively young man, he had lived the life of ease from the time he was born. His parents, both doctors, had been killed in a car accident several years earlier, leaving their money and substantial insurance policies to their only son. Rupesh, pursuing his master's in criminal justice, had been engaged to Anya, a woman he'd met in school. Convinced he was ensuring his future security, Rupesh invested with Taft. When his investments went south, however, his devoted Anya went AWOL.

I thought about Eric and his reaction when he discovered that my inheritance consisted of one big house and several hundred repairs. "I feel your pain," I said to the report in front of me. I understood the fury, and the desire for revenge Rupesh Chaven was going through. No doubt he was better off without his money-grubbing betrothed but that didn't make it hurt any less.

Could Chaven or Litric have killed Abe, believing they were targeting Bennett? Sure: Both were in or near Emberstowne on the day of the murder; both had come to court the day Bennett provided testimony; and both were of sufficient physical condition to get in, get out, and get away. The report provided photos; Litric's fit the suspect's description of middle-aged and average height.

Another handful of suspects were either not in town the day of the killing, or were too old or too frail.

The packet Fairfax had prepared included newspaper clippings on all my subjects. A photo taken outside the courtroom the day Abe was killed showed Jeremy Litric shouting and raising his fist at Samantha Taft. Mrs. Taft was shielded from the onslaught by her limo driver. How the Tafts could afford such luxuries when their investors were left destitute was beyond my comprehension.

Similarly, Rupesh Chaven had a documented run-in with the decked-out Mrs. Taft. In another headlined newspaper clipping, he was reported to have been questioned by police after the Taft household received threatening letters.

Handwritten in a distinctive cursive style, the missives were linked to Chaven, who did not deny sending them. He was quoted as saying: "There is no law in this country against expressing one's viewpoint. Everything I stated in those letters is true. I promise to see justice done. If Mrs. Taft considers that a threat, then perhaps she should be the one being questioned."

Litric and Chaven both suffered devastating loss. If they couldn't get to the Tafts—he in custody, she accompanied by bodyguards—it stood to reason that they might target Bennett instead. I decided to focus on these two for now. And then, in a moment of brilliance, I picked up the phone.

Fairfax Investigations answered after one ring.

I identified myself and requested surveillance on both Jeremy Litric and Rupesh Chaven. The woman on the other end of the line didn't question my intent. "I'd also like to order a report on another individual," I said.

"Subject's name?" the woman asked.

"Samantha Taft."

The woman on the other end tapped her keyboard. She asked for more information on Mrs. Taft, some of which I didn't have. "We will generate a preliminary report within twenty-four hours. Will there be anything else?"

"Thanks, no," I said, feeling like I was finally doing something constructive. I took a deep breath and opened my grandmother's personnel file.

"I'm heading to lunch," Frances called from the doorway. "Do you need anything before I leave?"

I assured her I was fine, but she came to stand in front of my desk, twisting her head sideways to check out the file. The woman was not exactly subtle. "You had no trouble finding what you were looking for?" she asked.

"None whatsoever. You're a peach."

She gave me a shrewd glance. "I'll be back in an hour."

I waited until she left. Then, finally alone with my grandmother's file, I dug in.

Chapter 23

I DROPPED MY HEAD INTO MY HANDS and stared down at the words I'd just read. "As of November 12, 1947, employment is terminated for Mrs. Sophie Careaux of the housekeeping department. As of this date, it is determined that her condition prevents her from adequately carrying out her responsibilities."

My mother had been born in February 1948. This meant Gram had been fired for being pregnant. That didn't exactly surprise me. Back in those days, before civil protections were put into place, capable people were terminated based on race, religion, or even their looks. No, this wasn't the eye-opener. What had taken my breath away was the note paper-clipped to the termination notice.

The flowery handwritten missive on Marshfield stationery was signed by Charlotte Marshfield. If I had my Marshfield ancestry right—and I did—Charlotte was the senior Warren's eldest daughter and the junior Warren's sister. That made her Bennett's aunt, a woman long deceased. Charlotte had died young, unmarried, and childless, leaving her brother, Warren, Jr., and his son, Bennett, the only heirs.

Apparently, the family fortune was something Charlotte kept close tabs on. Her note read:

My dear Mrs. Fitch,

I hope this communication finds you well. While I continue to be impressed with the quality of hired help your office provides my family, I have found a matter that is quite disturbing and I trust you will see to the timely correction of such. One of the young housekeepers you have engaged on our behalf, a Sophie Careaux, has proven herself to be far too eager to be of service to my brother, Warren. Mrs. Careaux, herself a married woman, has abdicated her wifely responsibilities in her constant inappropriate attentiveness. Additionally, she is with child. I am certain her husband would prefer she stay home to prepare for the birth of their baby. Please see to it that Mrs. Careaux is adequately compensated for the hours she is owed.

Sincerely,
Charlotte Marshfield

Was Charlotte suggesting that my grandmother had had an affair with Bennett's father? I did some quick math. My mom had been born in 1948,

Bennett almost a decade earlier. His mother had died when Bennett was very young, and his father, Warren, Jr., had never remarried.

This hurt my head. And my heart.

Charlotte's inferences led straight to another possibility. That my mother and Bennett were half siblings. All of a sudden, pieces of my life—of my mother's life that had never made sense—fell into place. *Chunk, chunk, chunk.* It was all there. All the time. I'd just never seen it.

Gram's infatuation with Marshfield. Her devotion to the home, the family. I'd always wondered how my mother had been born. By all accounts, Peter Careaux had disappeared for years at a time, carousing and taking up with women. Sometimes bringing them home to stay for a while. My mom never had anything good to say about her father. Never.

But what if Peter *wasn't* her father? Could that be why my mom and Aunt Belinda didn't resemble each other? My aunt was short and dark, my mother tall and blond. Like me. Like Bennett.

Blood rushed up to my face, and my breath came shallow and fast. If my mom was Bennett's half sister, that made me his niece.

I pressed my hands down flat on the paperwork in front of me and tried to focus. This was nuts. I was moving way too fast. There was no proof. I was clearly suffering from an acute burst of overactive imagination.

"Back early," Frances boomed from the doorway. I hadn't even heard her come in. She stared at me. "What's wrong?"

"Nothing," I lied. Like she believed that. "I just thought of something I forgot and need to do when I get home. Thanks."

If I'd hoped to dismiss her, she didn't take the hint. As she walked toward my desk, I had about two seconds to decide what to do. I didn't want to scoop up all the papers on my desk and shove them out of sight, but I clearly didn't want her to see the note from Charlotte. Frances was adept at reading upside down.

Abe had kept a ledger record of all acquisitions, their placement, and current status. It was a big leather-bound book, about twelve inches by fifteen, and about two inches thick. I grabbed a corner of this big book and yanked it on top of the paperwork, covering most, but not all. "I wanted to talk to you about this," I said. Breathing slightly easier now, I was nonetheless aware of Frances's skeptical expression. "We will eventually need to put all this information on a spreadsheet."

"You mean on the computer?"

I nodded, lifting the ledger's front cover. Opened, it hid everything else on my desk. "I know it will take quite a bit of effort, but once the spreadsheet is set up, it should be a breeze."

Frances's eyes narrowed. "Okay."

"Okay?"

"Yeah." Reaching for the ledger, she grabbed the cover and tried to close it. "I'll get started."

I grabbed the end closest to me. "But you don't know how to set up a spreadsheet. I'll have to show you."

"I've been working with the computer more than you realize." She tugged. I held tight. "I think I got the hang of it."

Pressing both hands on the ledger—hard—I didn't let it budge. "I want to go over a few things before you take it."

"You're busy. Let me have it now. I'll get it back to you later."

Frances's phone rang in the next room. "I guess you better get that," I said. "I'll bring this by in a few minutes."

Her look told me this wasn't over yet. But until I had a chance to sort all this out in my head, I wasn't prepared to share.

BRUCE AND SCOTT CAME HOME THAT evening to find me buried in paperwork. I'd opened every one of my mom's boxes and rummaged through the first dozen or so when my roommates complained that their way into the dining room was barricaded. "Why the sudden rush to clean?" Bruce asked.

Scott shoved one of the boxes with his foot. "You're still in your work clothes," he said. "Did you eat?"

I started to say that of course I'd eaten, but I hadn't. "Forgot, I guess."

"Stop." Scott held up both hands as I bent to lift another box. "Right now. Stop."

Behind him, Bruce wore a solemn look. "You never forget to eat. What's going on?"

Curiosity had banished all else from my mind. If my mother was truly Warren, Jr.'s daughter, I knew she'd have kept a record here to prove it. The treasure map from years ago suddenly sparked with reality. I couldn't stop myself from digging. Now two hours later, I was still at it, hungry, dusty, and worn.

I told my roommates about my grandmother's file and how I was convinced that if there were some familial ties between my mother and the Marshfields, there must be evidence of it here. "My mom never threw anything away," I said. "Neither did I." Looking at the mess, I felt disappointment slowly take over where my excitement had been. "I don't know what I expected to find."

Scott nodded. "First, food. Then all three of us will sort through this pile." He wrinkled his nose at the mess. "We'll get through it much faster that way."

Bruce prepared his version of a *croque monsieur* sandwich, and brought it, along with a tall glass of lemonade, into the parlor. "Here you go," he said. "While you eat, you can give us the details so we know what we're looking for."

Ravenous, I took a huge bite of the hot sandwich, and spoke around the mouthful, napkin at the ready. "That's just it. I don't know exactly what might be here. I just know that it is."

The two exchanged a look. I wolfed down the rest of my meal and cleaned up as they each took a box to sort. They read over items more carefully than I did. I had a tendency to skim. There were so many boxes that I'd unconsciously decided to do a quick overview and then—if necessary—go back in and search more thoroughly. I hoped it wouldn't come to that. I had a gut-level feeling that whatever proof I sought would jump out at me.

Scott sat cross-legged near the fireplace, studying pages from a manila folder spread on his lap. Bruce was on the wing chair, similarly absorbed in what looked like a scrapbook—turning pages slowly so as not to crack their yellowed edges. I picked my way closer to them and was about to open a fresh box, when my cell phone rang.

Muttering my annoyance, I made my way back to the kitchen and checked the display. I didn't recognize the number, and was about to let it go to voicemail, when it occurred to me that I'd given my number to Jack at the restaurant the other night, just in case. He hadn't called before his visit, but the idea that he might be calling now encouraged me to answer. "Hello?"

"Umm . . . Grace?"

I immediately knew this wasn't Jack. Male, hesitant, with a slight tremor, the voice was familiar, but only vaguely. "Yes?"

"Hi, uh, I don't know if you remember me . . ."

It hit me. "Percy?"

"Yeah, hey. Cool. You do remember."

I was about to ask why he was calling me, but I already knew. "Ronny Tooney gave you my number, didn't he?"

"I know this is weird for me to call you, but I don't know what else to do. Ronny says this is important."

I meandered to the doorway between the kitchen and dining room. Scott and Bruce had stopped reading and were both staring up at me, listening to my half of the conversation. "I don't really care what Ronny Tooney thinks," I began.

"No, y'see, this is important," Percy interrupted, talking fast. "That guy who gave me the money to make a scene in your mansion showed up at my house yesterday. Kinda scared me to see him again. I didn't think he knew where I lived. But he swears he had nothing to do with killing that old guy."

"And you believe that?"

A hesitation. "Not really."

"What did you tell the police when they questioned you?"

I could almost hear him shrug. "Not much. The guy gave me money, you know? Kind of a lot. I didn't want to get him into trouble when he was such a good guy to me."

"Did you at least provide a description?"

The delay in his reply gave me the answer before he did. "I was kinda vague."

"Percy," I said using my best stern-adult voice, "you need to go back to the police. You need to tell them every single little detail you can remember about this guy."

"You think?"

"Yeah, I think. I don't like the fact that he came to your house."

"Me neither."

"Call them now. They'll come out to talk to you."

"I don't want the police at my house."

Suspicion prickled the back of my neck. "Why not, Percy?"

"I just don't, okay? I'll talk to them, but not here."

"You'll go tonight?"

He hesitated again. "Will you go with me?"

I rubbed my forehead with my free hand. All I wanted to do tonight was sort through these boxes. I had no interest whatsoever in accompanying Percy to visit the police. "You're a big boy," I said, unintentionally invoking a double meaning, "Just drive over there now. I'm sure one of the officers will be happy to take your revised statement."

"I don't drive. I'll have to wait for a bus."

"Call your friend Tooney. He'll take you."

"Uh, no. He pestered the police so much he's afraid. He won't go with me." Percy waited a beat. "Please go with me?"

Without meaning to, I growled my aggravation. Curse that Ronny Tooney. What had he gotten me into?

"I'm sorry," Percy said. "It's just I don't know who to trust, you know? I thought maybe you would help me because you're part of the Marshfield group. And . . . you were nice to me."

It was already after eight. "Tell you what," I said, "I'll go with you after work tomorrow."

"Uh, can't do it tomorrow. Got a doctor's appointment."

"At night?"

"He's in another town. Takes me a long time to get there and back. And if I don't get the meds I need, I get into trouble. Even worse trouble than I got into at your mansion."

"Fine," I said. "Wednesday?"

Bruce and Scott stood up. Their eyes wide, they gesticulated wildly, clearly trying to get me to change my mind.

"You'll do that for me?"

"Yeah," I said, knowing this was something I had to do, or be sorry forever for not helping out someone less fortunate. "I'm tied up tonight, but I'll make time Wednesday. Where can I pick you up?" Back in the kitchen, I pulled out a pad of paper and pen.

He gave me an address just outside Emberstowne.

"Got it," I said. "I can be there by seven. Does that work for you?"

"I really appreciate this, dude," he said. "I mean . . . Grace."

I wanted to get off the phone, now. "Great. See you then."

"Do you think we could maybe grab a bite to eat while we're out?" His voice held a peculiar lilt. "You know, just you and me?"

"Let me guess, my treat?"

"Only if you don't mind."

I bit the insides of my cheeks and reminded myself to pay it forward. "Okay, but nowhere fancy. Just a quick bite."

"Excellent!"

"I gotta go, Percy. See you Wednesday."

The moment I snapped my phone shut, my two roommates descended. "You're not really going," Bruce said. "You can't."

Scott must have read the answer on my face because he said, "We're not going to let you go alone."

Bruce shot him a look.

"You can stay at the store Wednesday night," Scott said to Bruce. "The last hour is pretty quiet anyway. I'll meet Grace and we'll pick up Percy together." He turned to me. "What do you think?"

I gave him a hug. "I think you're the best."

Bruce affected a pout. "I think I deserve a hug. After all, just as you answered the phone I came across something very interesting in that scrapbook."

"You did?" I practically leaped over the boxes to get to the wing chair, where he'd left the leather-bound volume. I sat, pulling it onto my lap, thinking about how similar the book was to the ledger Abe and his predecessors had kept all these years.

Bruce reached to take it out of my hands.

"Hang on," I said. This wasn't just similar; it was identical to the ledger in my office. "I have something like this at the manor. The only difference is the pages inside." I fanned through them. "Abe's copy has lined pages . . . you know, for record keeping. But these are normal scrapbook pages." I closed the book again and ran my hand over the cover. "These books were made by the same manufacturer; they had to be."

"Then there's a link," Scott said.

"But not the only one." Bruce opened the book on my lap. "Your family was obsessed with the Marshfields," he said as he gently turned pages. He was right. There were dozens of newspaper clippings featuring Warren, Jr., all dated in the mid-1940s. "I thought it was all sort of normal—I mean, fans keep all sorts of paraphernalia on Elvis or the Beatles, but then I found this." He pulled a folded letter out from between two pages of photos. Addressed to my grandmother Sophie, it was typewritten on the official letterhead of Hertel and Niebuhr, and signed by T. Hertel, senior partner.

"This is the law firm that handles everything for the Marshfields," I said.

"I figured as much," Bruce said. "Read the letter."

I did, skimming so quickly I had to reread. In essence, the letter requested my grandmother's presence at their offices on March 1, 1948, at seven o'clock in the evening to sign documents that made her newborn daughter, Amelia, beneficiary of a trust for the home I lived in now.

Bruce said, "I think Marshfield bought this place and gave it to your grandmother. You said your grandfather—that is, your grandmother's husband—was a real jerk. If your grandma was hurting for money, this was probably a safe way for Warren Marshfield to help her out."

My brain was moving in slow motion. I still held the letter. "This is hardly proof."

Bruce leaned down to turn to the back of the book. Tucked in the inside cover was a sheet of yellowed paper, folded in thirds. Accompanying it was an old black-and-white photo with curlicued edges. "Does he look familiar?"

"That's Warren, Jr.," I said. I'd seen enough pictures of the Marshfield family to recognize them all. But I couldn't discern where the photo had been taken. "This must be on Marshfield property, but I can't figure out where."

Bruce nodded. "He's holding a baby. Your mother."

"We don't know that."

He unfolded the letter, and I read:

My dearest Sophie,

I thank you for the greatest gift any woman can give the man she loves. I know your feelings run as deeply for me as mine for you. I regret, with all my heart, that I cannot be with you. As you know I am forever disappointing my family and my father has made it clear that if I choose to follow my heart, I will do so absent his blessing. That would mean losing everything for myself, and for my young son. To recognize you would be to turn my back on all else. Sadly, I am not strong enough to face this fate. Perhaps, when he departs this earth, you and I will be together after all.

"It isn't signed," I said.

Bruce's voice was soft. "But you *know* who wrote it."

I did. I knew it from the flutter of my stomach

down to the tingle in my toes. The treasure map. After all these years, I'd finally found it. "But knowing something and proving it are two entirely different things."

Bruce looked ready to explode. "You don't call this proof?"

"Bennett seems to have taken a liking to you," Scott said. "Why not ask him about it?"

"Are you kidding? This morning he came in to fire me."

That took them both aback. "I fixed it," I said, not wanting to get into a lengthy explanation. "My job is safe for now. But there's no way I'm sharing this with him."

Scott folded his arms. "You should. You said he's a fair guy. Show it to him. Heck, then your job will be permanently secure. He might even offer you a share of the family fortunes."

"Not a chance," I said. "Do you have any idea how many people are trying to get a piece of him?" Since it was a rhetorical question, I continued. "I want him to trust me. Not to think I'm just another money-grubber, looking to stake a claim in his life." I was shaking my head the whole time I was talking. "I know what all this suggests. But it's circumstantial."

Scott blew raspberries. "You just don't want to rock the boat."

"Not true." I placed my hands flat on the pages of Marshfield history in the scrapbook. "If we were truly related to this family, why didn't my mother ever say anything? Do you think that's why she refused to sell the house? Because it was a gift from . . . from her real father?"

They didn't answer—they couldn't begin to get into my mother's mind on this matter—but I knew the reason she'd stayed mum. My mother was straitlaced, almost prudish. I'd often joked that I didn't know how she'd had children, because I couldn't imagine her letting our dad get close enough. To know that her mother—her *married* mother—had had an affair that resulted in my mother's birth would have been a difficult truth. She would never have told me. Not outright. But why hadn't she destroyed all the evidence? Sentimental weakness, perhaps? Sadly, I would never know the answer to that.

"It's your decision," Bruce said. "But keep an open mind, okay?"

I smiled up at them, my hands still on the precious artifacts on my lap. I could not tell Bennett. That much I knew for sure. I ran my finger along the corner of the black-and-white photo. Warren, Jr. had died before I was born. "Nice to meet you, Grandpa," I whispered.

Scott turned to face the roomful of boxes. "So now that we found what you were looking for, can we throw the rest of this junk away?"

Chapter 24

THE PRELIMINARY REPORT ON SAMANTHA Taft provided nothing unexpected. I didn't know what I'd hoped for—some indication that she'd hired a hit man? While there were plenty of news clippings, Internet postings, and photos of Mrs. Taft, nothing suggested she was more than a high-maintenance wife who somehow managed to preserve her standard of living despite the fact that her husband had bilked millions from unsuspecting investors.

Detective Rodriguez stopped by my office unannounced. "She didn't do it," he said without preamble.

I looked up from the stack of Fairfax reports on my desk. "Who are we talking about?"

"The stepdaughter. Ms. Singletary." He rolled his eyes. "You were wrong about her."

"I never suspected her."

"Oh no?" he asked, making himself comfortable in the seat across from me. "Then why did you tell us about her sneaking around? Was that just to shift the blame away from you?"

Rodriguez looked tired today. Not sleepy as much as worn out. And somehow, more approachable. "I was never really a suspect, was I?"

He shook his head. "We have to rattle people from time to time. You never know what will fall out."

"Speaking of rattling," I said, pulling reports from the bottom of the pile, "there are a couple of people who might be worth checking out."

"What? You think you're some kind of private investigator? You think we're not moving fast enough?"

Better to deflect that question. "I thought about who might want revenge on Bennett." Turning the files to face Rodriguez, I continued. "Jeremy Litric and Rupesh Chaven both lost a boatload with Taft."

Rodriguez stared at the reports. His deep brown eyes rose to meet mine. "A lot of people lost money with that creep."

"But these two lost more. Litric's family business has gone bankrupt, and Chaven's fiancé left him when the money ran out. These two are hurting."

"Where are you going with this?"

"Either one of them could have written those threatening letters. Either one of them could have broken in and tried to kill Bennett but killed Abe by mistake."

Rodriguez scratched his forehead and frowned. He took a few more minutes to skim the information from Fairfax. "This company you hired, they got all this information for you?" He waited for my acknowledgment, then nodded. "Not bad." He read silently for another minute or so. "Both these guys are educated. Litric's got a master's degree, and Chaven was going for his."

"So?"

"Those threatening letters weren't sophisticated. Whoever wrote them wasn't a university type."

"You don't think they were just trying to throw us off track?"

He chuckled. "Us, huh? Okay, kid. Us." Shaking his head again, he said, "Possible? Sure." He slapped his stomach. "But my gut tells me different. Whoever wrote the letters was in a hurry. They wanted money and they wanted it fast. They weren't worried about proper grammar."

Just then his radio squawked. He was up and out of his chair before I could say "boo."

"Gotta run," he said, making for the door. "But before I go—the main reason I stopped by was to let you know that Flynn and I are out of here for a while." Rodriguez read the concern on my face. "We've done all we can here and we're shorthanded back at the station. But I promise you, if something breaks, we'll be back in a heartbeat."

There wasn't much else to say. "Thanks, Detective."

"Oh, and can I get copies of those?" he asked, pointing to the files on my desk.

I waved. "No problem." I'd include Samantha

Taft for good measure. Maybe I'd be helping the investigation after all. I hoped so.

The moment I heard the outer door close, I snapped my fingers. It had completely slipped my mind to tell Rodriguez about my meeting with Percy tomorrow night. I would just have to connect with Rodriguez later when I got him these files.

WEDNESDAY MORNING, I STARED AT THE crisp envelope from RH Galleries with a combined sense of dread and anticipation. The owner of the gallery, Roxanne, and I had played phone tag all afternoon the day before. I'd intended to try her again this morning, but the mail arrived first. I tapped the handwritten envelope against the desk. This was way too quick. Which probably meant the painting was a fake. It was much easier to spot a fake than to authenticate an original. Still . . .

I picked up my receiver. "Lois," I said when the assistant curator answered, "I have a letter from RH Galleries in my hand."

I heard her sharp intake of breath. "What does it say?"

"I haven't opened it yet. I thought you'd like to be here when I did."

"Are you serious? Thank you!" she said and hung up the phone before I could respond. Less than a minute later she'd made it to my office, eyes bright. "Open it. I can't stand another minute of suspense."

I started to peel up the flap, then stopped. "Here." I handed it to her. "You do it."

"Really?" Her eyes couldn't get any wider. "It's got to be fake, don't you think? I mean, nobody could authenticate it this fast, could they?" She held her breath as she opened the flap, reverently removed the contents, and started to read. "Oh my gosh!" Her words came out fast and high. "It's real. It's a genuine Raphael Soyer."

I stood up to read over her shoulder. Roxanne had lucked out by connecting with a Soyer expert named Carson, who had personally cataloged all the artist's known works. He had a record in his files about a private project Soyer had done for the Marshfield family, but Carson had never seen the piece nor known its whereabouts. The elderly collector had attempted to contact the Marshfield estate several times, but had always been told that no such portrait existed. Roxanne claimed it was pure luck that she'd connected with him, but I knew better. Roxanne was shrewd and sharp. She'd known precisely where to turn.

"This is wonderful," I said. We would still have to order a second authentication, but right now we were golden. "Thanks, Lois."

She started to head back to her office, but returned to my desk. "Abe was a really nice guy, but he never shared this sort of stuff with us. He took care of all that himself. We found out later how things turned out. I just want to say thanks for letting me share in the moment."

"My pleasure," I said. And it truly was.

I picked up the phone and dialed Bennett. He seemed pleased to hear from me—a reversal from his mood two days earlier—and said he would be right down. I suggested I bring my news up to him, but he insisted on coming to the office. "I'll be here," I said.

When he arrived less than fifteen minutes later, Frances was away from her desk. Nonetheless, he shut the inner door before he sat down. "That woman is a busybody," he said.

I didn't want to disparage one of my employees in front of the boss, so I said, "But she's very good at her job."

"She is that," he agreed. "The woman knows more about everyone and everything than she should. She's almost always right, of course. But it's frustrating to have to deal with her."

I nodded. "I have news," I said, pulling up the letter from Roxanne, "about the painting we found in storage."

Bennett's face brightened. "And?"

"It's legit."

He slapped his hands on the desk, his face all smiles. "I knew it!" A half second later, he sobered. "Are you sure?"

"We have to get through one more hurdle, but it's

looking good. I'd say we're looking at a genuine Raphael Soyer."

"This is wonderful."

"It is." I hadn't ever seen him so cheered. Although perennially pleasant, he was rarely enthusiastic. This was new. And nice.

He surprised me by switching subjects. "Where did you come from?" he asked.

"Come from?" I repeated. "You mean where did I grow up?"

He nodded.

"I was born here," I said. "In fact, my mom used to bring me to the manor as a treat." I smiled and gave a self-deprecating shrug. "I think it was the beauty of Marshfield that inspired my career."

"But you didn't grow up in Emberstowne?"

I hadn't expected to discuss my family history with Bennett. Coming so close on the heels of my recent discovery, the conversation put me on edge. My face grew hot. "No," I said slowly, not sure where this was going. "I spent a long time in Chicago."

"That accounts for your flat vowels," he said, not unkindly. "What brought you back?"

I told him about my mom and how much she loved Emberstowne. I mentioned her getting sick and my coming back to take care of her.

"Your mother grew up here? What was her name?"

"Amelia Wheaton." I was attentive to any

change in his face—any expression of surprise or recognition.

Nothing.

"My dad was Lewis Wheaton."

"He passed away as well?"

I nodded.

"I'm sorry," Bennett said. "I don't mean to make you sad. I would just like to get to know you better. Abe and I . . ." He let the thought hang and it dawned on me, Bennett was lonely.

"My dad didn't grow up here," I said to break the silence. "That's part of what took us to Chicago for all those years."

"What was your mother's maiden name?"

I swallowed. "Careaux."

Bennett seemed to recognize the name but didn't express the sort of shock or outrage I might have expected, given the alleged relationship between his father and my grandmother. "Careaux," he repeated. "That's familiar. Did your grandmother work for the manor?"

"She did."

Bennett smiled as though reliving a pleasant experience. "I think I remember her. But I don't know her first name . . ."

"Sophie."

"I called her Mrs. Careaux, of course. I think she might have been a housekeeper, am I right?"

The soft cheer in his voice told me he was oblivious to our possible familial tie. Was I disappointed, or relieved? I couldn't tell. Part of me wanted him to know, but the other part of me realized that once the information was out there, things could get complicated.

"Yes, she worked here as a housekeeper. For a while."

My mind skip-stepped. Just like the Soyer painting, I had in my grasp what I knew was the truth, but until I took the final step to verify, I would never know for sure.

"What were you just thinking?" he asked me.

Startled, I shook my head. "Sorry, my mind wandered. I'm just surprised you knew my grandmother."

"Not well, of course. I was very young." He smiled at me in a compassionate way. "But it's nice to discover your ties to the manor."

If he only knew. "It is," I said blandly.

He sat back in his chair then, steepling his fingers. I watched as a thoughtful expression settled on his face. We sat there, silent for several minutes because it seemed wrong to break the spell. Finally, he took a deep breath and sat forward again. "I am pleased with how well you've taken control of the manor since Abe's passing."

I waited.

"Mind you," he continued, "I had my doubts. You're so . . . young. You're still just a girl." Holding up a hand to forestall any reaction, he added, "I know that probably isn't politically correct to say these days, but I claim all the rights my age and upbringing afford me."

Understanding his intention was to compliment, I said, "I'm happy to be able to help. And all I want is to do my best for Marshfield Manor."

"I've come to appreciate that," he said. "And that is why—despite my original misgivings—I want to take you a step further."

I had no idea what he meant. He pushed himself up from the seat and walked toward the other office. Instead of opening the door, he locked it.

Speechless, I waited while he made his way back. His eyes twinkled and he smiled. "You ready?"

I had no answer.

He crooked a finger and made his way to the fireplace. "Come here."

Dutifully, I followed. We stood facing each other with Bennett on the left of the fireplace and me on the right.

Squinting at me, Bennett said, "I believe you were acting in my best interests when you shared the secret room with the detectives. In fact," he said, glancing away as though ashamed to admit it, "the police told Terrence that they've determined that it is exactly how the killer got in." Bennett shook his head. "Who else could have known about that entrance?" he asked rhetorically. "Hillary swears she told no one but you."

I had no answer for that.

Full of cheer and energy, Bennett looked twenty years younger. He crouched in front of the fireplace and reached in, to the left of the damper. Running his fingers along the inside, he obviously encountered what he was looking for. He glanced up. "Come down here."

I did.

"Feel this ledge under here?"

I complied, my fingers taking up the spot where his had been. He smiled and exerted pressure on the back of my right index finger. There was a soft *click*, and he stood up. "Once it's unlocked, it's just a matter of . . ." he moved to the side of the fireplace and grasped the side of the oak mantel. With a flick of his wrist, he twisted the edge upward until it was perpendicular to the floor. "There you go. Now we open the door."

I saw no door.

Like a kid showing off a new toy, Bennett walked me over to the wall to the left of the fireplace. "Here," he said. He pushed at the paneled wall and it gave, easily. "Look."

The door was about two feet wide, just enough to squeeze through, but inside the compartment—and that's exactly how it felt, like a compartment—there were curved stone steps leading upward. I leaned into the dusty area and tried to look up, but the angle didn't allow me to see the final destination. This was cool. "Where does it lead?"

"A room just above."

Before I could say anything, he interrupted. "And before you think I'm a dirty old man making a lewd suggestion, I am not. You're young enough to be my granddaughter."

"I didn't think—"

"I'm telling you this because you and I may occasionally need to discuss topics we don't want overheard. We may not even want anyone to know we've met." He pointed to Frances's office. "This helped Abe circumvent such problems."

"And you're trusting me with this information?"

He wore a strange expression. "I am," he said slowly. "I can't say why, but I sense a kindred spirit in you." He shrugged. "I don't take my confidences lightly, so I trust you will not share this with anyone."

Touched, I crossed my heart. "I promise."

Chapter 25

WHEN BENNETT LEFT, FRANCES ASKED ME why my door had been locked. Whatever ideas she might have been brewing in that little brain of hers caused her eyebrows to jump around more excitedly than ever. With a straight face, I told her that Bennett and I had a few sensitive issues to discuss. She made a sound of annoyance and walked away.

Later that afternoon, I rearranged my desk four times in an effort to prioritize. Two semi-emergencies had popped up: A floor buffer in the basement had caught fire and initiated a sprinkler response; and a pregnant guest unexpectedly went into labor during a tour of the mansion. I ran down there and sat with her until the paramedics arrived. When I was notified that the woman had given birth to a healthy little girl en route to the hospital and named her Marsha, in honor of the manor, I made arrangements to send flowers.

Finally, after getting another couple of items scratched off my to-do list, I decided to take another look at my grandmother's file. I wanted to write down the exact dates of her employment. I thought it might be helpful to know as I sorted through the rest of the paperwork at home.

Contrary to my roommates' wishes, I hadn't chucked the remaining boxes. I still had a long way to go.

When I unlocked my desk drawer the folder wasn't there. I knew I'd put it away. I was *sure* I had. And yet . . .

I remembered having it out before Bennett came, but as soon as he was on his way, I swore I'd placed it safely in my drawer. I tried picturing my movements.

"Frances," I called.

She didn't answer. I got up and went into her office. Not there.

If I knew the woman and her busybody tendencies the way I thought I did, I had no doubt she would eagerly "borrow" the file from my office if the opportunity presented itself.

Her desk was a collection of tidy piles, each of them with a Post-it note stuck to the top with a to-do list written neatly on every one. She'd prioritized them, A, B, C, etc., but I couldn't find anything on her desk that resembled my grandmother's dark manila file. As I stood there, I allowed my gaze to wander over to the credenza behind her chair. There were four more stacks of files, and beneath the tallest one on the left I noticed a corner of a dark file sticking out. Just a little bit.

"Aha," I said softly, making my way around her desk to check things out. A bright pink note read:

"To do" and the stack appeared to be a collection of bills waiting to be paid.

I lifted the stack just enough to wiggle the dark file folder from the bottom. It was an old personnel file, and for a moment when I thought it was my grandmother's, my heart raced. But this one belonged to Rosa Brelke, and was, in fact, one of the records I'd read the other day. Frances hadn't returned it to the drawer yet. I wondered why not. I opened the file and paged through it again. Nothing of particular interest in here. I skimmed the dozen pages in her file, then stopped when I came to a typewritten letter addressed to Abe Vargas and signed by Ronny Tooney.

I lowered myself in the chair to read.

Half a minute later, the door opened and Frances walked in. Her surprise was evident, her annoyance plain. "What are you doing?" she asked, crossing the room in a flash. She didn't dare rip the folder from my hands though I could tell by the murderous look in her eyes that's exactly what she wanted to do.

"This wasn't in here before," I said, lifting the letter. "Ronny Tooney is Rosa's cousin?"

Frances stood in front of her desk, her lips tight.

"You took this letter out before you let me read the files."

No answer.

"Why?" I asked. "You said you thought Tooney was related to someone on staff. Why hide it now?

Don't you think I have a right to know? Don't you think the police have a right to know?"

Frances blinked several times, as though trying to come up with a reasonable excuse. I couldn't imagine one.

"Rosa asked me to," she finally said.

"And that explains this subterfuge?"

"This is really no big deal."

I stood. "It's a very big deal. And I intend to document this in *your* personnel record. Do you understand how completely wrong this is? Not to mention unlawful?"

"Rosa's scared. That's it. She was afraid she'd get in trouble because of Tooney. That doesn't make her guilty of anything. Doesn't make me guilty of anything either. Neither of them are suspects, so what's the problem?" Frances wiggled her head. "Why were you going through my desk, anyway?"

I'd forgotten, momentarily, about my grandmother's missing file. "I was looking for something."

"Did you find it?"

"No."

She pursed her lips. "Why don't you tell me what it is and I will attempt to locate it for you," she said it a tight voice.

No way. "Later," I said.

"Well then, if you're quite finished there, I'll get back to work."

306

I left a message for Rodriguez. Maybe this was just the break they needed.

AS ANNOYED AS I WAS ABOUT THE STILL-missing file and Frances's underhanded stealth, my mood was still buoyed by Bennett's revelation. Showing me the passage was proof he trusted me, and I vowed to do nothing to destroy that trust. I'd been the recipient of betrayal in the past and refused to inflict that pain on others.

At six o'clock, I left to pick up Scott for our meeting with Percy. The trip to the wine shop in Emberstowne would take about twenty minutes and the drive to Percy's about another fifteen. We weren't meeting until seven, but I always preferred to be early.

Emberstowne was charming, especially at night when the unseasonably warm evening air provided a perfect atmosphere for strolling and browsing. I snagged a parking spot on the street about a block from the wine shop and made my way over.

In a month or so the sidewalks would be busier, filled with couples out for a romantic evening, families pushing strollers, and buying ice-cream cones for their kids. But right now was when I liked it best. Not so busy, but with just enough activity to make things interesting. I wished I had the time and money to sit at one of the outdoor cafes and have dinner while I watched the world go by.

I glanced at my cell phone for the time and picked up my pace. I could probably afford coffee, but right now I couldn't afford the time.

The wine shop was smack in the middle of the busy section, flanked by an old-fashioned ice-cream parlor and a particularly excellent mystery bookstore. I hoped Scott was ready to go. The sooner I met with Percy and got this over with, the happier I would be. I smacked myself in the head as I walked, belatedly remembering that I had forgotten to talk to Rodriguez about this meeting tonight. I'd intended to connect with him when I sent the Fairfax reports, but I'd gotten busy, and asked Frances to send the copies for me. Darn.

I was about thirty feet from the wine shop's front door when who should emerge but Geraldine Stajklorski. Our unpleasant hotel guest carried two magnums of wine, and a shopping bag hung heavily from each arm.

There was no way I wanted her to see me, so I stepped close to the bookstore window and pretended to study the mysteries on display. Geraldine didn't notice me, but made her way unsteadily to her car at the far curb, struggling under the weight of her purchases. She loaded the magnums and bags into the trunk of a small gray sedan and I waited until she pulled away to enter the shop. Except for my roommates, the place was empty.

"You two just made a nice sale," I said. "What a great way to end the day, huh?"

Too late, I realized Bruce and Scott had been arguing. They looked up at me from behind the granite countertop, with forced "everything is just fine" looks on their faces.

"What's wrong?" I asked. "I just saw nasty Geraldine walking out of here with her arms full. Shouldn't you be celebrating?"

"Who?" Bruce asked.

I jerked a thumb toward the street. "Geraldine. That woman I told you about who took Marshfield Manor for a ride."

"She's outside?"

"She was just *here*."

Clearly puzzled, Bruce looked to Scott. "What are you talking about?"

"The woman with her arms full of wine," I said. "That was Geraldine Stajklorski." I didn't understand their confusion. "She must have used a credit card or something, so you had to have seen her name."

Bruce pointed to the street. "That was the woman you told us about? Are you sure?" The desperation in his voice scared me.

Scott gripped the counter, his face unnaturally pale. "The woman who just left was Dina St. Clair," he said shakily. "From *Grape Living*."

"No." My voice was low. "That's Geraldine Stajklorski."

The light began to dawn. On all of us.

Scott lowered himself onto a stool. Bruce dropped his elbows onto the counter and his head into his hands. "I had a bad feeling about her today."

"What?" I asked. "What happened?"

Scott's eyes went red and he looked away. "Maybe she uses a pseudonym?" he said, staring at the wall of wines behind him.

Bruce looked up. "She told us that the editors at *Grape Living* are still on the fence. They wanted a few more items to sample before they made a final decision." He glanced to Scott, who was still turned away. "Her manner today seemed off. She was in too much of a hurry. I didn't want to give her anything else from our stock. We can't afford it."

"She didn't pay for any of that?" I asked.

"I should have listened to Bruce." Scott's voice was soft. "She scammed us."

"We don't know that. Maybe she just uses two names." Bruce didn't sound convinced but he pressed on. "Maybe one is her married name and the other her professional name."

"Why don't you call your contact at *Grape Living* and check?" I asked. Pointing to the clock above the bar, I added, "They're on the West Coast, right? There should still be people in the office."

Bruce shook his head. "Dina *is* our contact with

Grape Living. We've never talked with anyone else."

"But you verified that she's their representative, right?" I asked.

Neither man answered.

"I mean, when she first showed up. You confirmed she was legit, didn't you?"

Their silence spoke volumes.

I wanted badly to ease my friends' pain. "Okay, so she's possibly gotten away with a few items. I saw her carrying two magnums and she had a couple of bags. That doesn't seem too terrible."

"What you saw her carrying was her last trip to the car," Bruce said quietly, as though he didn't want to rub it in Scott's face. "We loaded two full cases for her first."

My hand flew to my mouth. I wanted to ask what the heck they'd been thinking, but what good would that do? Instead, I said, "You don't *know* that she scammed you. Maybe everything is just fine. Call *Grape Living*, and see what they have to say."

Bruce and Scott exchanged a look of despair. We all knew exactly what the outcome would be, but Bruce dutifully made the call. He pulled out Dina St. Clair's business card—it looked genuine to me—and dialed the magazine's number. When the automated system answered, he punched in "Dina's" extension.

"Hello," he said, his face brightening when a real

person answered. "I'd like to speak to someone about your reporter, Dina St. Clair." A second later, he repeated, "St. Clair." He spelled it. His shoulders slumped as he turned to us. "They're transferring me to human resources. The woman I talked to doesn't recognize the name."

Ten minutes later, we had our answer. And one additional piece of information. The human resources person, after confirming that there was no Dina St. Clair, nor Geraldine Stajklorski employed by the magazine, mentioned that she'd received a similar inquiry earlier this week. Bruce informed the woman on the phone that it was possible that Dina St. Clair may have perpetrated fraud using *Grape Living* as her cover story. He said he had no proof but that perhaps the magazine would like to be aware of her antics.

The woman thanked Bruce and asked for his contact information. He provided it and hung up.

"I'm so sorry," I said.

Scott was clearly ready to lose it. When the front door opened to admit a middle-aged couple, he retreated to the back room. Bruce forced a smile and greeted the newcomers warmly. "Let me know if I can help you find anything," he said.

I looked up at the clock. Bruce caught me. "You've got that meeting with Percy," he said. "You're already running late."

"I can cancel."

"To do what? Hold our hands? No, we'll get through this."

I hated to leave, but I knew I needed to. "Don't tell Scott I went without him," I said. "I'll see you two at home later."

Coming out from behind the counter, Bruce approached the couple, who had pulled a bottle of port from the display. "Have you ever tried this with chocolate-covered blueberries?" They admitted they hadn't. "Ah," Bruce led them to the counter with the deft touch of a master salesman. "Then you are in for a special treat."

ZOE WAS ON DUTY AT THE HOTEL WHEN I called to ask about Geraldine. "I haven't seen her all day," she said.

"Don't let her leave the premises," I said. "Promise her anything. Just keep her there until the police arrive."

I tried getting in touch with both Rodriguez and Flynn, but could only leave messages asking them to call me. Scott and Bruce were planning to call the police, but I wanted to do all I could to help out, too.

The trip to Percy's gave me time to think. My heart broke for my roommates. I knew their financial situation, and it was just as bleak as mine. While we were lucky to have income at all, what we brought in was perpetually short of what was needed. Bruce and Scott had never been late with their rent, despite the fact that by keeping current they were often forced to delay repairs at the shop or on their car. I depended on their rent and my salary to keep our home in working order, but lately the house had become a veritable money pit.

Much like Taft's victims, Bruce and Scott had been lulled into a scheme that sounded too good to be true. They'd believed that *Grape Living* was interested in their little shop, just because a woman with swindling on her agenda told them so. They had seen what they wanted to see, heard what they wanted to hear. Geraldine Stajklorski, aka Dina St. Clair or whatever her name was, was clearly a con artist. And she'd taken my friends but good.

I thought about the roof repairs and my heart sank. I'd believed in my roommates' good fortune because they'd believed. In fact, as soon as the feature in *Grape Living* materialized, I'd envisioned asking Bruce and Scott for an advance on two months' rent, just so that I could afford to get the roof project started. Now that was out of the question.

Dispirited, I made the final turn onto Percy's street, wanting nothing more than to get in, get done, and get home as quickly as possible. As I drove slowly past small, ramshackle houses with ripped, upholstered chairs on their dirt front lawns and broken-down pickup trucks in almost every driveway, I started to have second thoughts. House numbering was inconsistent and it took me two passes to realize Percy's sat between a burned-out structure and a debris-littered empty lot. I pulled up to the curb thinking I probably should have waited until Scott was with me after all.

I considered turning back until I spotted a group of little kids playing tag across the street in another empty lot. Barefoot and unkempt, they ranged from about eight to twelve years old, running and laughing, completely carefree. If this area was safe enough for them, it was probably safe enough for me.

The moment I got out of my car they stopped running and stared. One of the little girls waved. I waved back. A boy jogged across the street. He pointed. "What's going on in there today?"

I didn't understand the question. "You mean at Percy's house?"

The kid shrugged. "Is that the guy's name? How come so many people are visiting him today? Does he sell drugs?"

"Other people visited? Like the police, you mean?"

"Not police. A guy came. And then a different guy and a girl. And then that guy came back without the girl."

"All of these people today?"

The kid nodded. "My mom tells me to watch out for drug houses. Is that a drug house? It looks like a drug house."

I had no answer for that. "I'm not here for drugs. I'm just here to talk to Percy."

That seemed to satisfy him. "Okay." With that, he turned and ran back to his group.

Chalk one up for substance awareness programs.

Percy had made mention of seeing his doctor about his meds. But drugs? That was a wrinkle I hadn't anticipated.

The structure's concrete stoop listed precariously but stayed put when I stepped up. I rang the doorbell but didn't hear chimes inside. No sound of movement. Guessing that the bell was out of order, as mine often was, I knocked on the front door. Scratched and scuffed, it looked as though a pack of dogs had tried to break in. Five miniature windows in a stepped-down pattern decorated the scarred maple. The lowest window was just about eye level, but far too dirty for me to see inside.

When my knocking produced no results, I tried rapping on the lowest pane.

Still no luck. I stepped off the stoop and made my way around a scraggly bush to the front. The first of the three windows there was broken, its top portion missing completely, the remaining bottom pane jagged, like a volatile business's profit chart. A bedsheet had been strung across all three in an apparent attempt at privacy. I checked the center window for cracks before rapping my knuckles against it. When the window didn't crumble, I rapped again, harder and longer. There was no way for him to miss the noise—if he was in there.

No movement. Nothing at all.

Cursing Percy for bringing me all the way out here and then forgetting about our meeting, I started to turn away.

The moan stopped me. I tilted my head, thinking it had been wind through the broken glass. But the evening was still.

Again, a moan.

I turned as it sounded once more, and realized it was coming from inside the house.

"Percy?" I shouted, stepping closer. "Are you okay?"

"Help."

No mistaking it that time. His voice was faint, but close enough. "Percy," I shouted again, "I'm calling for help."

I did. I pulled out my cell phone and dialed 9-1-1. I gave the dispatcher Percy's address and when she asked the nature of the emergency, I said I wasn't sure. Just that a man was calling for help. She said a squad would be on its way. "An ambulance, too," I said. Better safe than sorry.

From inside the house, Percy's voice warbled, "Please."

When I turned, I nearly knocked over the little boy. He'd appeared right next to me, his friends gathered a few feet behind. "What's going on?" he asked.

"I don't know. I think the man inside needs help." I judged the distance from the edge of the stoop to the window. I might be able to stand on the upraised edge and see inside just enough to know what was going on.

"Did you call 9-1-1?"

"Yes," I said, trying not to let my impatience show. "They're on their way."

"Did you try the front door?" the kid asked, moving up onto the stoop next to me.

I spun. "What?"

"Nobody locks their doors around here," he said as he twisted the knob. It turned. "See?"

"Don't," I said, blocking him from going in. "You don't know what's in there." I pointed across the street. "You and your friends go over there and wait."

"Awww . . ."

My ears strained to hear sirens, but the neighborhood was silent.

"What if he's dead?" the kid asked. "Huh?"

"He's not dead," I said, taking up the entire doorway to prevent the kid from getting past me. "Now go down to the sidewalk at least, okay? I'll go check on him."

The idea of entering Percy's house on my own was not part of the plan, but I was the adult here and I felt pressured to set a good example. "Listen," I said to the ringleader, hoping that by wrangling his cooperation I would prevent him

318

from taking any chances, "I'm going inside. If I scream or yell, or don't come out, you call the police for me, okay?"

"I thought you already did that."

Precocious kid. "A second call might get them to show up faster."

"Maybe. They take a long time to get here, usually. Mom says it's because we live in a un-in-cor . . . corpry . . ."

I didn't have time to listen to the kid's civics lesson, earnest though it was. "I'm counting on you," I said and stepped into Percy's house.

It smelled bad. Like hold-my-hand-against-my-nose bad. Just inside, I stopped when I heard animated conversation, belatedly recognizing the pace and canned laughter of a sitcom. The entryway was tiny—a closet-sized foyer with a second, inner door. Dingy and blistered from years of neglect, it apparently led to the living room. I stifled a gag reaction when my fingers made contact with its sticky doorknob.

Immediately inside, the smell intensified. Next to the door, a small television tilted precariously atop a giant plastic garbage bin, the bright blue light flickering into the darkened room. The sitcom's familiar background music swelled and I took one more step in.

Across the room, Percy stretched across a threadbare print sofa, one arm draping lifelessly to the floor, looking like a couch potato in his finest hour. Except his face was contorted in pain. And his shirt was red. Soaking red. Just like the puddled patch of carpet next to him.

Panic spurred me forward. "Percy," I shouted. Fighting down fear that whoever did this might still be around, I crouched next to him. "What happened?"

Tears trickled down the sides of his face. He didn't answer.

"You'll be okay," I said, lying through my teeth. There was no need to seek out a pulse, his chest rose and fell in rapid, panicked breaths.

He tried to speak but most of what he said was garbled. It sounded as though he was saying "same" or "sam."

"The same guy?" I asked. "Was it the same guy who paid you?"

"Same." Percy blinked hard, twice. Might have been agreement. More likely was pain.

"Stay with me, Percy," I said. "Come on. You're going to get through this."

"Please." His voice was strangled. "Don't . . . let me . . ."

I knew what he was asking. "I won't."

"Don't leave . . ."

"I'm right here."

Help arrived within minutes, though it felt like months. The police pulled me away from Percy as they and the paramedics took efficient control. I waited outside, leaning on my car, shaking.

Rodriguez arrived, told me to stick around, then went inside. He emerged about five minutes later. "I caught the call," he said. "What happened?"

I told him everything, including Percy's attempt to talk. "I think he was trying to tell me it was the same guy."

Rodriguez nodded and took notes.

When I'd finished giving my rendition, I asked, "Was he shot?"

"Looks like. We'll have to see if it's the same caliber as the one recovered from Abe Vargas's body."

"Will Percy survive?"

Rodriguez looked up toward the darkening sky, then at me. "Hard to say. He's lost a lot of blood."

Suddenly remembering, I looked around. "There may be witnesses. There were kids playing out here all day. They said that a lot of people came to visit Percy today."

Rodriguez scribbled. "So how come I didn't know you were coming out here?"

I apologized. "I intended to tell you."

"You should have."

In just over one week, I'd twice come upon victims who had been shot. "What's going on around here?"

Rodriguez fixed me with a sober look. "I wish I knew."

Remembering my earlier conversation with Frances, I told him about the relationship between

Rosa Brelke and Ronny Tooney. The detective didn't seem terribly impressed and I commented on that. A corner of his mouth tugged upward. "Half the people on your staff are related to each other."

"Yeah, but—"

"I'll check into it," he said. "I promise." He asked me where I'd been just before coming out here. That reminded me, and I told him about Geraldine Stajklorski, also known as Dina St. Clair.

He frowned. "Do you believe this individual is involved in either of the shootings?"

"No," I said. "Just bad timing. But Bruce and Scott are my friends. Who should they talk to if they want to file a complaint?"

Rodriguez expelled a breath of frustration. "When it rains, it pours." He started a new page of notes. "Give me the details."

"I'm sure my roommates can talk to someone else in your department. You've got so much going already."

Weary eyes met mine. "There ain't nobody else. Me and Flynn are all we've got. Now, spell this woman's name for me."

I did, giving him the best information I could on what I knew of Geraldine Stajklorski. While we'd been talking, the paramedics had been busy inside. I kept an eye on their comings and goings and sucked in a breath when it took four men to carry

Percy out on a gurney. He wore an oxygen mask over his face and had an IV attached to his arm.

"He's still alive, then," I said.

Rodriguez grimaced but said nothing. "Back to this new development. Anything else you can tell me?"

I spotted the ragtag group just beyond the barrier of flashing lights. "See that tall kid?" I said. "Check with him. He seems pretty smart."

"You and I will talk again later," he said, and trotted off to question the children. As he approached, the oldest one swaggered forward with an air of self-importance.

Two squads—which probably accounted for the entire Emberstowne police fleet—parted to allow me to drive away.

I shook all the way home.

Chapter 26

THE FOLLOWING MORNING, I GOT IN TO Marshfield extra early. I didn't care to see or talk with anyone until I got a better grasp on my emotions. I intended to immerse myself in work and not look up until the day was over, but my soul apparently had other plans. The minute I sat down, my energy dissolved. Leaning forward, I rested my arms on the desk and simply stared out the window.

I'd really wanted to talk with Scott and Bruce last night when I got home, but the house had been dark and quiet with my roommates behind closed doors. Whether they'd turned in for the night, or just didn't feel like talking, I didn't know. I longed to tell them about Percy—to share the terrible experience with them—but they were handling a loss of their own. I couldn't—I wouldn't—intrude.

I don't know how long I stared out the office window, but I was startled back to reality when Frances sauntered in. "Good morning," she said. If I'd expected sheepishness or discomfort on her part after our discussion yesterday, I was mistaken. She placed files on my desk with the utmost care, raking me up and down with her gaze as she did so. "How long have you worked here?" she asked.

"Why?"

A shrug, as though it was no matter. "You're shrewder than I gave you credit for."

I had no idea what that meant, but clearly no compliment was intended. She stared at me a moment longer before pivoting and prancing away to answer her phone.

"It's for you," she called from the other room. "Detective Rodriguez."

I snatched up the receiver. "How is Percy?"

"Hanging in there," he said. "But it's touch and go."

I nodded, even though I knew he couldn't see me. "Thanks for the update."

"He's got a guard watching over him so no one tries to finish the job, you know?" Clearing his throat, he continued, "And we've finally got additional manpower coming in to assist with the Vargas murder. On another matter, I plan to talk with your friends about this scam woman later today or tomorrow."

I sat up. "Wait," I said. "Didn't you pick her up at the hotel?"

"Your friend Stajklorski checked out," he said. "Left yesterday."

"But—"

"Yeah," he said, anticipating me, "the hotel staff is surprised, too. Her room was completely vacated. And stripped. According to the manager, everything that wasn't tied down is missing.

Bedsheets, pillowcases, ice bucket. You name it, she took it."

"That little conniving . . ."

"I hear you. We'll see how much we can get from the hotel staff. With any luck, they'll have her license plate. But I'm not holding my breath. Gotta go."

"Thanks." I hung up and rubbed my eyes.

I felt better that at least Percy wasn't dead, and that con artist Geraldine Stajklorski was on the detectives' radar, but there were still so many loose threads. Too many. I took a deep breath and slowly let it out.

I decided to focus on Rupesh Chaven and Jeremy Litric. Their files, along with that of Samantha Taft's, were not on my desk. I tried to remember where I'd put them, and snapped my fingers. I pulled open the left-hand desk drawer and reached down to pull them up.

Litric, Chaven, Taft. And . . .

My grandmother's personnel file.

I gripped it tightly, surprised and relieved to have it in my possession again. I must have stashed it away with these other files when I cleaned off my desk yesterday. I didn't remember doing so, but it wouldn't be the first time I'd accidentally misplaced an item I was certain I'd put away. I'd suspected Frances, and was very, very glad I hadn't voiced my doubts aloud.

"Did you say something?" Frances asked from the doorway.

I glanced up, taken aback by her venomous stare. "No."

Accusingly: "I heard something."

The phone rang on her desk. Neither of us said a word as she spun to get it. "Just a moment," she said. Back in the doorway. "It's for you. Again."

I reached for the receiver. "Thanks."

Frances spoke under her breath, "You're welcome, Mizz Marshfield."

"What did you say?"

"The phone is for you."

"After that."

She affected a look of innocence. "Nothing at all."

The light on the phone blinked. I had no idea who was waiting to speak with me, but at the moment, I didn't care. I stood. "Why did you call me Ms. Marshfield?"

She splayed a hand across her chest. "Why would I ever call you that?"

"That's what I'm asking you."

Pointing, she said, "That's the Mister on the phone. You better answer it."

I did. Bennett had heard about the incident at Percy's house and was calling to see how I was. "You could have taken the day off," he said. "I would have understood."

"During my ninety-day probationary period? Not a chance."

His voice deepened. "After everything that has

happened these past couple of weeks, I wouldn't be surprised if you were the one who wanted out. You have been called upon to go above and beyond . . ."

Bennett probably didn't realize how close he was to hitting the mark. I kept telling myself, however, that once we got through this difficult period, my routine here at Marshfield would resemble that of a curator and not that of a homicide cop. "I'm doing okay," I said. It was true. More or less.

"Good. Keep me updated."

He hung up.

I returned to studying the files on the investor/victims and on Samantha Taft. I had one hand resting at an angle on top of the reports in front of me, obscuring most of Mrs. Taft's name. All I could see was "Sam," and I felt a tiny trill of excitement. Last night, I'd been certain that Percy had been trying to say "same." What if what he had truly been trying to say was "Sam"? Samantha?

Frances hovered. "The hotel called while you were on the phone."

I looked up. "About Geraldine?"

She nodded.

"What a mess," I said. "Send a memo to all departments to keep alert for her. I doubt if she'll come back now, but I don't want to take any chances. The woman is ruthless."

"What made you think to check on her?" Frances asked. "I mean, she was unpleasant, for sure, but we never expected this. What made you start this investigation?"

I didn't want to get into the details. "She scammed friends of mine," I said, hoping that would be the end of it.

"Oh," she said with peculiar inflection. "Then you knew her from before."

"No," I snapped. "I didn't know her. Not until she lodged her complaint. Yesterday I discovered that she was running a scam on friends of mine."

"Uh-huh."

"Do you have something to say, Frances?"

When she shook her head, her neck waddled. She flashed an angry look and returned to her office.

Not a minute later, my cell phone rang. I pulled it up, my heart sinking when I read the display. "When it rains, it pours," I said, mimicking Rodriguez, and got up to shut the door between my office and Frances's. "Hello, Liza," I said.

"Hey, how's it going?"

I didn't have time for her this morning. "I'm really busy here. What's up?"

"Are you in a bad mood?"

I didn't answer.

"I hate to give you news like this over the phone," she said slowly.

I didn't want to hear that she'd blown all Mom's money on a business venture that went bust. I'd had enough of scams lately. Too many stories of people losing everything they owned. I didn't want to hear that she'd been arrested and needed bail. I didn't want to hear any of it. "Then don't," I said.

She laughed.

And that's when I knew exactly what she had to tell me. And of everything, I didn't want to hear that, most of all. "Good-bye, Liza. I gotta go."

"Wait, please."

I don't know why I didn't flip my phone shut at that moment. Maybe some long-lost sisterly affection made me hesitate. Maybe for one single instant I hoped her news really wasn't all that bad.

"I'm married," she said.

My breath caught. I couldn't speak.

"He wants to talk with you."

"I don't—"

The moment I heard Eric attempt a wavering, "Grace?" I slammed the phone shut and onto my desk, seething for a long moment before I could speak. "Have a good life," I said between clenched teeth. "You two deserve each other."

I was rattled. So much so that my skin itched from the inside. I needed to break away—to get away.

I'd hit my breaking point. From the lack of progress on Abe's murder investigation, to Percy's attack, to Geraldine eluding our grasp, to this kick in the gut, I'd had it. I stared at the Taft investor information for a long moment. Burying myself in tasks would bring blissful oblivion. But I knew that no matter how hard I tried to concentrate, at this point I wouldn't be able to absorb a single word.

I got up and opened the door, headed for the hallway.

"I'm going out," I said to Frances.

Frances looked me up and down. "You're not taking your walkie-talkie?"

"No," I said, daring her to criticize me. "I won't be gone long." All I needed was ten minutes of quiet, alone, with no chance of anyone interrupting my solitude.

"The Mister wants us to keep our walkie-talkies with us all the time."

"I won't be gone long," I repeated, more slowly this time.

She arched her brows. "All righty, then," she said, her tone clearly communicating disapproval.

Three minutes later, I was outside with the warm sun on my upturned face. Closing my eyes, I took a deep breath of the fresh, green, spring scents. I let the breath out, willing my body to release its tension. Opening my eyes, I made my way to the entrance of the maze. I'd originally intended to lose myself in there for a little while, navigating the tall greenery. Just as I was about to step in, however, I thought better of it. Feeling the way I did, the last thing I needed was to feel hemmed in or trapped.

Instead, I turned toward the low ridge where Jack

said he'd stood when he spotted the killer running from the mansion. I took long, fast strides up the small hill. Air deepened my lungs, but I continued to push myself, little beads of sweat forming near my brow. Had I been wearing more comfortable shoes or a less businesslike outfit, I would have been happy to run. With everything built up inside me, I knew the only way to exorcise my frustration was to push myself physically.

At the top of the hill, I turned back to stare at the mansion. Glorious, magnificent, it deserved to be named one of the country's crown jewels. I could see my office window from here, and I stared at it longingly. I thought I had everything planned out so perfectly: Learn all the mansion's workings from Abe and then take over seamlessly when he retired. But here I was, tragedy having pulled me into a role far more complicated than I had anticipated. Abe's murder had changed all our lives, certainly not for the better. I wished, with all my heart, that he was still here. All of a sudden, I wished my mother was still here, too.

With only the breezy wind to keep me company, I heard and felt every breath as I fought to remember why I'd wanted to work here. Below me, tourists meandered. I spied a young mother holding her little daughter's hand as they stared at the house and took in its exquisite grandeur. I wondered what the little girl was thinking right now. That had been me once upon a time. Those childhood moments had defined me, had helped shape the person I'd become. I knew I wanted to be part of Marshfield from the moment I first visited.

Looking back now, I wondered how much of that longing was influenced by my mother's secret. Why hadn't she ever told me about our ties to Marshfield? Were they real? She would know, wouldn't she? Why wasn't she here to answer my questions? Why was my house falling apart? Why couldn't I have a sister I could depend on?

I felt very alone.

Maybe it *was* time to give up.

"Hey there."

I yelped and spun, startled to see Jack trudging up the hill behind me. Gripping a hand to my chest, I said, "You scared me."

"Sorry," he said, looking not very sorry at all. He closed the distance between us. "What are you doing out here?"

I tried to force a smile, but it fell flat. "Clearing my head."

"It's been a tough go for you, hasn't it?"

Wrinkling my nose, I looked at the house again. The majestic, gorgeous mansion that had towered over these grounds since the late nineteenth century. "The manor won't collapse if I'm not here to oversee things, will it?" I asked.

"What are you saying?"

"It's too much," I said simply. "I thought I could handle it. I can't. I'm crying 'Uncle.'"

"You are handling it. Darn well, if you want my opinion."

I smiled at his attempt to cheer me up. But what else could he say? "I underestimated how much Abe's murder and its aftermath would affect me," I said. "I thought because I didn't know him well I could just press on, be a good soldier, and lead the troops back to normalcy. But I'm in over my head."

"We're all in over our heads, Grace." His brows came together and he took a step closer. "Did you ever consider that? No one here knows what to do. We've never encountered anything like this. We're all fumbling in the dark."

"But I'm the one who's supposed to run the place."

"And you've been doing a hell of a job."

I narrowed my eyes. "Is that a compliment or a cut-down?"

His voice softened. "You're making a difference here. I'm seeing evidence of that everywhere. Little things are changing. The questions you ask, the departments you visit, your unflagging enthusiasm when it comes to making things right—these are all having an effect on the staff. People are *thinking* more these days, and responding less by rote. They're beginning to take ownership of their positions. And that's what you've been working for, right?"

I nodded.

He was on a roll. "It's not going to happen overnight, but I'm seeing attitudes changing. You're too close to the situation to see the effect you're having. There's a sense here, finally, that better times are ahead. And almost everyone on staff believes that change is necessary."

His words cheered me more than I cared to admit. He'd hit, exactly, my hopes and dreams for this place.

"But you can't stop now," he cautioned. "Or everything you've worked for so far will be lost. Just hang in there, okay? If not for yourself, then for all of us." The genuine concern in his eyes took my breath away.

"Thanks," I said, my throat too tight to say anything more.

He tucked his hands into his pockets. "You know," he said, looking out over the grounds, "maybe Saturday night you and I could meet up at Hugo's again, and see if the music's any better this time."

I smiled. "I'd like that."

I'D BEEN OUTSIDE FAR LONGER THAN TEN minutes, but for the first time in days I felt renewed—that everything would be okay—and as though all the troubles I'd been juggling might get sorted out after all.

Plus I had a date. With Jack.

When I returned to the office, I stopped short.

335

Bennett had pulled up a chair to talk with Frances. His elbows on her desk, he leaned forward. At my entrance he twisted around, his eyes clouded like he'd been recently hurt. Frances met my stare, a tiny smile working at her lips. "Here she is now," she said.

I stepped forward, my good mood dampened by the obvious tension in the room. "Bennett, I didn't know you were here."

He stood. "I gathered as much."

Still seated, Frances piped up, "Mr. Marshfield came down here to talk about all your recent excitement over the past few days."

"Of course." I started to move toward my office door. "Come in, please. I'd like to bring you up to date on Percy and on Geraldine."

He stared at me for a long moment. Turning to Frances, he said, "I will be upstairs if anyone needs me," and walked past me.

"Bennett," I said.

He didn't answer.

"What's happened?" I asked. "Is something wrong?"

Turning, his eyes narrowed as though searching for answers in mine. "I'm far too tired for weighty decisions today," he said. "Far too tired." Without another word, he left.

I pounced on Frances the moment the door shut. "What did you say to him?"

Brows up, eyes wide, she blinked. "He's the

owner. He's entitled to know what's going on around here."

"What did you tell him? Specifically?"

She pursed her lips. "To expect a court order."

"From whom?"

Frances stared up at me in disbelief. "Who do you think?"

I held my hands out trying to grasp what was going on. "I'm totally confused here, Frances. What in the world are you hinting at?" But even as I said the words, I put it together with her "Mizz Marshfield" comment earlier. Frances must have gotten a look at my grandmother's file. I gritted my teeth. "You had no right to go through my desk."

"I didn't," she said with a smirk. "You left it right on top. Like you wanted me to find it."

"Why did you tell Bennett?"

She barked a laugh. "You had him fooled. You had us all fooled. Somebody needed to warn the Mister that you weren't the sweet, helpful soul you pretend to be."

"I would never have told him."

"Sure, you wouldn't."

There was no reasoning with this woman. "It's all circumstantial, Frances. You can see that much. Why would I jeopardize my job here with no proof?"

"Jeopardize your job? *Pheh*. When you think you can finagle inheriting the entire estate? I don't think so."

My euphoria was long gone. In its place I felt only frustration, helplessness, and fury. "I'll set this right," I said. "You'll see."

Trying to decide my best course of action, I returned to my desk. A moment later I heard the outer door close. I got up to check. Frances was gone.

Although I knew it would be better to wait, to rehearse just the right words to explain, I couldn't stop myself from grabbing the phone and dialing Bennett. His line rang. And rang. He had apparently shut off his voicemail, and I let the *whirr* repeat twenty times before I gave up. I tried reaching him on the walkie-talkie, on his direct channel. No answer.

I didn't blame him for being upset at the possibility that his father may have had an affair with my grandmother, but I did blame him for listening to Frances's ugly whispers. He knew how much she liked to gossip. Why couldn't he see that she'd distorted the facts?

I thought about his lament about everyone trying to get a piece of him. He now thought of me as one of them. My throat hurt. He'd begun to trust me. But now . . .

Unable to help myself, I tried calling Bennett again, both on the phone and on the walkie-talkie. Still no luck. I tried reaching him elsewhere. Terrence hadn't seen him, nor had anyone else.

On a hunch, I took a walk down to the Birdcage

room. I looked around the bright area—searching—and coming up empty yet again. The sun filtering through the topmost shades, and the harpist plucking out notes of a soft song gave the area a quiet calm. Tourists sat at tables, drinking tea and enjoying finger sandwiches. This is where it had all begun. Where Percy had started us down a tragic spiral. Where Bennett had warned me that I was on probation.

Just today—just an hour ago—I'd been willing to give up this job, to cave in to the pressures surrounding me. But now, the idea of losing my place here made me physically ill.

With no way to reach Bennett, I returned to my office, determined more than ever to figure out who might have killed Abe. For the briefest of moments, I was tempted to use the hidden staircase by the fireplace and confront Bennett in his rooms. I knew, however, that accessing the secret passage—a tangible example of his trust in me—would send the wrong signal at this point. I needed to give him the time he needed to cool off. Then I'd approach him, through normal channels. He was a rational man, wasn't he? He had to listen to me. He just had to.

Chapter 27

FRANCES DID HER BEST TO MAKE ME FEEL uncomfortable Friday morning. Shooting me scathing looks whenever I crossed her path, she whispered into the telephone at every available opportunity, switching to stony silence whenever she spotted me. No doubt she was eagerly spreading word of my impending release.

Bennett still wouldn't answer his phone. Worried for his safety, I checked with Terrence and discovered that Bennett had dismissed his bodyguards. "You're kidding," I said. "With Percy being shot, it's obvious the killer is still out there."

"You're preaching to the choir," Terrence said with steel in his voice. "He and I have gone 'round and 'round with this. He's sick of being treated like a child—his words—and he refuses to cooperate. Tell you the truth, Grace, I think he believes that if he ignores the problem, it will go away." Terrence heaved a deep sigh. "He wouldn't be the first."

"If you see him, please ask him to call me."

"Will do."

That afternoon, I looked up from my Taft project, bleary-eyed, when my cell phone rang. Liza again. I silenced the ring, and waited for the chirp of a voicemail. Nothing. Good. I had nothing to say to her. Not now. Maybe not ever. When the phone rang again moments later—Liza—I shut it off completely.

I stood up to stretch then wandered to the window. Tomorrow night was my "date" with Jack at Hugo's. What had put me in such a good mood just yesterday was causing me angst today. Although I very much wanted to go out with him, my mood was so dark that I feared I would be miserable company.

Grabbing my walkie-talkie, I decided to check in with some of the staff. Jack had told me that my visits had been helping morale and that people felt good knowing their efforts were appreciated. Attempting to put Bennett's displeasure with me out of my mind, I headed out to do my job.

Frances stopped me. "Where are you going?"

"Is there something you needed?"

"It's just . . . I'm leaving early today." She glanced at the grandfather clock. "In about five minutes. I left a note on your desk last week."

She had, and I'd forgotten. But I wasn't about to admit that. "No problem. If anyone needs me, they can reach me here." I held up the walkie-talkie.

"Taking it along this time, are you?"

I ignored her and left the room.

LOIS AND TWO OTHER ASSISTANT CURators were in the process of acquiring an antique paperweight that had recently become available through one of our European channels. They updated me, and while there Lois and I discussed the ultimate placement of the Raphael Soyer painting. I suggested a location in the former Smoking room, but Lois preferred one of the second-floor bedrooms. We both looked forward to making that decision upon the painting's return.

Outside, I made my way over to visit Earl. "How's it going?" I asked him.

He pulled a Starlight mint out from his deep pocket and handed it to me. "Well enough for a Friday."

I took a moment to gaze out over the grounds. "Just beautiful," I said. "You've made spring come alive."

"Nah," he said, "Mother Nature takes care of that. I just make sure we give her 'nuff to work with."

"Is Jack around?"

"Took off," he said. "Always leaves early on Fridays."

A tall young man hustled over, his blond hair dripping sweat, his coveralls stained down both sides as though he had a habit of wiping dirty hands on his legs. Out of breath he said, "Hey, Earl," and jerked a thumb eastward. "The damn tractor died on me again. Mind if I go scare up some help from maintenance?"

"You go ahead," Earl said. "Tell them I'm warning 'em, they better fix it right this time."

The young man was about to take off when Earl grabbed his arm. "Hang on, Kenny." The elderly gardener turned to me. "You think maybe you could help us out, Grace? Maintenance keeps telling us that old tractor is fine, but it breaks down about once a week. Maybe if you talk to them?"

"Sure," I said but my mind was not on heavy equipment. "You're Kenny?"

"Kenneth to my mom, but yeah."

"Are there any Kennys on staff?"

"No, ma'am. We got two Bobs and two Jims, but I'm the only Kenny."

"But," I stopped myself before the words came out. Jack had said that he saw a man running from the mansion at the time Abe was killed. He'd also said that he'd originally thought it was Kenny. This young man standing in front of me was tall, lanky, fair-haired, and no more than twenty-five years old.

Rodriguez was looking for a man between thirty-five and fifty, under six feet tall, and a little bit overweight. Not like Kenny here. Not at all.

"But what?" he asked.

"Nothing." I scratched the side of my head. "I'll talk with maintenance," I said. Distracted, I thanked them both for their time and walked away.

If only I'd had a chance to talk with Percy. He'd all but admitted he'd given the police an erroneous description. What had the killer really looked like? From the description Rodriguez had, I was surprised he hadn't ever seriously considered Ronny Tooney as a suspect. Because unless I'd received bad information from Rodriguez, Ronny Tooney fit.

Fit *exactly*.

But then, who had Jack seen running from the mansion? Should we be looking for an accomplice? Rodriguez had gotten the description of the middle-aged man from our housekeeping staff. Had Tooney been involved from the very beginning?

I walked quickly, but my mind raced faster.

Rosa might very well have known about the secret room and staircase adjacent to the study. In fact, with all her years in service to Marshfield, I would have been surprised if she *didn't* know. What if she'd shared that information with cousin Ronny? That could easily explain how he had been able to get in without being seen—and get out without being caught.

Back inside, I knew better than to confront Rosa directly. If my suspicions were correct, the moment she smelled my interest she'd report it to Tooney. My heels clicked down the tile steps as I formulated a plan. So much information had been provided by hearsay. The only person who told me himself that the killer looked like Kenny was Jack. Now that I'd met Kenny, I needed to get the rest of my facts straight.

If Rosa was somehow protecting Tooney, I

intended to find out. And the only way to do so was to exploit the weak link.

Making my way to the basement, down through the labyrinthine hallways, the cacophony of busy washers and dryers and the scents of hot cotton and bleach were my guides. Three women folding gold-crested navy blue towels chatted as they worked.

"Excuse me," I said over the din of the laundry machines. "Is Melissa around?"

Yvonne tapped one of her companions on the shoulder and pointed. When Melissa spotted me, she gave a nervous wave. Would my presence always inspire such trepidation in the staff? If Frances had her way, I might never find out.

I gestured for Melissa to follow me to a quieter location. "I'd like to ask you a few questions," I said. The staff break room was two doors away from the laundry room, and empty. I ushered Melissa close to the windows. That way, we would be far enough from the door so no one could overhear.

Melissa looked ready to throw up. "What's wrong?"

"You and Rosa were upstairs when Abe was killed, right?" I knew that already, but I wanted to ease into my interrogation.

She nodded.

"And you told the police that you saw a man up there."

345

A quick nod.

"What did he look like?"

She shook her head. "I try not to think about that."

"I understand," I said softly. "But there is a killer out there. Someone who might have killed again."

Her hand flew to her chest. "Who?"

I held up a finger. There was a flash of fear behind her eyes that told me she was hiding something. I wanted to find out if Rosa had asked her to keep quiet. I wanted to find out if it was, indeed, Ronny Tooney who had disappeared from the room so quickly after shooting Abe. My instincts told me to push, but the last thing I needed was for Melissa to go running to Rosa. So I chose my words carefully.

"I know about the secret room," I said.

She flinched.

I thought, *Bingo.*

Too late, she tried to deny comprehension. "I don't know—"

"Sure you do," I said keeping my voice low.

She swallowed.

"It's never too late, Melissa," I said, "to make things right."

"I have to go," she said.

I tried to stop her, but she was out of the room before I could react. I followed, but only halfheartedly. Cornering her would do no good right now. I decided to try again later after giving her a chance to realize I was right. I circled back to the laundry room. Yvonne looked up.

"Where's Rosa?" I asked.

She shrugged. "Gone for the day, I think."

Frustrated, I returned to my office.

As promised, Frances was gone. "Does everybody here leave early on Fridays?" I asked aloud. The grandfather clock in the corner ticked, but that was no answer at all.

I refused to give up, despite the fact that I seemed to do no more than perpetually spin my wheels. Despite the fact that most of the staff saw me as an ogre. Despite the fact that my assistant loathed me. Despite the fact that Bennett was probably planning to fire me first thing Monday morning.

Returning to my inner office, I pulled out the hefty Taft file again. If I came up with a clue that brought Abe's killer into the limelight—if I was able to help bring that person to justice—then maybe Bennett would realize what a gem he had in me.

Ronny Tooney didn't strike me as a billionaire in disguise, but he might have invested with Taft just the same. The more I thought about it, the more it made sense. While most victims of the Taft scam had lost millions, the vast majority of those people had maintained their standard of living.

Tooney was not a wealthy man. If he *had* invested with Taft—a question I planned to have answered tonight, if it killed me—he'd probably invested a modest sum. To someone like Tooney, a hundred thousand dollars was a fortune. What if he'd lost it all? Was that reason enough to kill?

Suspicions dancing in my mind, I opened the record report to the last page, to work my way up from the bottom. One thing bothered me and that was Tooney himself. Except for his sudden appearance in the passenger seat of my car, and his propensity to skulk around, he didn't strike me as a killer. He didn't have an edge. In fact, he seemed rather pitiful.

But it was Tooney who had sent me to meet Percy. And from what I understood, the shooting had occurred less than an hour before I got there. What if I hadn't been running late? Had the killer planned to take me down, too?

I turned the page, working backward, not finding Tooney's name among the smaller investors. There were about four thousand people who lost less than fifty thousand dollars each—small change in this business. I finished going over that list and moved up to those who had invested less than one hundred thousand, then those who invested less than two hundred and fifty thousand. As I moved up in dollar amount, the number of names grew smaller.

I leaned back and stretched, wondering if my efforts were as futile as they felt.

When my desk phone rang, I let out a little yelp

of surprise. I let it ring one additional time to allow my nerves to unjangle, then blinked to try to make out the clock across the room. I couldn't tell the time. After nine. Maybe even close to ten. I'd been at this for hours and hadn't come across any Tooney in the list. Nor for that matter, any Brelke either.

I answered. "Grace Wheaton."

"Ms. Wheaton?" A man's voice. Soft drawl. "This here's Bo in security."

"Good evening, Bo," I said, trying to place his face. Unfortunately, I still hadn't learned all our employees' names.

"Well, I can't say rightly that it is a good evening. We think there might be an intruder on the property. Have you heard anything out of the ordinary?"

"Not at all," I said. I stood, ready to spring into action. To do what, I had no clue. "Where was the intruder seen?"

"Take it easy, ma'am. This might be a false alarm. But we need you to stay tight in your office 'til we give the all-clear."

"What about Mr. Marshfield? Have you alerted him?"

"Already done."

"What about the rest of the staff?"

"Pretty much everybody's gone home," he said. "'Side from you, a few maintenance guys, and us in security, there's almost nobody here. So you just stay there in your office and wait 'til you hear from me again."

As soon as he hung up, I locked the outer door.

Back at my desk, I stared at the phone. Bo had called rather than raise me on the radio. Could that mean that the intruder had somehow compromised our dispatch system?

The idea of a stranger trespassing in the mansion unnerved me more than I cared to admit. I felt helpless and alone, not to mention frustrated. I wanted to ensure Bennett was safe, but calling him at this hour just to satisfy my curiosity was out of the question. Not that he would answer anyway.

Pacing my office didn't do any good, so I forced myself to return to my task. I opened the next section of investors: those who lost less than five hundred thousand. Just like the millionaires, this bunch numbered in the dozens rather than the hundreds. Again, I worked my way up from the bottom, looking for Tooney—a needle in a haystack.

And then I came across "Jepson, Samuel."

Jepson? Where had I heard that name before? I repeated the name aloud. Closing my eyes and whispering the name again, I willed my synapses to make the connection I *knew* was there. Backtracking through the days since Abe's murder, I tried to re-create my activities. Why did I equate this name with housekeeping?

I sat up. Samuel Jepson was Melissa Delling's

husband. The one Frances claimed had left her. The same husband who remained on Melissa's health insurance. I traced my finger along the report, which listed him as a Taft investor. Samuel Jepson had lost $358,000 in the Taft Ponzi scheme.

A fortune for almost anyone. I remembered Frances gossiping about the always downtrodden Melissa. Her husband had told Melissa to quit Marshfield to start a family. Then, without explanation, Melissa was back at work.

I bolted from my chair to pace the office.

Frances had assumed Melissa's husband had left her, but what if that wasn't the case at all? What if he'd given all their money to Taft? Had Taft promised him millions?

I stopped at the window. I'll bet he had.

For the first time, I wished my gossipy assistant was here. She would know the best way to find answers to all these questions. And she'd get them in a heartbeat, I had no doubt.

My impulse was to race out of here—to take this information to Detective Rodriguez—but the security staff's warning tamped down that urge. That didn't mean I couldn't call him, though. I picked up the phone, my mind still sorting through the jumble. Percy hadn't been saying "same," he'd been saying, "Sam," after all.

Fingers tingling, I tapped the detective's number. I got Flynn. "This is Grace Wheaton at Marshfield

Manor," I said all in a rush. "Where's Detective Rodriguez?"

"Gone for the day. We've been splitting shifts. Trying to cover more ground that way."

"I think I know who killed Abe Vargas."

"Oh, do you now?" he drawled.

"I do. I've been going through the list of investors. Remember that girl who was outside the study when Abe was shot?"

"Ms. Wheaton, I know you believe you're helping . . ."

"Listen to me," I shouted. "I think her husband killed Abe."

He sighed deeply. "I've been on duty for less than two hours and already I've got three disturbances reported. Friday night gets busy 'round here, you know? Maybe you can come in Monday and we'll talk about it."

"Are you kidding me? I am not waiting until Monday."

"Well then, I don't know what to tell you."

"Wait, did you say disturbances?" I asked. "You mean the one here at Marshfield?"

"Nope. Couple of the bars in town—"

"What about the intruder?"

"Come again?"

"Here at Marshfield. A security guy called a little while ago to make sure I stayed in my office until the intruder was apprehended. You don't know anything about that?"

"Can't say that I do. But I'll be sure to check on it right away. You have yourself a good night." He hung up.

"Thanks a bunch," I said to the dead phone.

Thus dismissed, I resumed pacing, stopping long enough at the wide window to stare out into the pitch-black night.

I wanted to be home. Right now. I didn't want to bother with the twenty-minute drive, but just be there. Frustrated, I blew out a breath and thought about how I might get in touch with Rodriguez tonight. I opened my Web browser and called up the local white pages, hoping to find his number.

Unlisted.

Ronny Tooney seemed to have everyone's phone numbers on speed dial. Maybe I should call him. Yeah, right. A half hour ago, I was sure he was the killer, now I was considering asking for his help? No way.

Pushing myself away from the window, I started for the phone intending to call security for an escort to my car, when I heard the unmistakable sound of a key turning in the outer lock. Panic kicked in, freezing me in place. Logic told me it had to be Bo, come to release me. Fear told me that Bo would have phoned first.

Should I call out? Hide?

Immediate, profound terror immobilized me. My feet absolutely could not move. I opened my mouth, but nothing came out. It didn't matter—in the short second it took for my mind to process all this, the outer door creaked open. The intruder was inside the room.

"Ms. Wheaton?"

I recognized Bo's soft drawl, and let out the breath I was holding. "In here, Bo," I said, making my way to Frances's office. So intense was my relief, I nearly laughed out loud. "For a minute there I thought—"

Bo wasn't alone.

"Melissa?" I said, looking from her to Bo and back again. "What's going on?"

Standing a couple of steps behind Bo, she bit her lip. My brain took its sweet time processing the situation, but my gut had gotten the message loud and clear. "You're not Bo," I said.

The lanky blond man smirked. "You're right, ma'am, I am not."

He looked just like a Marshfield security guard. Wearing the dark pants and pale shirt with insignia. And a holster, with a gun. Even a nameplate that read *Bo*.

He pointed to my office. "Why don't we all go in there and have ourselves a nice discussion?" Turning, he barked an order. "Mel, shut that damn door."

Meekly, she complied.

I called upon what little courage I could. "Get out of here now, before I call security."

"Your security's useless. They're all busy right

now anyway." Samuel Jepson winked. I wanted to slap the smug look off his face. "And, 'sides, I got my own security, right here."

He pulled up a sleek semiautomatic, waving it casually. "I'm going to make this real easy for you, darlin'."

Somehow I didn't believe that.

"You're going to pick up that phone right now and call Mister Moneybags. Tell him it's important that he come down here to see you right now."

"The hell I will."

"Tell him you know who killed Abe."

Scared as I was, I folded my arms. "I refuse."

"You gonna argue with me?" He waved the gun. "Pick up the damn phone."

"Why do you want him down here?"

"You really have to ask?" Pointing the gun at the phone, he raised his eyebrows. "Now."

I lifted the receiver and dialed, praying Bennett's refusal to speak to me would hold out just a little longer. Jepson brought his ear close to mine to listen along. A mouth breather, Jepson's breath nearly knocked me over. This close, I was tempted to try to wrestle the gun from his hand. But my chances of overpowering the guy were nil. He might be lanky, but he had muscles. I wouldn't last a minute.

"It's still ringing," I said unnecessarily. "He must not be there."

"He'll answer."

As we stood there listening, my mind repeated a mantra completely opposite than that of just a few hours earlier: Don't answer. Don't answer.

Five rings. Six. "Still nothing," I said, absurdly hoping that Jepson would just give up and go away. Melissa, near the doorway, was no help at all.

He muttered under his breath. "Old man probably goes to bed early. Hang up." He walked away from me making angry noises. "How am I supposed to get him down here?"

Melissa spoke. "Maybe we should all go up there."

Jepson's gaze snapped up. "Don't be stupid. We have to do it here." He pointed to the ground. "We *planned* this out. We can't change it now."

A man on the verge of a breakdown, he paced like a wild animal in a too small cage. In movies and books, the hero always gets the bad guy to talk. But those characters probably weren't shaking the way I was. They could probably even think straight. I was having no such luck. My mouth was sandpaper and I thought I might pass out. Summoning as much strength as I could, I cleared my throat. "Where did the money come from? The money you lost with Taft?"

He spun, and pulled the gun up. "Do *not* interrupt me while I'm thinking."

"We won a lottery," Melissa whispered. "Not a real big one. But a lot for us."

Jepson didn't seem to notice that she was talking.

She watched him as he walked back and forth, and continued whispering. "Sam thought we could be millionaires. That Mr. Taft said it was a sure thing . . ."

"Shut up!"

Melissa flinched and backed closer to the doorway. No wonder she always wore a haunted look: Her husband was a controlling lunatic. Melissa, I knew, was my only chance at freedom. I inched toward her.

"Do *not* move." Jepson's voice was a growl. In his eyes I could discern no hint of kindness, no measure of compassion. He was going kill me right where I stood, if it suited him. I just had to make sure it didn't.

His lips were thin, his skin pasty. Holding up the set of keys he'd used to open the outer door, he turned to Melissa. "Will any of these work upstairs?"

She shook her head. "Rosa and Beth have the only sets. They never lend them out."

"Damn," he said again. "I don't want to have to go all the way down to the basement to get up there."

I turned to Melissa. "You're the one who told him about that secret room and staircase, aren't you? Who told you?"

She opened her mouth to answer, but stopped when Jepson glared. To me he said, "I bet you got keys to the old man's rooms, don't you? Give 'em to me."

"I don't."

He shot me a look of impatience. "Mel, they gotta be in the desk. Go find the keys, will ya?"

Melissa scooted past, not meeting my eyes. Although I was so panicked I could barely stand upright, I thought maybe if I could get her to look at me, I could make her understand how wrong all this was. She rooted around in my desk. "I can't find them," she said.

Jepson spoke through clenched teeth. "Look harder."

She tried. She went through every drawer. I remained as still as possible, glaring at Jepson. What I most wanted was to avoid broadcasting the fact that my keys were in my purse on the shelf below the desktop. I tried to think of bunnies, flowers, and marshmallow men—anything that would prevent my face from giving the location away.

"I can't find them," Melissa said again.

Looking ready to explode, Jepson brought both hands up to massage his head. The gun pointed skyward and I considered my chances at overpowering him while the lethal weapon was directed away.

Too late. "Okay, you . . ." He lowered the gun at me. "Sit in that chair."

I took the seat behind my desk, wishing it had

been outfitted with a silent alarm button. My walkie-talkie—my only chance now—sat just to the left of my blotter. I averted my eyes, but Jepson caught me. He grabbed the radio and shoved it into his pocket. "Don't even think about it," he said. "And while I'm at it . . ." He yanked the phone, pulling the cord out from the jack with a *pop*, leaving the little connector still in the wall. He strode into Frances's room and I heard him render that phone inoperable as well.

"What now, Sam?" Melissa asked when he returned.

He spun. "I'm thinking, okay?"

With his shoulders pulled back, his breath came in short pants, and he looked ready to shoot either of us if we so much as blinked. His Adam's apple bobbed, and he ran his free hand through his cropped hair. After the briefest of moments, he turned. "Here's what's going to happen," he said to Melissa. "I have to go all the way down to the basement to get into that stairway. There shouldn't be anybody around. And with this uniform, I'm cool. It's going to take longer than I planned, but there's no help for that." He seemed to be convincing himself as he spoke. "While I go upstairs to get the old man, you stay here and guard her."

"Can't we just all go with you? Can't we—"

"Are you an idiot? Three of us roaming around this place at night? You don't think she'll start making noise? What do you think's going to happen then?"

She backed away at his rebuke. "But I don't want to stay here alone."

Lowering his voice, he ran his free hand along her shoulder and down her arm. "Listen to me, honey. You're doing an important job by staying here."

"But—"

He placed his index finger on her lips, then used the same hand to reach under his pant leg. Pulling out a second gun, he handed it to her. This one was a revolver. "You remember how to do this, right?"

"No, Sam." She backed up. "I can't."

I could see by the look in his eyes he wasn't hearing her. Still holding two guns, he asked me, "What do you have in here I can use to tie you up?"

Like I would tell him. I shook my head—my best effort at looking helpless. Given the circumstances, it wasn't all that hard.

"Damn," he said again. "Look in the drawers, Mel. Hurry up."

She hadn't gotten through the first drawer when his expression brightened. "You," he said to me again. "Take off your panty hose. We'll use that."

I held up my hands. "Not wearing any."

"Nobody under forty wears panty hose anymore," Melissa said helpfully.

"Shut up."

He scanned the room. I watched indecision work across his face. Again I worked hard not to broadcast my thoughts. He pointed the gun at me. "Get in front of the desk. On the floor."

I did as told and sat, afraid to do anything but agree.

"And you, Mel, you stay across the room. All the way across. She can't move without you seeing her." He handed her the weapon. "You point the gun at her the whole time. If she tries to get up, don't think twice. You just shoot. Got it?"

Melissa nodded.

He took her elbow and led her to the corner opposite mine. "You've got a clear line of sight here, Mel. Shouldn't be any problem for a crack shot like you."

As he said this he stared at her, as though daring her to disagree. But I caught the alarm in her eyes.

"I asked if you got it," he said. "You got it?"

She looked around his shoulder at me then back up at him. "Yeah, I do."

"Give me ten minutes. Less than that. Shouldn't take me long to get up there, and bring the old guy down." Before he left, he spoke softly. "I'm counting on you." She gazed up at him with such a look of total trust and adoration, I felt my stomach lurch. "You're my girl, aren't you?"

She nodded.

"I won't be long at all," he said. "And when we're done here, honey, we're getting away from

361

all this. Nothing will touch us ever again. We'll be safe, together. You want that, don't you?"

This time a more vigorous nod and a tiny smile.

He held up a finger. "You're going to do this. For me." He leaned in and they kissed. "So sweet."

I wanted to retch.

Right before he left, he pointed the gun at me yet again. "Don't try anything."

He shut the outer office door and I heard him fumbling with keys. When the lock turned, Melissa flinched, then faced me. "Please don't move, okay? I don't want to shoot you."

I didn't have time to waste. Scared as I was, I stood up. "You can't shoot me," I said, trying to talk to her like I might a frightened child.

"I have to," she said, shaking. "He told me to."

Jepson was probably halfway down the hall, maybe even at the staircase. Why had Bennett dismissed his guards? Right now their presence could mean the difference between life and death. Terrence had beefed up the other patrols, and I prayed that one of our crack guards would recognize Jepson as an intruder: Shoot first and ask questions later.

But I couldn't count on that.

Melissa's eyes teared up. "I can't let Sam down. Not again," she said.

"Again?"

"I'm the one who gave him the idea. I made him talk to Mr. Taft about our money."

Her lips set in a tight line, she squeezed her eyes shut against the memory.

The moment she closed her eyes I rushed her, knocking her sideways with a *whoof* that might have come from either of us. The gun clattered across the floor and she clawed at me, reaching for it. With her back against the wall and me trying my best to wrestle her arms down, we had to be a crazy sight. The girl might have been mealy-mouthed and timid around Jepson, but in hand-to-hand combat she was a vicious mountain lion. Wedging her hand under my chin, she shoved my face upward, grunting when I managed to grab a handful of hair and yank. I couldn't hold out much longer and we both knew it. I was taller and heavier, but this chick was all muscle.

"Melissa, stop," I said. My throat extended, my voice came out as a rasp. "You don't want to do this. I know you don't."

Her arm slacked for less than a second. Just long enough for me to knock her sideways to the floor. I scrambled away, grabbed the gun, and pointed.

"Please, Melissa. Just please . . ."

She held up her hands and started to cry. "Don't let him get hurt," she said. "He's all I have."

I doubted that, but this was no time for philosophical arguments. "You're worried about him?" I ran to the desk, dove for my purse, and came up with my keys. I hated to use the gun as a threat, but I had no choice. I forced Melissa into

363

Frances's office. "Figure out a way to call security," I said. "And then the police. Right now. Tell them what's going on."

"I can't."

"Melissa, it's your only chance."

Without waiting for her answer, I slammed the door in her face and locked it.

She banged on the heavy oak, calling to me from the other side. "What are you doing?"

I ran to the room's far side and crouched by the fireplace. Concentrating on working the lever the way Bennett had shown me, I didn't answer her. It took a minute until the lever finally clicked. One down. Standing, I twisted the mantel edge until it was perpendicular to the floor and I felt something give.

Blowing out a breath of relief, I pushed open the hidden side door while Melissa sobbed from the other office, begging me to keep Sam safe. "Call security," I shouted to her. "Hurry."

This was my only chance.

Terrified, but determined, I started up the curved stone stairway.

Chapter 28

I WISHED I'D HAD THE CHANCE TO TRY out these stairs before. Maybe then I would have some idea of where I was going. Right now I was literally fumbling in the dark. The gun in my right hand was heavy but I had nowhere to put it. Keeping my finger off the trigger—anything that startled me could cause me to accidentally shoot—I ran my free hand on the cool wall and hoped my feet wouldn't trip me up. With no illumination and the stone steps each about half again as tall as a regular riser, I moved as fast as I could. The thought of Jepson racing up to Bennett's room made every step feel like I was moving in slow motion.

At the top of the stairs was nothing. Nothing at all. Just three solid walls. I reached the pitch-black summit and felt around, realizing this was a tiny area, about two foot square. Running my hands along the three sides of the enclosure, I pushed, hoping for something to give. Why had I never thought to ask if there was a lever I needed at the top?

Breathing hard, I closed my eyes, willing them to adapt to the dark. When I opened them again moments later, my heart raced. A faint outline to my left, just a little lighter than the surrounding gloom, provided the answer I needed. I ran my hands along the perimeter, and nearly cheered aloud when my left index finger encountered an indentation with a tiny nub inside.

I pushed. It didn't give.

"Come on," I whispered. Pushed again.

Still nothing.

I did another sweep of the outline, wanting to rush but forcing myself to take my time and do it right. And that's when my right hand found a similar smooth indentation along the top of the outline.

Taking a deep breath, I pushed both nubs at the same time. When nothing happened I wanted to scream. Instead, I remembered Hillary and Bennett showing me mechanisms that had required two steps. "Okay," I said. I used my left hand to press the nub on the edge and my right hand to press the nub on the top.

The *click* was soft, but solid. I placed my hand on the wall and it gave. I eased through the opening, grimacing when the hinges creaked but there was nothing I could do about that.

The room was dark and I didn't have any idea where I was. I glanced around quickly, not recognizing anything. Taking a tentative step forward, I tried desperately to get my bearings. I knew I must be on the south side of the residence, the same side of the corridor as the study. The stale scent of old cigars and the grouping of chairs around a small table made me believe this was a game room or . . . yes. I bumped into the corner of a billiard table. Game room. Got it. Turning to my left, I made my way to the double doors.

I held the gun in my right hand, pointing skyward. Not the safest way to carry it, but it would have to do. I'd fired guns before and knew how to handle them. This wasn't a semiautomatic, and I'd double-checked. The cylinder was full.

I opened the leftmost door and slid into the hallway. Out here, night lights illuminated the floor in small patches, and it took me a half second to assess where I was in relation to Bennett's room.

I moved quickly to my right, taking long strides. I passed rooms I'd never seen and fought down fear as I picked up speed. I had two choices. Wait for Jepson in the study and shoot him when he emerged, or go directly to Bennett's room, warn him, and call security. I didn't think I could actually pull the trigger on Jepson so this was a no-brainer.

I raced past the study and bolted into Bennett's sitting room, out of breath. It was dark, as I'd expected. "Bennett?" I called out. I made my way to his bedroom. "Please, wake up. It's Grace. We need—"

He was in bed, but I could tell by his voice he hadn't been asleep. "What? Who?"

"It's Grace," I said trying to speak slowly, but moving quickly to his side. "Someone's coming—"

Before I could get the words out, Bennett wheeled his legs over the side and got to his feet. Standing in front of me, he pointed to the door. "Get out, now. I'm calling security."

"Yes, please call security," I said, looking around for a telephone.

He grabbed the revolver out of my hands. "My God," he said, examining it. "A gun?"

Too late, I heard scuffling in the hallway. "Get down," I said. Shoving Bennett away, I raced back to the doorway, and peered around it just as Jepson arrived in the sitting room, his gun at waist level. He slowed long enough to cock an ear toward the bedroom door.

"What the devil is going on?" Bennett boomed.

Jepson turned at the sound and sprinted toward us.

The moment he crossed the threshold, gun extended, I clasped my hands together and slammed my arms down on his. The gun went off, but I'd knocked his aim so that it fired toward the ceiling. With that split second of surprise working to my advantage, I jammed my knee into Jepson's side. He hadn't expected an ambush but recovered fast enough to twist toward me, gun pointed. My ears were still ringing when another shot went off. And another.

I called out to Bennett, but couldn't hear my own voice. The next thing I knew I was on the floor. It got suddenly dark and then I heard nothing at all.

Chapter 29

WHEN I AWOKE, THE FIRST THING I noticed was that it hurt to open my eyes against the brightness. I thought I heard someone say, "She's awake," but I couldn't be sure.

Another voice: "Don't go to the light," then, "Woo . . . woo . . ."

My mouth was dry, my lips cracked, and when I finally got my eyes open, my first word, "Scott?" came out groggy.

Scott and Bruce stood on either side of my bed. But I wasn't home. And no hospital was decorated like this. "Where am I?" I asked.

My roommates exchanged a look I didn't understand. "How are you feeling?" Bruce asked. "What do you remember?"

I tried to sit up, realizing too late that my right arm was bandaged between the elbow and shoulder. Not only that, it was sore as all get out. Nothing made sense. "What happened? Is Bennett okay?"

Scott patted my hand. "Why don't you rest a little longer and maybe when you're fully awake—"

"I'm fine right now," I said, levering myself to a sitting position using only my left arm. Not fun. "And I need to know what's going on." As I sat up,

I looked out the wide window to my right. "I'm at Marshfield?" I said incredulously. But the softness of the sheets and the lush surroundings told me I could be nowhere else. "This is surreal."

Bruce lifted a glass of water with a bent drinking straw to my lips. I sipped quickly, bathing my parched throat with cool, heavenly water. I swallowed, then sipped more.

"Not too much. Take it slow," he said then added: "All of this makes perfect sense. But since you aren't going to let us out of here unless we explain, I guess we'll just have to." He put the water down, then pulled up a Louis XIV chair and sat, clearly eager to dish the dirt. "First—what's the last thing you remember?"

"No," I said. "Before that, I need to know—how is Bennett?"

From a corner of the room, I heard his voice. "I'm doing just fine, Gracie. Thanks to you."

Gracie? No one had called me that since I was a kid.

He stepped forward to stand behind Bruce.

"You're not angry with me anymore?" I asked.

His eyes tightened for the briefest of moments, then he smiled. "How could I be? You saved my life and risked yours doing it." He waved a hand at Scott and Bruce. "You catch up with your friends. We'll talk later."

As soon as he left, I turned to my roommates. "What day is today?"

"Saturday."

My mouth was beginning to feel normal again. "You mean all this happened last night? It feels like I've been out for days."

"Hours, actually. It's just past six in the morning. You were sedated while they sewed you up."

"What?" I said. "Talk. Now." I wiggled forward, coming to a sudden and startling realization. "My clothes are gone," I said, pointing to the pale pink nightgown I wore over what felt like appropriate undergarments. "Who did this?"

"Bennett had a nurse here with you. She took care of your incidentals."

Thank God.

"Okay," Bruce began. He looked up to Scott who was still standing to my right. "Jump in whenever you want." To me, he said, "From what we've been able to put together, Jepson shot you, and Bennett shot Jepson."

"Jepson. Where is he?"

The two men exchanged a look. This time I understood completely. "Jepson's dead?" They nodded. "What about Melissa? Where is she?"

Scott interjected. "She's under arrest and giving her statement now."

I sat up. "I have to talk to the police. Jepson was controlling her. I don't think she realized what she was doing."

Bruce placed his hand over mine. "That may be, but she knew enough to allow Jepson access to the

371

mansion. That's how he was able to get in and kill Abe and almost kill you. She's not so innocent here."

I sat back. They were right. "Are you guys on a first-name basis with the detectives, or what? How did you get all this information?"

Bruce fidgeted in his chair. "As a matter of fact, we are buddies with the cops now. They picked up Dina St. Clair in Tennessee and she's being brought back here to face charges. That is," he added, "after she faces charges in Tennessee, Kentucky, West Virginia, and Maryland."

"For pulling scams?"

"She targets small businesses. All kinds of businesses. It's a real living for her."

"At the expense of innocent, trusting people," I said. "What else?"

Bruce's grin was wide. "Remember how you made us call *Grape Living* to check on her, and that's when we found out how badly she'd taken us?"

I nodded.

"Well, turns out the magazine feels responsible, so they're sending out a real reporter to do a story after all."

"Are you serious?"

Scott held up a hand. "This won't be a feature spread like the one Dina promised. This will be a lot smaller, maybe just a paragraph or so. But they promised a picture." He held up his thumb and index finger close to one another. "An itty-bitty picture."

Bruce was grinning. "But it's still *Grape Living*."

Their good mood was contagious. "So why am I here?"

"Bennett insisted. Once the paramedics and police came and sorted everything out, he refused to let you out of his sight."

"Wow." I looked at my arm. "Did I lose a lot of blood? Why don't I remember any of this?"

"That's normal. You must have blocked it. I'm sure it will come back."

"I didn't faint," I said, feeling suddenly pathetic. "Did I?"

Bruce stood up. "Tough girl like you, faint?" He winked at Scott. "Not a chance."

They left me alone then, with still too many questions left unanswered. I stared out the window and tried to use the sun's movement to figure out exactly where in the mansion this room was located. Clearly I was in Bennett's private residence.

I knew I should rest, but I couldn't sleep. I'd slept enough.

I wiggled out of the giant four-post bed and lowered myself to the ground. There was a sling on a table next to the bed. Gingerly, I fitted it around my neck and arm, sucking in a breath at the instantaneous shooting pain. Biting my lip, I took a slow barefoot tour of the room, allowing my breath and heartbeat to resume normal speeds.

Were I to design the perfect space, this would be it: a window seat with cushions overlooking the grounds to the south; a cloud-covered mural ceiling; cheery salmon-colored walls; and thick rugs on the wood floor. I recognized a real van Gogh on one wall, and a John Singer Sargeant on another. I made my way over to a wing chair and sat.

My solitude was short-lived. Almost the minute the clock struck seven, Rodriguez and Flynn were outside my door, requesting a statement. They didn't have a lot to add to the story Bruce and Scott had told me, but I did glean two important pieces of information: Percy was going to be fine; and the strange paper the threatening letters had been written on had been found at the Delling/Jepson household.

"Did you find a music box?" I asked, and explained why I wanted to know.

"Found it just in time. It was boxed, ready to be mailed to an address in Europe. Probably some collector. We're following up."

I gave my official statement and they left. About twenty minutes later, I heard a familiar voice behind me: "Am I bothering you?"

I turned. It hurt.

Jack stood in the doorway, holding a bouquet of heavy-headed pink flowers held together by a makeshift grip of aluminum foil. "Peonies," he said as he crossed the room and handed them to me. "For our hero."

When I reached to take the flowers, my arm didn't seem to hurt so much. "They're beautiful."

He took the chair opposite mine. "I picked them from the gardens."

"These are perfect," I said, bending my head to smell them. "I love them."

At that, he sat up a little straighter. "Everybody here is buzzing about what went on. Lot of rumors going around, too."

"I'll bet."

Clearing his throat, he pointed to my arm. "You obviously need time to recover."

Our date. Tonight.

He looked crestfallen. "You forgot."

"No, I didn't forget," I said. "But I'm not completely myself yet. They tell me today is Saturday. But I feel as though I've been out of touch for a week." I sighed. "The sooner I get home, the better."

"Tough being cooped up?"

From the doorway: "Excuse me." One of the butlers arrived, carrying a tray. Just like in the movies, it had a bud vase and a single rose. This one, pale yellow. The butler placed the tray on the low table in front of me and stood straight. "My apologies," he said. "I was unaware we had guests." Turning to Jack, he asked, "Would you care for breakfast, sir?"

"Thanks, no," he said standing. "I need to get going."

The butler, dismissed, left immediately.

"Hang on," I said to Jack. "Let's see what's in here." I lifted the silver dome to find a steaming plate of scrambled eggs, hash browns, biscuits, fresh fruit, coffee, and two kinds of juice. Additionally, the staff had added a note to ring for whatever I needed.

"I should ring?" I said laughing. "I could get used to this life."

Jack smiled. "I'll bet you could." He started for the door, but turned and waved. "We'll talk soon."

I hoped so. There were many things I wanted to learn about him. So many questions. He was an intriguing fellow, this Jack Embers. And I wanted the opportunity to get to know him better. "I'm looking forward to that," I said.

"So am I," he said and then he was gone.

Chapter 30

AS BEAUTIFUL AS MY SURROUNDINGS were, by three o'clock I was itching to get out of there. I had called Bruce and Scott and left a message asking them to bring me some clothes so I could go home, but neither had called me back.

I poked my head out into the hallway, looking both ways down the corridor. "Hello?"

No answer.

I returned to the window and stared out over the grounds. "I need to go home."

Bennett had snuck up on me again, and I jumped when he asked, "Don't you like it here?"

Was everyone going to surprise me from the doorway?

"Thank you," I said, "for taking such good care of me."

He gestured to the two seats Jack and I had vacated earlier. "The least I could do."

As we sat, I decided to broach a difficult topic, "About what Frances has been telling you . . ."

He leaned forward. "Just one question: Is it true?"

In a million years, I would not have expected to be having this conversation with Bennett, especially not while wearing a long pink sleep shirt and bare feet. I took a deep breath. "I don't know."

He raised an eyebrow. "Frances thinks you might have doctored your grandmother's personnel record."

"I didn't," I said, my anger flashing. "But if believing that makes everybody happy, then so be it."

He leaned forward, elbows on his knees. "I really want to know, Grace. Frances hasn't yet shown me anything. I got the story secondhand. And, knowing that woman the way I do, I shouldn't have jumped to conclusions without checking the facts first. My apologies. I admit, I've become jaded over the years. So many people try to prove a familial relationship. They're out for money, prestige . . . whatever that elusive thing is that makes people happy." Lost in his own musings, he seemed to forget I was there. Bringing himself back to the present, he said, "Tell me what you found."

I shrugged. "I just looked up my grandmother's file because I was nosy."

He laughed. "That you are."

"In it was a letter from your aunt, suggesting that my grandmother Sophie might have gotten too . . . close . . . to your father."

He nodded.

"My grandmother was fired," I continued. "She was pregnant." I held up a hand. "That's certainly no proof, to be sure. But things started to make sense all of a sudden . . ."

"Go on."

"At home I found a picture of your father, holding a baby. And a letter, unsigned, that said he couldn't leave his fortune, or young son." I pointed. "I thought he might be talking about you," I continued. "I kept digging and found the document that awarded the house to my mother."

"The old Careaux house."

"The trust was prepared by your law firm."

He nodded. "My father loved that old house. Drove past it all the time. I always wondered about his fascination with it." Looking pensive, he said, "Now I see what you mean about things falling into place."

I waited.

"So, what now?" he asked. "Should I expect a court order for a DNA test?"

For the first time, I smiled. "No."

He seemed genuinely surprised. And that surprised me.

"No?" he asked. "Why not? You have enough evidence to support a claim against the manor. Why not get the final proof?"

We had both scooched forward as we talked, and I placed my hand on one of his. "What good would that do? If your father is really my grandfather, he knew about his daughter. And he provided for her. Just as he chose to provide for you. You have your inheritance, and I have mine. I don't plan to make any claim against you."

His eyes narrowed. "Do you have any idea how much I'm worth?"

"I run the manor, remember? Of course I do."

"And you're willing to give that up?"

"I can't give up something that was never mine to begin with," I said. "And here's the thing: If we're related, it's on your father's side. It's mothers who carry mitochondrial DNA. We could take a test and still not know any more than we do now."

He nodded.

I went on. "And . . . I like believing that we may be related. A test may take that all that away."

"You're a strange girl," he said.

"Is that a compliment?"

He smiled then but his eyes grew red, and tears pooled in their pale blue depths. "I miss Abe," he said.

I patted his hand. "I do, too."

He swallowed. "I told him once that I would never let anything happen to him. I failed at that, didn't I? Failed completely. But he didn't. He took a bullet for me." Bennett wiped his eyes looking embarrassed by his show of emotion. "And now you did, too."

I didn't know what to say to that.

After a moment, he composed himself. "Gracie," he said. "May I call you that?"

"I like it."

"This has been a very tough time. I haven't been terribly kind to you, you've had to deal with the wrath of Hillary, and the cattiness of Frances. You've even been shot . . ." He took a breath. "I wouldn't blame you if you left here and never returned. But I've come to recognize that you're exactly right for Marshfield Manor." He gave me a pointed look. "You belong here. Is there anything I can do to convince you to stay on?"

Overcome by the enormity of everything that had happened, relief washed over me, taking my breath away. But even stronger was the awareness of all I'd accomplished in these crazy couple of weeks.

Bennett waited for my answer, looking anxious, little knowing how determined I was to hold on to his hard-won trust and my newfound strength. "I'm not so wild about having been shot," I said, "but these have been the most exciting weeks of my life. I wouldn't trade this job for the world."

An award-winning author, Julie Hyzy also enjoys writing short stories, many of them mysteries and science fiction. Julie was born in Chicago, but loves the history and grandeur of Washington, D.C.

Center Point Publishing
600 Brooks Road • PO Box 1
Thorndike ME 04986-0001 USA

(207) 568-3717

US & Canada:
1 800 929-9108
www.centerpointlargeprint.com